THE PAGE

THE
PAGE

M. JONATHAN LEE

Copyright © 2015 M. Jonathan Lee

The moral right of the author has been asserted.

Apart from any fair dealing for the purposes of research or private study, or criticism or review, as permitted under the Copyright, Designs and Patents Act 1988, this publication may only be reproduced, stored or transmitted, in any form or by any means, with the prior permission in writing of the publishers, or in the case of reprographic reproduction in accordance with the terms of licences issued by the Copyright Licensing Agency. Enquiries concerning reproduction outside those terms should be sent to the publishers.

Lyrics reproduced by kind permission of Frank Turner.
© & (P) 2013 Xtra Mile Recordings Limited.
Lyrics reproduced by kind permission of Hallelujah The Hills
© 2012 Reverse The Tape Decks ASCAP

Matador
9 Priory Business Park
Kibworth Beauchamp
Leicestershire LE8 0RX, UK
Tel: (+44) 116 279 2299
Fax: (+44) 116 279 2277
Email: books@troubador.co.uk
Web: www.troubador.co.uk/matador

ISBN 978 1784622 633

British Library Cataloguing in Publication Data.
A catalogue record for this book is available from the British Library.

Typeset in Aldine by Troubador Publishing Ltd
Printed and bound in the UK by TJ International, Padstow, Cornwall

Matador is an imprint of Troubador Publishing Ltd

For Nikky
A girl who takes tolerance to unparalleled levels

Hellhound in the foyer
Fooled again by mannequins
We escape again
From the straight jacket
It's alarming, man
But it's nothing you can't stand
You're a full grown human man

Hello, My Destroyer, Can I Destroy You?
Can I Destroy You?
Can I Destroy You?
And then right on cue
You could destroy me too

– Hallelujah the Hills

Time it will change us but don't you forget:
You are the only brother I've got.
I'll see you when I see you.

– Frank Turner

about three months earlier

one

The rain wasn't falling. It was forcing itself out of the shadow of the moonlit clouds and smashing down to the earth below.

The tall, lean figure of a man exited through the door, leaving the relative warmth of the building behind him. He strode forwards intently towards the scattering of cars part-hidden in the darkness of the car park. From inside the pocket of his trousers he pressed the button on his keys. The car awoke, momentarily lighting the dim scene with a flash and emitting its chirpy beep. The man pulled open the door and sat in the driver's seat. He removed his gold, half-rimmed glasses and wiped the rain from his forehead.

A few moments later he was followed by a short and very slightly overweight woman. The woman, no more than sixty years of age, looked flustered. From the warmth inside she had swept her belongings into her bag and quickly headed outside after the man. She pushed open the door and stood for a moment, half inside the pub and half outside. Until now she hadn't noticed it was raining. She stood for a while under the porch, taking in the scene. The car park was fairly quiet with maybe five or six cars dotted around its vastness. Large trees surrounded the area. The heavy rain on the leaves weighed down the boughs, pointing accusatory fingers at her. Across to her right, the brightly lit sign of the pub swayed backwards and forwards, making a repetitive creaking sound. Usually, in this kind of weather she would wait under the canopy, protected from the rain, whilst the man brought the car to her. She knew tonight wasn't usual. Tonight, if she was going to get in the car at all, she would have to make her own way there. Tonight, it wasn't going to come to her.

The engine of the long black car began to spew grey smoke which glowed red as it wound itself through the rear lights. To save time she folded the top of her handbag over instead of zipping it and, grasping it tightly in both hands, headed towards the lights. The rain continued to fall, soaking her with each step. Her journey toward the lights was not as fast as that of the man; her high heeled shoes wouldn't allow that.

The passenger side mirror allowed the man to watch her get ever closer. It was too dark to make out her expression, but it was obvious to him she was struggling to make her journey through the rain toward him. He smiled.

When she was about ten feet away, the man shifted the gear stick into reverse and accelerated at speed. The wet gravel crunched as it was displaced by the wheels. Startled, the woman paused and the man swung forwards, brushing her arm with the wing mirror. Abruptly, the car came to a stop. The woman's soaking face, lit by the car's interior lights, was now in his view.

She took a step back and pulled the door handle. The door clicked open and the woman threw her handbag into the passenger foot-well and climbed into the passenger seat. She let out a loud sigh and reached into her bag. From it she pulled a small packet of pocket-sized tissues and pulled down the sun-visor to use the mirror.

The man retrieved his glasses from the dashboard in front of him and looked at her. His face was expressionless.

She was aware he was watching but ignored him and began to remove the make-up that the rain had helped to distribute around her face. She licked the tissue and carefully wiped away the track marks which led from her eyes like black tears. She would not return his stare. This time, for once, she would be strong.

That evening the conversation in the pub had not gone exactly how the woman had expected. It had gone *exactly* how the man expected. He had been preparing for this for some time.

The woman had been trying, as the man had requested, to 'book an appointment' with him for a number of weeks. He was busy at work. He didn't have time for a drink. She had waited patiently, rebuffed over and over but tenaciously persevering like a summer wasp. Each time she was refused his time, she would return with unrelenting persistence. She would get her moment. She would have her say. The man believed he knew what the woman had to say and internally conceded he would allow her 'her' moment. Just not yet. First, he needed time.

One evening a number of weeks earlier, he had finally relented and suggested they go to a country pub to have the conversation the woman so desperately wanted. She was unsure why he had picked this particular pub over any of their usual, more local choices. However, due to the nature of what she had to say and the fact that they were likely to bump into friends or perhaps clients, she felt that on this occasion she could allow this.

They shared the usual small talk on the ten-mile journey, each knowing that they would speak about something much larger when they arrived. At the pub the man ordered his usual whisky and water, the woman her small Chardonnay. The pub was long and thin, with the exterior stone visible in places. The cream walls were lit with mock-Victorian gaslights which housed amber-coloured light bulbs that jumped and crackled in a predefined pattern. The man directed her to a small, quiet corner which he had selected on his previous solitary visit. He hadn't noticed the light bulbs that day, as it had been a busy lunchtime with bright sunshine streaming through the chipped white window frames.

The woman had considered ordering a large glass of wine but decided against it as she wanted to be completely clear when she said what she had to say. She had rehearsed the conversation over and over in her head for as long as she could remember. It had forced her awake on too many nights over so many years whilst he lay asleep beside her. She was therefore somewhat startled when the man spoke first, scattering her rigidly prepared conversation structure like dominoes.

"I know why we're here, Margaret," he said in a headmaster-like tone.

"You do?" she replied, already struggling to remain steadfast.

"Yes, I do, Margaret," he replied, repeating her name for gravitas.

She immediately knew that she had lost control of the situation. She was used to this tone, that unwavering, quietly spoken 'you are nothing without me' tone. It was one of many other characteristics she had got used to during their thirty or so years of marriage: his condescending looks, his controlling nature, his ability to make her feel like she physically shrunk when he spoke to her. She couldn't remember whether it had always been like this. The feeling of well, just drowning. Being caught in a funnel of rapidly reducing sand, spinning helplessly toward the narrow chute at the bottom. The life being sucked from you. A feeling of pure misery. Pure misery. No, she concluded, she couldn't remember any other feeling as far as the man was concerned. But more recently she had begun to feel alive. It was a physical feeling, as if something inside her had burst and sent shockwaves from the centre of her body to her furthest extremities. To her fingers. Her toes. Her own mortality and her own happiness were now paramount. She could not continue to live this way. These thoughts flooded into her mind and mentally she returned to her script. She would not be overpowered. Not this time.

"Well," she said, "then you'll know I've been unhappy for some time."

His eyes narrowed. "Margaret, if I could just stop you there..."

That tone.

"...define 'some time'."

Margaret shuffled slightly in her seat. "I can't tell you exactly how long, Michael," she conceded, "but a long time."

"That isn't very helpful, Margaret, now is it?"

She willed herself to be strong. "Well, I'm not sure that the exact length of time is important..."

"I have to disagree," he whispered. "I have to disagree."

The conversation continued, Margaret asserting herself in bursts as she tried to make her points and state her feelings to her husband. Each time it ended in the same way, a feeling of defeat. A feeling of being utterly overpowered by a carefully chosen, small technicality. Michael was not going to make this easy. But Margaret was not going to stop.

A waitress approached to offer more drinks, which Margaret eagerly accepted – this time a large glass. Michael wouldn't have another. Not tonight. Michael's eyes widened and he beamed at the waitress, showing his slightly yellowed teeth.

"Got to watch this one!" he said, passing her a ten-pound note.

The waitress smiled and reached into her money belt for change.

Michael shook his head, indicating the waitress's search for coins should stop.

"That's for you," he said, winking.

The waitress smiled and left.

Margaret was unsure whether she'd said everything that she wanted to say. She had never been able to discuss any of this with anyone. She had lived with these feelings inside her head; feelings that had slowly gnawed away at her for so long. So, so long. She had often thought that perhaps if she had someone to confide in, she may have been able to make sense of it all. But this simply hadn't been possible.

She knew that their only daughter, Jane, was unlikely to say anything bad about her father. She'd often considered Jane to be her only real friend, but had concluded that however close they were she was not the right person to speak to about the way Michael made her feel. It was well, just too close. She couldn't speak to any of her friends because her friends were 'their' friends. It wasn't possible to speak to her female companions because they were somehow behind the shield of their relative husbands. And their husbands were Michael's colleagues, ex-colleagues or business associates. The dinner parties and evenings at restaurants they had with such friends were always pleasant enough, but they were rarely about Margaret, rarely about the women. No, they were about the men, and their new cars, and their business deals, and their name dropping and their money. About which clients they were working for, about rumours, about fee income. True, on occasion the women were left alone to chat unencumbered by the men. But these situations were always brief, toward the end of an evening or perhaps whilst clearing the dishes away, and the men were never far from earshot. On a handful of occasions, when she felt she could stand it no more and when the Chardonnay had disappeared a little too quickly, Margaret had mustered up the courage to discuss how disposable Michael made her feel. But almost instantaneously an alarm bell had rung in her mind and she would quickly backtrack, realising that she certainly didn't know these women well enough to confide. And anyway, it appeared that they and their husbands all adored Michael. The Michael they saw.

Michael stared at a meadow-scene watercolour and yawned before slowly turning his head back towards her.

"So, in summary, Margaret, you're unhappy and have been for some time. Yes?"

That tone.

Margaret took a sip from the large glass that the waitress had delivered earlier. It remained near-full.

"Yes," she replied, looking up through the top corner of her eyes, her head bowed.

"And what is it exactly that you wish to do?"

The shockwaves struck and she lifted her head. In her script Michael made the decision on their marriage; she hadn't considered the onus passing to her. Well, if this was her decision she would just say it. It was time. Another quick sip, the wetness ensuring the dryness of her lips didn't interrupt the next sentence.

"I think we should separate, Michael."

"Separate, Margaret, or divorce?"

"Divorce." The words crackled from her dry throat. She took a further sip and repeated more resolutely: "Divorce."

"Right. I see no reason to stay here any longer."

Michael stood. He looped his navy woollen scarf around his neck, put on his grey waterproof walking jacket and slowly and precisely zipped it to just below his chin. He then turned and left.

Margaret fluffed her hair, fruitlessly trying to restore it to how it looked before her journey to the car. It wasn't working; her previously neat salon-set hair sat like a sodden dark-grey dishcloth. The wipers continued their metronomic dance across the windscreen, trying to keep up with the demands of the heavy rain.

The car was still and silent aside from the ticking of the engine. Michael appeared to be in no rush to move it forwards; instead he chose to continue to stare at his wife.

Margaret felt uncomfortable; she hadn't considered this stage in her overall plan. She slid the door back across the mirror of the sun-visor, switching off the light it provided, which made the car slightly darker.

Slightly eerier.

She looked straight ahead and noted there was nobody around. Nobody outside in the dark, slightly foggy evening. The woodland that surrounded the car park from every side gave her the sense that she was in the centre of some bleak amphitheatre. To her left were the lights which shone through the half-closed curtains in the windows of the pub. But the lights were becoming blurred from the condensation which was building on the inside of the car windows. For a moment, she considered going back into the pub and making alternative arrangements to get home.

Michael seemed to sense this fleeting thought and all of a sudden, from the corner of her eye, she saw his hand move, pushing the gear stick into first. The car crept slowly forwards. A slight ripple of relief passed through her as Michael's head turned away from her. She returned the sun-visor to the roof of the car and stared directly ahead, their vision now focused in the same direction.

The car moved slowly towards the edge of the oval car park, following the perimeter instead of the more direct route across the almost empty space. It approached the area furthest from the pub, furthest from the exit, creeping slowly into the darkest area of the car park. Then Michael reached down very precisely and put the car into neutral. His head turned and again his eyes narrowed.

Margaret looked at him directly. She could just make out his eyes in the near-darkness, the moon reflecting the shine from his pupils. She could see enough to deduce that they had changed. The shine was simply a creation of the moon. They looked empty, vacant. The stare lasted only a couple of seconds, until Michael snapped back into reality, put the car back into gear and headed towards the exit.

They reached the junction with the main road and paused alongside the tall wooden sign which invited people to the warmth of the Ring O'Bells. The wind outside had increased and the hand-painted silver bell on the sign swung violently. Silently tolling in the black night. The silence was broken momentarily by the click-click of the indicator signalling that they were turning right, away from the direction of home.

Michael turned out of the car park and joined the unlit main road, at which point he quickly accelerated. Margaret wasn't sure where they were heading but knew that Michael was familiar with this sparsely populated but affluent area of the Oxfordshire countryside. She was aware that, sporadically, at the roadside were entrances to long, sweeping drives winding their way up to mansion-like farmhouses set in acres of land. She was aware of this because Michael would proudly tell her of the latest new client he had obtained in small villages around the area. And, of course, he would tell her of the money these clients would bring to his firm of solicitors.

The car continued to gather speed, accelerating at pace before slowing abruptly to safely navigate the tight, twisting bends. Inside the car it remained deathly silent. The Eagles (which had accompanied them on the outward journey) no longer played. To Margaret, the choice of silence indicated Michael now had control, and today she would simply not relinquish it.

They sped along the country roads, the rain continuing to

smash relentlessly against the windscreen, making visibility ever more difficult. The tall hedgerows on each side of the vehicle made Margaret feel increasingly entombed. From time to time they would approach a small hamlet and Michael would slow the car right down before accelerating quickly, rendering the 'Thank You for Driving Carefully' road sign a blur.

Margaret reached down into her bag and retrieved her mobile phone. She clicked the button on the top and the screen lit brightly. She awaited the bars to indicate that if she needed to make a call, she could. The phone would take her attention away from the weight of the silence in the car. It would also give the impression that this journey was not affecting her and that she had other things to do.

The car continued at pace through the darkness.

No signal.

She was used to Michael driving at speed; 'using the power of the vehicle' he called it. She had lost count of the times over the years that she had asked him to slow down. The times that she had told him she was scared. But at those times, he would simply accelerate. Enjoying her fear. Enjoying his utter domination of the situation. But today things seemed different. His hands gripped the steering wheel ferociously. His face, lit by her phone, was contorted. His eyes had definitely changed. Now he didn't seem to be driving the car. Rather, he was trying to tame it, to keep it under control. His face reminded her of a rodeo cowboy as the horse kicked and jarred beneath him. Total focus, total concentration. This scared her.

And now they were on a straight road. Ever quicker. Ever faster.

Then brake.

A bend.

Swing to the left.

Swing back to the right.

And accelerate again.

Wet twigs discarded by trees cracked under the tyres. Water splashed up from the road, coating the windscreen before the wipers sent it back to earth. Faster. Ever faster.

Margaret gripped the handle on the passenger door tightly with her left hand. The palm of her right was beginning to hurt as it encased her mobile phone. She glanced down. Still no signal. This was too fast. Much too fast. Her entire body clenched so tightly that her muscles hurt.

Accelerate.

Brake.

Swing left.

Swing left again.

Accelerate.

Accelerate.

Accelerate.

Accelerate.

It was time to speak, time to say something. Time to relinquish control.

"Michael!" she shouted. "Slow down."

Silence.

Michael pushed his foot toward the floor.

Faster.

The wipers struggled to cope with the rain.

"Michael, for God's sake, slow down. Please."

The 'please' was an open admission that signified to them both that her control was now lost. But now Margaret didn't care. She was scared. So many times throughout her marriage she had felt afraid, but never like this.

The car swung again, gathering pace.

Quicker.

Faster.

"Michael, this is ridiculous. It's not safe!" she screamed. Tears welled and then exited her eyes. "It's not safe!"

Silence.

Quicker.

Faster.

"Michael, what are you doing? What do you want?"

Michael slowly turned toward her.

"Margaret," he said calmly and deliberately, "I never want to hear your fucking voice again."

about now

two

The lift jolted to an unsteady stop and the ping that sounded signified that Michael had reached his floor. He was pleased to leave the lift after noticing the dark wet stains under the arms of his olive shirt in the floor-to-ceiling mirrors that covered three sides of the interior. The doors slowly opened and he dragged his small suitcase onto the white marble floor. He reached into his pocket and retrieved the black plastic triangle to which the key was attached. Matching the white number on the triangle to the sign on the wall, he headed right, in the direction of his room. The corridor was brightly lit by the sun, which shone in through an opening at the far end. Michael could see the cloudless blue sky and hear the sound of laughter and playful screams coming from the pool area three floors below.

When he reached his room he pushed the old steel key into the lock. The door clicked open and he dragged his suitcase into what would be his home for the next seven days. Leaving his case at his feet, he sighed loudly and sat down on the double bed. He stared around the room, wondering why he had been harangued into this holiday in the first place.

It had been Jane's idea. She was the one behind it; in fact, she was the one who had eventually booked the flights and the hotel. She should have picked up on his lack of enthusiasm to leave the family home. She should have noticed his obvious inertia when she brought round brochures and emailed him links to various far-flung destinations. He was aware that his daughter was only trying to do what she thought was best for him under the circumstances. It was unlike him to agree to anything that wasn't his idea, and yes, perhaps she had caught him in a rare moment of weakness. She had been so enthusiastic, and an escape from the situation at home had in some ways appealed. Now he was here, though, things were different: he had no control over whatever may be happening at home. Now he wished she'd minded her own business. If she had, he wouldn't now be stuck in some fucking holiday resort, alone and so far from home.

He removed his gold half-rimmed glasses, placed them on the terracotta-and-lemon-striped top sheet and wiped away the drips of sweat from his face. Pushing his thumb and forefinger deeply into his closed eyes, he paused for a few seconds. At this point all he could see was darkness, which momentarily allowed him a short escape from his surroundings. He felt small droplets of sweat race down his back, which reminded him that he needed to change out of his shirt. He opened his eyes and replaced his glasses, mentally resolving that now he was here he might as well make the best of it.

He wandered over to the patio doors at the far end of the room and pulled them open. The baking heat from outside burned the hairs in his nose. He removed his shirt and folded it neatly over the back of a cream wicker chair on the balcony. Stretching out his arms in front of him as far as they would go, he placed his hands on the pine wooden rail which lay across the top of the balcony wall, and leaned forward. It was, he conceded, a spectacularly beautiful day. The sun sat far above him, slightly off centre, beating down onto the pool area below.

There were three pools in total. The main pool was octagonal and was surrounded by row after row after row of white plastic sunbeds. There were tightly packed together, with little space to walk between them. At first glance it appeared that all were in use. Michael let out a sigh again; this type of resort was certainly not what he was used to. A second, much smaller children's pool was set just off the far end of the main pool. This area was to be avoided at all costs. Little brats running around, shouting and screaming and crying. This was not a place that Michael would spend any of his time. Over to the right, however, there was a small rectangular pool in an area that from above appeared to be cordoned off by a thick rope. The rope drooped in the centre before rising again to meet each thick wooden post set neatly around the pool. Michael noted there were twenty posts in total. This area seemed much more appropriate. Instead of plastic sunbeds, there were large wooden frames of a similar size to a single bed. As the area wasn't overpopulated, it was possible to see the thick cream padded mattresses on the vacant beds. A man stood at the entrance to the area, smartly dressed in a white short-sleeved shirt tucked into navy shorts. To his right was a large stack of white towels. As Michael watched a slim, dark-skinned women in a yellow bikini approached the man and appeared to exchange some kind of ticket for a towel. The man led her to a bed, outstretching his arm. The woman nodded, smiled and placed the towel on the vacant bed. The man smiled back and returned to the entrance.

The heat of the sun was beginning to redden the skin beneath the white hairs on Michael's forearms. He returned to his bedroom in search of sun-cream.

Jane was aware that her father would now have arrived at his destination. She hoped that he liked the place she had chosen. She knew her father was difficult to please at the best of times and she felt a wave of anxiety flutter through her chest. She reached into her handbag for her phone. Pressing the keypad, she scrolled through until she saw her father's name on the screen. Her finger hovered momentarily over the green 'call' button. No, she concluded, she would call the next day. Today he would have to fend for himself.

Michael lifted the suitcase onto the bed and unlocked the gold padlock. He unzipped the case, opened the lid, unhooked the chrome clasps, which were joined by elastic stretched across the inside of the case, and slowly began removing the items one by one. He just wasn't used to this. Had Margaret been here she would have been doing this task whilst he retreated to the balcony with a glass of wine. He pictured her removing the items and hanging them neatly in the wardrobe. Each on its own hanger, in colour order from light to dark. Light to the right, dark to the left. Just how he liked it. She would inform him where his underpants and socks were and ensure that they were neatly folded and placed in the drawers perfectly. She would remove all the toiletries and arrange them in the bathroom, in order of use from left to right. The shaving foam first, then the shaver, the deodorant, the aftershave, the balm. Shampoo and soap would be on the side of the bath, waiting, ready. His electric toothbrush, his toothpaste, his floss; all next to the sink. Where he needed them. Then, with a smile, she would come out onto the balcony to inform him that the unpacking was complete. If she was lucky, he would look up for a split-second from his book and nod silently.

Due to the circumstances he had no choice but to perform this task alone. He removed his wash bag from the case and stood, pausing for a second. His brown leather sandals squeaked on the tiled floor as he shuffled his feet into the bathroom. There, for the first time since he left home that morning, he was confronted by his own face. The bathroom was typical for a hotel of this type. The toilet was directly in front of him; the bath, complete with pristine white shower curtain, was to his right. On his left were two sinks, which quickly became four in the long mirror that stretched to the ceiling along the entire length of the wall. It was here that he saw himself. He had aged. There was no doubt about it. The events of the last few months had seen his short, neatly cropped salt-and-pepper hair edge its way ever closer to salt. He noticed that the skin beneath his eyes had gathered heavily and, as if doing the opposite to his hair, had darkened to near black in colour. His ice-grey eyes hadn't changed, though. They were the same. He stared deeply into them, trying to see through them to understand what had happened within his mind. The eyes stared back, as if challenging him to look away.

"Michael Sewell," he whispered, shaking his head slightly.

He unzipped the black leather toiletry bag and began to remove the items from it, carefully placing each in exactly the right order.

three

Michael left the lift and walked quickly past the light-green wicker chairs which filled the large expanse of the reception. It was fairly empty, save for one or two seats taken by people whose holiday was now at its end. They waited quietly alongside their cases for the bus to arrive to take them to the airport. Michael made his way to the reception and flashed his key fob. The receptionist smiled and passed him a ticket for the private pool area. He took it and turned away.

He followed a sign post which indicated that the pool area was off to the right. As he rounded the corner a small boy, no more than five years old, tore toward him, laughing and screaming loudly. His face was thick with ice-cream and he was naked aside from a pair of blue swimming trunks and some brown ankle-length boots whose laces danced as he ran; an unusual combination of attire. As he approached he twisted his head to face in the opposite direction to the way he was running. Michael had seen the collision coming but had no time to stop it. The child, unaware that Michael was approaching, hit him face to thigh, caking a mixture of ice cream and some kind of red syrup from around his mouth onto Michael's pressed cream shorts. At the same time, Michael felt the weight of the boy land on his big toe, which was exposed through his sandals. He grimaced. The child bounced back slightly, his face an inch or two away from Michael's groin. For less than a second, Michael considered hitting the child with the back of his hand. Instead he raised his hand and pushed the boy's face firmly away. A hollow sound indicated his head had hit the marble floor. At that moment, the child's parents, who had obviously been his focus moments earlier, rounded the corner. They were greeted by a crying child as they came into view. The child lay still on the floor.

"He ran into me and fell," said Michael.

The father knelt down beside his child.

"Oh dear. Are you okay, Rhys?"

The little boy snivelled, stretching his arms toward his father.

"Come on, little fella; let's pick you up."

"Sorry," said the mother giving a look that said 'oops'. "He's just excited."

Michael raised his eyebrows.

"Oh dear, sorry about your shorts," said the mother, glancing down at the cheek-sized patch of raspberry juice.

"You know what kids are like," said the father, smiling.

Yes, I fucking do, thought Michael. I know only too well what they're like. They bring nothing but misery.

The father scooped up the child from the floor and stood upright. He was tall, a similar height to Michael.

"You should watch where he's fucking going," Michael said calmly, staring directly through the mother.

"There's no need to speak to us like that," she said.

"He pushed me," the child snorted, holding back his tears. Snot was added to the ice-cream and red juice combination on his face.

"That's not true: he fell," said Michael.

The mother looked at Michael.

"He pushed me over," repeated the child.

Michael shook his head, his eyes fixed on the mother.

The father interrupted: "I don't know what happened here, and, er, well, it's not good to make up stories, Rhys…"

The child's mouth opened wide and the crying began once again. The father hugged him tightly.

"Just say sorry to the man, Rhys."

"Let's just go," said the mother.

Michael pushed between the mother and father in his path, forcing them to separate to let him through. He said nothing and walked away in the direction of the pool area.

Michael showed his key to a disinterested dark-skinned man, before making his way down a covered sloped walkway to the pools. He took determined strides through the abundance of sunbeds, avoiding eye contact with their occupants. He repeatedly had to change his direction, stepping over drinks or inflatables or children. From time to time someone would pull a bag out of his path to assist his passage and smile weakly. He ignored this. He knew which pool he was destined for.

He reached the area cordoned off by ropes and was greeted by a man leaning on a pile of towels at the entrance.

"Welcome to the Tropicana Court, sir. It sure is another beautiful day!"

The particularly poor mock-American accent annoyed Michael, though he managed to slightly extend the corners of his mouth upwards.

The man took Michael's ticket in exchange for the loan of a towel and showed him to a sunbed in the far corner of the enclosure.

"Have a great day!" said the man, hovering alongside the bed.

Michael said nothing and sat down. He placed his black leather bag on the bed alongside him and unzipped it, looking for his sun-cream and book. The man watched. The black leather bag, around the size of a small loaf of bread, went everywhere with Michael.

The various pockets and zipped sections were perfect for his organised mind. Margaret and Jane giggled on occasion, nicknaming it his 'man bag'. Michael didn't see the joke.

He retrieved his book and placed it alongside him on the white towel mattress. The sun-cream was harder to find. His hand swept around inside the bag, feeling each item and then discarding it as its shape didn't match what he was looking for. His room key, his glasses case, his wallet. As he searched he was surprised to see the man was still standing alongside his bed. He looked up and frowned.

"Anything else you need, sir?"

"No."

"You sure?"

Michael reached into the bag and pulled out his wallet. He pulled out a five-euro note and pressed it firmly into the man's outreached hand.

"Have a good day, sir," said the man.

Jane fingered her phone again. Only a few hours earlier she had resolved not to phone until the next day. But she knew her father and she knew that she would be far more settled if she heard that everything was alright. It was her father's first holiday alone since Mum. She knew that her father would never say that things were going well; it wasn't in his nature. But regardless of his words she could tell from the inflection in his voice whether he was generally satisfied, generally buoyant. Again, she brought his number up on the screen, and again her finger hovered over the green button. No, he would have to wait. If anything was wrong, he would most certainly call her. She scrolled down to the next number and telephoned Matt; if he wasn't too busy at work, he would take her mind away from worrying about her father for a few moments.

The sun-cream wasn't in the bag and after a thorough search, which included emptying the bag out in full, Michael slowly began to put all the items away. He prided himself on his meticulous planning, and to forget any individual item necessary for his day was a failure. This wouldn't have happened if Margaret had been here. She would have brought her own bag with her. And if he had asked for any item, it would have been there for him. At the precise moment he needed it. True, in the past she may have forgotten to bring something, but Michael's reaction on discovering this would mean that it never happened again. Margaret quickly learned to check and double-check everything before they left for any kind of day out. He felt the anger rise in him. Margaret should be here.

The heat of the sun was already reddening his pale, thin legs and he realised staying in the sun without the cream would be simple stupidity. He glanced over his shoulder toward the main pool and decided the return journey to his room was intolerable. He got up from his sunbed and made his way to the bar.

"Hello again."

"Hello," said Michael, his chest tightening at the prospect that he now required something from the man.

"What can I get you?"

"I seem to have forgotten my sun-cream. Do you sell any here?"

"This is a bar, sir."

"I can see that."

"We sell drinks and snacks. We don't sell sun-cream."

"I understand," said Michael, realising that there was a game to be played. "Whisky. Double. Ice."

"Okay."

The barman fixed the drink with the usual performance of

tossing and catching the bottle and then propelling ice cubes into the air before catching them in the glass. Michael sneered. Following the performance the barman placed his drink on a paper coaster on the bar.

"Fifteen euros." He placed the receipt on a small silver tray and slid it onto the bar. The barman smiled. "So you need sun cream too, man?"

Michael stared at the whisky, refusing to answer. He knew the barman already knew this, and *he* wasn't enjoying this game at all.

"I have my own sun-cream you can use."

Michael looked up.

"Yeah, it's right here." The man turned and grabbed the bottle from the bar behind him.

Michael's eyes narrowed. He was thinking.

"You're welcome to use some," said the man, passing the bottle between the beer pumps to Michael.

"Thank you," said Michael quietly, reaching and taking the bottle. The man's grip remained and for a short moment they both held the cream.

"Twenty euros."

Michael sat on his sunbed. It was hard to keep the rage he felt from escaping through his mouth. He swallowed. For a moment at the bar he had considered turning away and simply walking back up to his room. It would have been worth the walk so that the hateful man didn't beat him in the game. But he had glanced across at the seemingly endless mass of bodies around the main pool and decided to concede. For now. He smiled to himself, pleased with the knowledge that he had used vast quantities of the cream. Without losing eye contact once throughout, he had silently applied handfuls of the cream to his body, allowing large quantities to drip through his fingers to the floor. He hadn't actually lost the game; he had won. And if the man believed otherwise then he would see. In time.

four

Michael placed the book down by his side. He had been reading for around two hours and sweat was trickling down his body. The sun beat down unmercifully and the heat from the occasional strong gust of wind hit him as if he were being blasted by a giant hairdryer. He rose and wound the wooden handle at the end of the bed, which pulled the cream fabric canopy across the top of the bed frame to block out the sun. It now resembled a four-poster bed. He lay down on his side, now completely in the shade aside from his left leg, which he pulled in, closer to his right. He removed his glasses and placed them on the wooden table at his side and closed his eyes.

He hadn't been asleep long before he heard the flip-flap of footwear approaching. He didn't sleep the same since losing Margaret. It was now a kind of half-sleep where one part of his mind shut down to let his body rest and the other stayed awake like a sentinel on guard. Always aware, always prepared. A voice dragged his mind's restful side into line with the sentinel.

"Another drink, sir?"

Michael opened one eye slowly and then the other and looked up. He was relieved to see it was a different man this time.

"I will, yes. Whisky and ice. Double."

"Okay, just gimme a moment, sir."

Michael sat on the edge of the sunbed shaded by the canopy. In the distance he saw tall, barren mountains spotted with collections of small white buildings. He decided that was where he would head in the evenings. The journey from the airport had taken him along a busy urban road overshadowed by the huge hotels which suffocated the coast. The area was swarming with families and he was relieved when the taxi had taken a route off to the right and away from the mass of people. He calculated that he was perhaps a mile or two away from the busy centre, which he had no intention of visiting. On arrival at the hotel, the receptionist had kindly informed him that a free bus would take him to the centre whenever he wanted. He had informed the woman in no uncertain terms that he would not need it. When Jane had booked the holiday she had managed to keep him away from the busy hustle of the town centre. She had at least got that much right.

The waiter approached and handed him his drink along with the tab. He settled the bill with a couple of crumpled notes from his wallet. He sipped at the whisky, staring into the distance at the numerous hills which stood in the shadow of mountains. He had intended to ask the waiter which restaurants on the hillside were worth visiting, but he couldn't bring himself to get into a conversation. His Spanish was good enough for him to hop into a taxi and find his own way.

A child shrieked in the main pool and Michael's fist clenched slightly. There was no possibility that he could survive a week here surrounded by these false people and their abhorrent children. These people who believed that taking a holiday away as a family somehow solved all the problems lying in wait for them at home. These people for whom a little sun was somehow enough to get them through another fifty-one weeks in the dire drudge of reality. He needed to be alone.

A gust of wind whipped up across the small pool area. Michael quickly placed his hand to his side to stop his book flapping. Plastic cups scattered across the tiled floor around him. The few other people on the beds nearby clutched their items as a pile of napkins made their way, one by one, across his line of sight.

The wind dropped but soon increased again. Across the pool, a book that lay on a table adjacent to a vacant sunbed quickly flipped opened. Seconds later it spewed its pages into the bright sky, each detached from the now non-adhesive spine. Pages littered the area, scattering on the floor. Pages dodged and twirled in the sunny sky, corkscrewing in the wind before gently landing on the surface of the pool. As Michael watched the papers dance before him, one flew across and stuck to his white-haired torso.

The wind subsided and Michael watched the forty or so pages bob and ripple on the surface of the pool. They reminded him of rectangular lily pads, their weight just enough to keep them on top of the pool water.

Suddenly, the wind whipped up again, blowing the plastic cups around his feet. This was enough for Michael. He drank remainder of his whisky and pulled the page from his chest. His own book flapped again, and he grabbed at it before shoving it into his bag. Then he stood, turned and posted his feet neatly into his sandals. Realising he was still gripping the scrunched-up page in his hand and looked around for somewhere to dispose of it. The wind whipped up again, sending the plastic cups rolling. He clutched his black bag under his arm, undid the press stud on the side pocket and shoved the screwed-up paper inside. He firmly pushed the press stud closed and scoured the scene. It took him less than a second to decide the quickest route and then he turned and began his long strides back to the quiet of his room.

five

Jane fingered the rim of the porcelain Forever Friends mug. She was sitting at the far end of the cream sofa. Her eyes fixed on the skirting-board.

"He'll be fine," said Matt – who, having changed out of his suit, had paused to watch his wife on his descent down the open staircase in the lounge.

She looked up and smiled weakly.

"He will. He'll be absolutely fine," Matt repeated, passing her on his way to kitchen. "Another coffee?"

"Er, yeah, I suppose."

Jane pushed herself up off the sofa and followed Matt into the kitchen.

Matt filled the kettle.

"I don't know what you're worrying about."

Jane leaned against the frame of the kitchen door as if unsure whether to go in. She stared at the black-tiled floor.

The small kitchen was perfectly clean. Nothing was out of place. The slightly frosted glass cupboard doors had been polished to perfection. The black granite work surfaces had no smears. Even the piles of post, which were usually haphazardly tucked behind the Dualit toaster, had been filed away. The only letter which required attention had been attached to the magnetic whiteboard, alongside the strip of passport photos of Jane and Matt which slightly covered the picture of Margaret beaming brightly on her only daughter's wedding day.

"I know," Jane replied, giving the impression that she didn't. "It's just…"

Matt scooped the coffee into the cafetière. "It's just what, love?"

Jane pondered her response. She and Matt had been here so many times before. She knew that he cared enough to listen, but she didn't want this conversation to become yet another one about her father. She paused, long enough for Matt to speak.

"You're worried about your dad, aren't you?"

She looked up, pushing her long dark-brown hair away from eyes. She smiled nervously.

"I've told you he'll be fine."

"I know," she repeated. "I'm just being silly."

Matt smiled. He ran his fingers through his hair which instantly flopped forwards again, refusing to be pushed out of the way. The kitchen light caught his hair, illuminating the copper flecks in the blond. The kettle clicked and he poured the boiling water into the cafetière, attached the lid and plunged the tiny dots of coffee to the bottom.

Conversations about Jane's family had been like this for as long as Matt could remember. He and Jane had met at university more than ten years previously. Against the will of her father, certainly, Jane had decided to become an art student. Matt had studied computer science. Although Michael had never said it to him directly, he knew that he disapproved of this choice of subject as well.

Matt and Jane had had hit it off immediately. Mutual friends in the student union bar had introduced them whilst they spent an afternoon drinking. They had smiled at one another across the table and, although usually shy, the beer had given Jane the confidence to point out that the artwork on Matt's Green Day t-shirt matched exactly the sticker on the side of her art folder. Aside from their love of alternative rock, they were anything but peas in a pod. Jane could speak for hours about texture and light and how art was simply taking an unseen part of the brain and turning it into something physical for the world to see. Matt would nod and smile at the right times, his more logically tuned brain understanding little of what she said. But there was something in the way that Jane spoke. How her mouth moved, how her freckles seemed to grow on her tiny nose when she was excited. How she seemed to physically glow when she was happy. He spent a long time wondering what exactly she saw in him and at times, when they had drunk too much, he would ask her. She would resolutely refuse to answer his question, saying that he should know, saying that those types of questions could destroy them.

They went to gigs, they got drunk, they talked and they had sex. This pattern heightened Matt's fear. Surely this couldn't last forever? Surely when university ended and they had to get on and have 'proper lives', as Michael called it, then the bubble would burst? This thought propelled itself regularly into Matt's consciousness. Each time it did, he somehow managed to avoid dealing with it.

And then, university was over and the bubble didn't burst. Overnight they joined the real world and everything continued as before. Certainly, the attendance at gigs, the drinking and the sex all reduced slightly. But the talking never did. The talking stayed the same. And over time, Matt began to realise what Jane saw in him. She liked his dependability, his kindness, his logical mind and, above all, the fact that when she talked, he listened. The only subject of discussion on which they couldn't manage to agree was her family – more specifically, Michael.

Matt poured the coffee. Black for him. White for Jane. He returned the milk to the fridge and turned to her.

"Are you going to sit down?" he said, motioning to the two tall stools at the breakfast bar.

Jane moved from the door and climbed onto a stool. Even in grey velour jogging bottoms and a simple white vest she looked radiant.

Matt slid his elbows down the work surface and came to rest opposite her.

"So…" he said, inviting her to continue the conversation.

"You'll think I'm stupid," said Jane rhetorically.

Matt raised his eyebrows and gave her a slight 'go on' smile.

"Well, I've been thinking about Dad all day – you know, alone on holiday for the first time."

The pristine condition of the kitchen had made this obvious.

"And well, I'm worried about him. He's never been away without Mum, ever. I just hope he's okay and he doesn't feel lonely and likes the resort and…" Her speech was becoming more rapid, words cartwheeling over one another. "…I know if we were there, or I was there, or Mum, then…"

"Hey." Matt reached over and put his hand on her cheek. He noticed the tears welling in her eyes. "It's okay."

Jane sniffed and shook her head.

"I know. I told you, I'm being silly."

If anyone at all in this whole world can cope on holiday for the first time alone, Matt thought, it's your bloody father.

Matt had first met Jane's parents a few months after they began dating. Jane had excitedly taken Matt from the relative safety of the university campus to her parents' home. She was eager to show him off. Her mum had been pestering Jane to introduce

Matt. From that first meeting Margaret had always been cordial and kind to Matt. Michael, it was quite clear, didn't approve.

But Michael had a way of making those around him feel that he did approve of Matt. That the words he spoke were simply misinterpreted and those listening had simply misunderstood his intentions. He openly made underhand comments about Matt and then instantly persuaded his audience that his words weren't meant to be interpreted the way that they had been. To everyone, he gave the impression that his wife and daughter meant everything to him. An ever-loving father and husband whose sole purpose in life was to protect his family. Although he used short sentences, the inflection in the way he spoke gave the impression that the words he spoke were genuine. It didn't quite ring true to Matt; the words lacked any depth or feeling. Words read from an autocue, selected and devised purposefully so as to always show Michael in the very best light. However, when Michael spoke about his interests outside of his family, his voice seemed to take on a truer tone. There was something tangible there. When Michael spoke of work and clients and money and power, there was feeling. Feeling that was missing in his family conversations. Money and the power that it brings were much, much higher up Michael's list of priorities.

Matt despised how Jane and Margaret let Michael behave in the way he did. Interrupting their sentences with snide comments or gestures which would cut them dead. Listening for a moment or two before correcting some aspect of what his daughter or wife were saying. The superior tone which led all conversations quickly back to Michael. But for some reason unknown to Matt, his future wife and her mother *did* allow him to continue in this way: a permanent invitation that allowed Michael to behave in any way he chose. Whenever Matt questioned Jane, she would churn out the same unconditional answer: "Well, that's just Dad's way." And when he asked Margaret, he should have expected the almost robotic "It's Michael's way".

Had he had the confidence to tackle 'Michael's way' earlier in the relationship he wouldn't have found himself over the years being sucked into this ridiculous charade. More crushingly, he wouldn't have found himself using the same words when making excuses for Michael to his own family and friends.

This wasn't to say that Michael was completely unlikeable; he wasn't. At times when they were talking Matt had felt accepted, like he had made it through some invisible barrier. In these conversations Michael's tone suggested he was speaking from on high to where Matt was grounded below. But Matt accepted this on the basis that he had been entrusted with Michael's only daughter and it was paramount that he treasured her.

At family meals or drinks at the local pub, Michael would sometimes greet Matt with a sharp pat on the back. When Jane was around he would seemingly listen to what they had been doing, how work was, the usual. There was always a slight air of disapproval, but rarely overt enough to ruin an occasion. And of course Margaret was always there, a conduit to keep the conversation flowing or if necessary strategically switch a subject when she felt like it may not suit Michael or the conversation had gone a little too far down a certain path.

There had been times when the 'women' (as Michael referred to them) had gone off to bed and Michael and Matt had stayed up drinking. It would always be at the suggestion of Michael that they shared one of Michael's thirty-year-aged whiskies. Matt had interpreted the fact that he was sharing a bottle of Benromach, or some other unpronounceable whisky, as evidence that he was accepted. Worthy. As the tiny measures were poured from the bottle time and time again, Matt may see a flash of Michael's stained teeth for a second or two as he threw his head back and laughed. It was for these moments that Matt felt it was worth keeping the family equilibrium. Although these situations were rare, Matt felt a rush of incredible elation when something he said brought about this reaction from Michael.

He felt like he was getting somewhere.

He had been finally recognised as a member of the family.

But the elation would be invariably short-lived and the conversation would become serious again as Michael realised he had let his guard down. He would remove his glasses and slowly place them on the arm of his high-backed chair. And then, focusing his steel-grey eyes directly on Matt, he would take Matt's hand in his.

"You'd never hurt my daughter, would you?" he would say.

"No, of course not," Matt would respond, his eyes filled with sincerity.

Michael would increase his grip on Matt's hand and Matt would shake his head, repeating his promise over and over until Michael's grip became looser. Then Michael would smile and pour another measure each, and Matt would smile and drink his whisky, and know that, as far as getting closer to Michael, he was back where he began.

Jane and Matt held hands across the breakfast bar, his thumb repeating an up and down pattern on the outside of her hand.

"He'll be fine, I promise."

Jane smiled a distant smile. Matt finished his coffee.

"I'm just tired. It's just, well, he's been so different since, Mum. So negative and distracted and…I'm really worried about him."

It was true; Michael had been negative and distracted. But no more than usual, Matt thought. He had seen little change before or after the accident.

"Come on, drink up. Like you said, you're just tired."

He smiled at her. This was no time to get into a dispute about her father's personality. So many thoughts had built up inside that he worried that if he did begin to speak, he may never stop.

six

It had been a fitful night for Jane. Not so for Matt, who had slept soundly alongside her. Jane had turned to cuddle him on occasion but found herself pushed back across to her side of the bed. She had concluded that he must be exhausted and decided to leave him untouched on the other side of the bed. Jane had tried to get comfortable but hadn't managed it. It was as if she had a mental tick-list of the actions she needed to carry out before sleep could eventually throw its warm arms around her and envelop her until her mind stopped whirring. Each time a thought would jump into her mind she would act on it, convincing herself that if she completed that task then sleep was just moments away. If she just switched positions, or emptied her bladder, or had a glass of water that would help her to meet her dreams. But completing the tick-list hadn't worked, and instead she had stared into the darkness of the room for several hours.

She hadn't slept properly for some time now and her friends had convinced her that a doctor's appointment would probably be in order. Jane had considered it, but wasn't the type of person who gave up on a problem by simply medicating it. It didn't match her personality. The only time she would truly settle was when she worked through the problem. Her mind would rotate, and she'd visualised the problem that she was trying to solve in the middle of her mind, like some heavy stone centrepiece in a darkly lit gallery. She would look at this problematical monolith from the outside in, and rotate her line of vision around it, trying to change her perspective, trying to get a new angle on it. Searching for the solution. She would approach it time after time, night after night. And when she thought she was close to solving it, it would quickly metamorphose into a longer or rounded or more contorted shape and she would have to start over. Usually, after many weeks of sleepless nights she would finally corner the problem, finally allow it to shape-shift no more. And then it was tamed and it became the correct shape to file away in her mind. It was an exhausting process but it was the only option which made her feel she had confronted and overcome the issue.

She sat upright, her back cushioned by several pillows against the wall, and watched the illumination of the red digital numbers on the clock which sat on the bedside table next to where Matt lay. Without diverting her stare, she watched time pass by as the numbers made their way to the pre-set moment when the clock filled the room with its woeful, intermittent buzz. Six o'clock. Greeted by the sound of hell.

Matt turned his head away from her, dragging his face along the pillow one hundred and eighty degrees toward the clock. His fingers flicked the switch to 'off' and his right arm flopped down toward the floor.

"Morning," said Jane.

"Hwmwmmm," he said, leaving his mouth open on the sheet.

Jane put her hand on his wide, naked back.

"Time to get up."

"Hwmwm, I know."

"I'll get you a coffee."

Jane climbed from the bed, relieved that the day had at last started. She pulled on her pyjamas and went downstairs.

She pulled up the wooden blinds in the kitchen, the morning sunlight causing tiny specks of silver in the black work surface to dance. It was quite a nice start to the day. It looked cold, but the sun had already thrown its light on a small quadrant of their averagely sized, yet perfectly tidy garden. The grass glistened and a small plopping sound came from the tiny pond in the corner. The pond was covered by a stiff plastic net which Matt had put down in preparation for the one that never came. Butterflies quickly fluttered in her chest.

She flicked on the kettle and whilst it sloshed and bubbled she picked up her phone, which had been charging on the side through the night.

One message.

No missed calls.

She had half-expected that her father may have rung to say that he had arrived safely or that the hotel was of an acceptable standard. The message was unlikely to be from her father. It was very rare that he texted people because he didn't approve of it. Indeed, he had stated on more than one occasion that he was 'opting out of texting' on the basis that 'the country was fucked and society had long since lost the art of conversation'. She entered her PIN and flicked to her inbox. It was Martha. Jane glanced at the message time: late the previous night. It started with an apology should the text have woken her. Jane smiled; chance would have been a fine thing. Martha was wondering whether, at short notice, Jane could come in to work in the shop that day. The only other staff member had called with a pressing family matter and wouldn't be able to get into work. Martha would understand if Jane couldn't come in. Jane smiled. She loved Martha and loved the shop. She had nothing else planned that day and work would help her take her mind off things. She texted to say that she would be there for opening time.

Jane carried two mugs of coffee into the bedroom and placed

them on the long waist-height chest of drawers at the end of the bed. Matt came out of the en-suite, rubbing a towel through his hair. He smiled weakly.

"Knackered."

"Uh-huh."

"Did you sleep okay?"

"Yeah, not bad." It was easier to respond in this way; he wouldn't worry.

"Good," he said, pulling on his boxer shorts and collecting his cup. "Thanks for the coffee, gorgeous."

Jane smiled back, a smile which started at the back of her eyes and danced into the spotlight at the front. She quickly stopped herself, wondering what she would do without him. It wasn't a thought she wanted to consider that day.

"What's the plan today, lady of leisure? Back to bed? Day on the sofa?"

"No, Martha texted. I'm going into work."

"Oh, okay."

He buttoned his shirt and pulled on his tie. He dried his hair again, before using his wax stick to give it the same look it had when he first awoke. He took a large gulp from his coffee and kissed her on the cheek.

"I might be late tonight," he said as he made his way down the stairs. "We're really busy."

Jane was used to hearing this. It had become an increasingly regular occurrence over the last few months.

The front door clicked and Jane, suspended in time for a short moment, walked aimlessly over to the window. She leaned her elbow on the windowsill and stared outside. It was only six thirty; she had two hours before she needed to leave for work.

Michael awoke. He had slept fairly well. Better than for a long time.

The taxi driver had been unable, or perhaps unwilling, to give Michael any guidance whatsoever as to a good restaurant. This had caused Michael to take an instant dislike to all Spaniards. Michael had attempted a number of conversations which had been met with a stony silence. In the end, Michael had simply pointed to the next restaurant they had seen and left the taxi. The meal had been average and he had let the waiter know. 'Overpriced and needlessly complicated' was how he described it. The waiter had nodded a bemused 'okay' type look and taken the bill away. Michael had, however, enjoyed the bottle of local Tempranillo along with an after-meal whisky and the customary shot of schnapps. The relative disappointment of the meal was tempered slightly by the sprawling view from the mountains down to the bright lights. Yes, they had made his evening more memorable. He weighed up the evening and was satisfied that his three per cent tip was enough to encourage them to do more food-wise but also gave credence to their efforts on the non-cuisine side. His journey back down the mountain had been a little hazier than on the way up. When he returned to his room he retired straight to bed. He had tried to finish the last few chapters of *The Chamber* before sleeping, but his eyes had mixed the words together into a kind of papier-mâché-style black-and-white mush. He had quickly relented and flicked the switch on the lamp, turning the room from light to dark.

He rolled over in bed and let out a loud satisfying yawn. He could already feel the warmth from the morning sun radiating through the balcony doors. Pulling back the sheet, he swung his feet over the side of the bed on to the floor. He linked his fingers together and stretched, pushing his palms out in front of him. It felt good.

After Matt left, Jane left the window and retreated to her studio. She sat on the varnished wooden floor. She felt the cold of the wall on her back through her white cotton pyjamas. Her second coffee of the day sat between her legs alongside her mobile phone.

The room was a reasonable size but the large sash window at the far end to her right made it feel bigger. The walls were a perfect blast of white. On every available wall space were her pictures. To her left, just past the door, was artwork that took her back to university days. Great splashes of colour thrown on differing sizes of canvas in a Pollock-esque style. Blues, reds, yellows mixed together to blend into greens, purples and oranges. She had termed this her 'primary collection' and she had been rewarded with a first class honours degree for it. On the wall to her right were her more experimental pieces, fusing bits of fabric and foil to create a more defined three-dimensional effect. Again, her bright signature colours lit each piece with expert style. On the wall she was sitting against were more pictures, this time on much smaller canvasses, each measuring no more than a foot square. These were extremely detailed pieces. Pictures from everyday life which had been painted with such precision they could have been photographs. Her subjects again bursting with colour; traffic lights, Smarties, tropical fish, a box of children's pencils. She had termed this her 'study of society' collection.

Directly ahead were her easels. There were three. Two of the easels had large wooden frames holding canvasses of similar sizes. Works in progress. The third was smaller. This was her favourite easel; it was fast approaching its fifteenth year. They had been together a long time and in many ways they had been through a lot together. Sometimes she would sit in front of it, staring at the tiny splashes of paint which had strayed from her brush. Each tiny fleck represented some moment in time from her past. Each splash of colour represented a small piece of her life. The easel was covered in these moments of significance to the extent that the original wood frame was only visible at the very top and where the legs met the floor. Layers of bright colours had built up on top of one another over the years. More recently, however, some had been covered with specks of a more aphotic nature.

This easel held her current painting. It had taken her around four months to complete, from the moment she visualised every aspect of it in her mind to the moment it actually became real. And alive. And tangible. Jane was open about her work and because of this many of their friends had seen it evolve. The majority would stand in front of it and smile, complimenting her on yet another success. But Jane couldn't understand them. To Jane it was like she'd mixed eggs and milk and butter and sugar in a bowl and then been complimented on her wonderful cake. How could they love something that was so incomplete? Matt didn't understand her work either. As she spent hours finding the right colour and texture to paint an area the size of a thumbnail, he would lean against the doorframe and shake his head, smiling.

She stared at the painting, stripping it back layer by layer, trying to find the something about it which didn't match the vision in her mind. There was nothing. Each colour, each brushstroke was just as she had imagined. But it wasn't right. It was just so ugly. So uncomfortable to look at. To take in. The deep purple background held a thud of black and brown kidney shapes which swam on top. Across the centre was a maroon triangle which began straight-edged from the left before trailing to splashed paint where its point should have been. Dark grey water bled vertically from the top of the canvas, obscuring the shapes below like prison bars. The picture glared across the room at her.

The buzz of her phone diverted her eyes. She looked down as

it playfully moved across the polished floor. It was her father. She grabbed the phone and hit the green button.

"Dad, hi. How are you?"

"Hello, Jane."

"Hi, Dad. Good to hear from you…"

"This was a bad idea, Jane."

Her heart sank. "Oh…"

"The hotel is full of fucking kids. Running and screaming."

He paused in the way she hated. The way which made her unsure whether it was her turn to speak or he had more to say.

"Oh…"

"…and shouting and…" He sighed. "It's just fucking hopeless. I'm not sure you could have sent me to a worse place."

"I'm sorry, Dad."

"I'm thinking of coming home."

That wouldn't be a good idea, Jane thought. He had been in their lives so much in the past three months. The break was designed to do him good, and do her and Matt good.

Until the death of her mother, she had rarely seen Michael. He was always with clients, or playing golf or out with friends. He hadn't time to come and see her; he was abroad visiting a vineyard or on a client's boat or at one of his profession's many black-tie events. She understood that after the accident her father would change. Without her mother he would have different needs and perhaps a different focus. She also understood that their roles would change forever. But in some ways in the period after the accident he had stayed very much the same. Still the same attitude. Still the same tone. Still the same person. Just there more. A lot more.

Too much more.

In the days after the accident, Michael had begun to appear

unannounced at Jane's house. This was unusual, but as Matt had pointed out, the whole situation was unusual. Michael had lost his wife, Jane her mother, and perhaps, as Matt had logically stated, Michael needed the closeness of his only living relative. Michael would arrive at the house and sit down on the sofa and just stare. He would refuse any offer of drinks or food and simply stare ahead at the wall before him. Jane would sit alongside him and sob or share a story or memory. Michael rarely responded. He seemed to be in some state of shock. He appeared to liven up slightly when Matt arrived home from work. Exchanging greetings, and perhaps a few sentences more. Then, after an hour or two had passed since his arrival he would stand and pull on his long grey Mac, fasten his shoes and leave. On occasion he may do this whilst Jane was in another room and she'd return to the lounge to find him gone.

The intensity of the first week following the accident lessened over time and Michael's need to be around his daughter waned slightly. After the cremation, he appeared at Jane's house less regularly. But he did still arrive a few times a week, ignoring Jane's request that he telephone in advance to let them know he was coming. At his insistence, he had a key, and would let himself quietly into the house. Then he would remove his shoes and coat in silence, listening to the voices coming from the kitchen. Several times, Jane had walked from the kitchen to the lounge only to be startled by his presence. He would be just standing there, motionless, in the hallway. She had no idea how long he had been there. When he realised that Jane had noticed him, he would simply greet her and sit down on the sofa. It appeared that he was waiting for something. Jane wasn't sure what that was.

Jane wound her finger around one of the pull strings which hung from the front of her pyjama bottoms.

"It's only your second day, Dad."

"I know what day it is, Jane."

She held the phone away from her ear, shaking her head. At that point she noticed the time.

"Dad, look, I'm really sorry but it's past eight and I have to leave for work in half an hour."

"You don't work Tuesdays, Jane."

"Well, I've been asked to work today. Sarah's not in."

"Hmm…"

"Look, Dad, I'm sorry, I really have to go. We'll speak…"

Michael had hung up.

seven

There was no possibility at all that Michael was going to enjoy the day ahead. He had decided that at the moment he had hung up on Jane. He stood on the balcony, ignoring the pool below. Instead he gazed above the high rises in the distance and toward the horizon. He followed the jet stream of a silent aircraft in the blue sky until it disappeared from view. "What the fuck am I doing here?" he thought aloud. He felt his muscles tense. He had no idea how he had been persuaded to make this journey abroad by himself. He cursed himself for being carried along by Jane's enthusiasm; that he should have a break, to 'get away from things' at home. Life had changed for the worse since the crash, much more so than he could have ever imagined.

He had never been a man for over-emotional outpourings but he had been suffocated by them for the last three months. The cards and flowers he received were all very nice; they could be discarded easily enough. Thrown into a black bin liner along with his memories. But the telephone calls and, worse still, the visits were intolerable. Friends, colleagues and, perhaps most difficult, Margaret's friends telephoning to share their feelings. Telling him that they couldn't imagine the pain he was going through. Telephoning him to say that *they* had done nothing but cry over Margaret and they wanted to share this with him. To comfort him, to let him know that that they were thinking of him. That he wasn't alone. Pah! he thought; what did they want from him? He had found it hard at times not to simply hang up the phone or ask them to leave him alone. But he was aware that doing so would only be read as a sign that 'Michael isn't coping very well' and the calls would increase in their regularity. It had been no wonder he had spent more time with Jane. Yes, people could still reach him on his mobile at her house, but there he was equipped with the very genuine excuse that he was spending time with his daughter. This seemed to appease those making contact, and over time the calls subsided. Plus, spending time with Jane served a second purpose. It allowed him to be near her so he could see how she was coping and, more importantly, let her share her feelings and thoughts about life before and after the accident.

He didn't buy for one minute Jane's excuse about having to leave for work. She was never called in at short notice. She just didn't have a reason he shouldn't pack his bags and come home immediately. He knew she didn't have a reason because he knew that he was much cleverer than she was. He felt the fury rise up inside him again. If he did go home now, he would only have to see her and be disappointed with her once again.

He considered for a second whether he could somehow increase his working hours again. This was not really a possibility as he and his fellow partners had spent the last two years winding him down to a day a week in preparation for his retirement. His substantial pension had been agreed. The vast majority of his workload transferred to younger members of the firm. He would look ridiculous if he were to change his mind now. And being a figure of ridicule was something that he simply would not contemplate.

He slid his hand along the balustrade, feeling the warm heat that it radiated. It was still early and aside from one or two people covering sunbeds with towels the pool area was completely empty. A gentle ripple spread from a water outlet, quickly spanning the pool. He would go for a swim, then a walk in the mountains away from people after breakfast. He span around, suddenly in a hurry to get into the pool before it became populated, catching his finger on the rail. It stung.

Jane arrived at the shop with eight minutes to spare.

"Hi, Jane. Super-thanks for coming in today," Martha beamed. Her theatrical yet almost-childlike demeanour never failed to cheer Jane. "Looks like Janey needs a hug!"

Martha opened her arms, revealing a huge, multi-coloured necklace which appeared to be made from Christmas tree baubles. They hung festively above her equally huge breasts. A pink vest displaying a repetitive pattern of unicorns struggled to keep them at bay, so for backup a purple mohair shawl was fastened by a hook at the neck. Her costume was finished with a black belly-dancing skirt bejewelled with gold and silver-tipped slippers.

They hugged, the hairspray in Martha's black, cropped hair slightly prickling Jane's neck.

"What's the matter today, Janey?"

"It's Dad," she sighed.

"Well, who'd have guessed?"

Martha led Jane to the purple chaise-longue next to the till and signalled with a wagging prod that she would put the kettle on.

From the outside, *Les Celestins* appeared to be nothing more than a small curiosity shop and there was no indication of the cavernous interior that lay within. The shop was enormous. Two large windows were separated by an oversized wooden door. The giant stuffed swans in the window, draped with vibrant pink boas, gave no hint of the contents within. Certainly, the huge kingfisher, complete with deerstalker style hat, offered no more in the way of clarity. Having stepped through the door you were immediately hit by a scent which suggested just how old the shop was. It was musty and the atmosphere was somehow dry. The ceiling was painted a deep red, clashing pleasantly with golden architraves and coving. And at eye level, all around you were simply books. Floor-to-ceiling books. There were no walls to see. Just books. Almost all second hand. Huge wooden shelves climbed from the scuffed oak flooring high above to the ceiling, which bowed in the centre. Visitors got the distinct feeling that should the shelves be removed the whole building would simply fall in on itself. Immediately ahead was a stairway which led to an upper floor. The stairway was also oak which was partially covered by a carpet that ran up the centre, proudly displaying naked female bodies in its tapestry. Various tables of differing heights and sizes were randomly scattered around each floor. Some displayed books, some others items which Martha found interesting. A Van der Graff generator on one, a 1960s' toaster on another. Martha had inherited the bookstore from her father when he passed away ten years previously. He, in turn, had inherited it from his father. Between various stints as a model, a dancer and an actress, Martha had always returned to work in the shop. Even back when it was simply Hartley's Books.

Jane loved the shop. As soon as she set foot in it she felt that she had been transported into her own little fantasy. She also loved the way Martha ran it. She kept it interesting. She loved that on the upper floor, near the front window, Martha had created what she termed her 'rainbow section'. This was a bookcase, probably ten foot or more in height. The books, which had been hand-selected simply based on the colours of their spines, were displayed in a perfect span from red through to violet, with each book getting a slight shade lighter. On the more quiet days, Jane would stand in front of the rainbow section and drink in the colours. Jane had mentioned to Martha that although it looked beautiful it wasn't very customer friendly because it was impossible for people to find a book there when there was no discernable order. Martha responded by designing a 'Not for Sale' sign and sticking it to the front of the shelf.

As for the rest of the shop; well, it was pretty much in order. The books simply ran in alphabetical order by title regardless of whether they were fiction or non-fiction. It would have been more sensible, of course, to have them alphabetically by author and divided by genre, but Martha enjoyed watching people have to participate in what she had nicknamed the 'treasure hunt'. It happened on more than one occasion daily.

A customer would arrive, asking for books by, say, John Banville.

"Which one would you like?" Martha would ask.

Sometimes the customer would know the title and Martha would kindly let them know that all books were in alphabetical order by title. She wouldn't take them over to the book or even point them in the right direction. "If you want something badly enough," she would say to Jane, "you have to put in some effort yourself."

Other times the customer would be unsure of the title, or perhaps had received a recommendation for a particular author and was buying for the first time.

"Do you have any idea of the title?"

"No, I'm sorry, I don't," the customer would invariably say.

"Okay, well, I'm going to treat you today."

Martha would then give the name of one book by the particular author requested. As usual, she would then kindly inform the customer of the alphabetical arrangement of the bookstore. The customer would sometimes just purchase the book that they were sent to find. However, a good proportion of the time the customer would read the blurb and find it not to their taste. They would then return to Martha.

"Do you have any other books by this author?"

Martha would take the book and carefully open the front few pages. She would run her long, polished nails down the list inside of the other books written by the same author.

"Which one would you like?"

The customer would select another title that caught their fancy. Martha would retain the first book, motioning that she was going to return this one to the shelves as the customer obviously wasn't interested in it. She would remind the customer about the alphabetical nature of the shop and send them off once again. She'd giggle as she watched them head upstairs and downstairs in search of an unknown treasure.

When Jane first began working at the shop she was astonished that anyone could deploy such a haphazard method to run a bookshop. But then she realised that Martha wasn't running a bookshop. She was living out a fantasy of running a bookshop. This was all a performance and she was the lead role. And it wasn't as if she needed the money. Her father had left her far more than simply the bookshop. It wasn't long after that Jane realised also that people didn't come to the bookshop specifically for books. They came for the performance. The entrance fee was simply leaving with a book. It was an experience that suited everyone.

Michael had to admit to himself that the swim in cool water of the empty pool was enjoyable. As he swam up and down the length of the pool, he felt the muscles in his whole body relax. At each turn at the end of the pool, he closed his eyes and let all his thoughts gently ebb away. Immersed, he felt somehow weightless and the heavy burden he was carrying seemed to be carried instead by the water. He began to count the number of strokes it took to get from end to end, until he could seamlessly time when he needed to open his eyes and take a glance at the bright world around him. This focused routine enabled him to push away the dark thoughts attempting to creep in.

After the swim he dried himself lightly and lay back on a sunbed, allowing the hot early-morning sun to complete the process. He gazed at the mountains and decided to head out somewhere quiet for breakfast. He remembered that Jane had paid for breakfast in the hotel to be included when she booked the holiday. But there wasn't a chance he was going to sit amongst the families and listen to their tedious and vapid morning chatter.

Martha carried the drinks over to where Jane was sitting. Her arrival snapped Jane's distant stare back into the present.

"Thanks," she said, taking the steaming coffee from Martha.

"What's he been doing now?"

Jane dabbed her eyes on her sleeve. Martha pulled a crumpled tissue from inside the top of her bra and handed it to Jane.

"I'm just being silly," said Jane, embarrassed to be having the conversation.

"No, Jane, darling, you're not."

Jane explained the telephone call and how worried she was about her father. She explained that she felt responsible for him now. She didn't explain that she had never felt this reciprocated by her father, or that she felt guilty for having helped him begrudgingly. She didn't need to explain this.

Martha took her hand and held it between their two faces, gently squeezing it. The bright halogen lights from above momentarily caused hundreds of colourful, dancing stars to reflect from the giant glass rings that adorned her fingers.

"He's been through a tough time," she said. "You all have."

Jane nodded.

"But his happiness isn't your ultimate responsibility. It's his, darling." She smiled. "And, Jane darling, focus on you first. You've also had a loss. He must understand that. When you're ready, focus on him."

A man appeared outside the shop door. He was smiling and tapping his watch.

Martha released Jane's hand, smiled back and waved.

"Let's open up," she said.

Jane sniffled. She gripped the tissue in her left hand and wiped her eyes on her sleeve.

eight

Michael had changed quickly in his room (khaki chino shorts, lemon linen shirt) so as to avoid any possible conversations with diners as they left the breakfast room and spilled into the hotel lobby. He applied his ten-hour sun cream (he wouldn't make the same mistake again) and stuffed his wallet and room key into his pocket. He avoided the lift (potential conversation, enclosed space, no escape) and headed down the stairs.

A man was tending the flowers in the hotel atrium, pouring water from an old plastic watering can. He turned and nodded at Michael. Michael ignored the gesture and walked briskly out of the hotel and onto the street outside. Whilst in the taxi the previous evening he had noticed the wide mouth of a dust track which seemed to lead away from the holidaying population. The sun shone intently down on the barren track beneath his feet.

Somewhere around an hour had passed when he happened upon a small row of buildings. The houses were single-storey, their white paint slightly dirtied and chipped by the elements. At the end of the row was what looked like a small café. Outside sat a man in a navy corduroy hat and grey shirt. He looked at Michael impassively. There were three tables on the pavement outside the café and Michael took the one furthest from the man. The legs on the white plastic chair momentarily buckled until Michael levelled them on the broken flagstones below.

The café was sparse. From the angle that Michael was sitting at, he could just see inside. A white Formica counter bowed, its edges peeling away in places to expose the chipboard beneath. On top was a large plastic tub containing various sandwiches and pastries, each suffocated by cling-film, making it difficult to see the contents clearly. Behind the counter was a metal coffee machine which had a delta of rust running from spout to drip tray. Inside was dark, lit only slightly by a naked bulb hanging above the counter. There was no natural light, save that which entered through the thin doorway. At that time of day the café was entirely blanketed in shade which, judging by its appearance, seemed fitting.

"*Café?*" said the man.

Michael turned his head. Michael noticed the peak of the man's hat was slightly torn, discharging its white stuffing like a pan bubbling over. His grey hair mimicked this, natural curls pushing from underneath the hat around his ears. His skin had the appearance of cured meat.

"*Café?*"

"Yes. *Sí.*"

"*Solo?*"

"*Sí.*"

The man pushed himself up from his table and ambled toward the doorway.

"Oh, and *magdalenas.*"

The man nodded and went inside.

A few minutes later the man returned and placed the coffee on the table spilling some of the liquid into the saucer below. He nonchalantly tossed down a plate and left. Michael smiled as he bit into the sugary pastry that the man had delivered. For the first time in three months he was beginning to enjoy himself. Settled in the stillness of the surroundings he was ensconced in. There was no traffic. No noise. No nothing. Just the warmth of the morning sun.

A year earlier he would never have imagined himself in this scene.

It could never be said that Michael and Margaret had not enjoyed his success. They had holidayed at the most expensive, salubrious places in the world. They had travelled on cruises around the Caribbean more times than he could remember. They had visited each continent several times. In fact, it had become difficult to find somewhere new to visit. Of course, Margaret never chose the destination. A client or professional contact would suggest a place to Michael, and he would make the idea his own. As always, Margaret would comply without complaint or question. Thank God that they had Margaret's mother on hand to take care of Jane whilst they were away. Each time he informed Margaret of the holiday they were taking she would smile agreeably and thank him for 'all the special things' he did for her. Never had he even observed a glimmer of her not wanting to go where he suggested. She simply complied. And that suited him.

But now, he found himself alone on holiday without her for the first time. And look where he was. He was not surrounded by equally successful people, talking about wine and clients and money and places-you-just-have-to-see. He was not surreptitiously checking what brand of watch they were wearing. He was not formulating his next sentence to climb the conversational hierarchy whilst half-listening to what they were imparting. He was alone with his own thoughts, with no-one to interrupt him. He was rarely alone with his own company and it didn't feel right. It had to be said that Margaret was not like the people Michael would usually surround himself with. She was not remotely interested in money or status. She had spent the best part of thirty years in these circles. Black-tie dinners. Awards ceremonies. She had learned to mould, though; to listen to the conversations and nod at the appropriate times. And over the years, she played the ever-loving wife whilst neatly fading into the background. Her husband's friends and colleagues liked her. She knew this because they would tell her. Over sprawling dinner tables they would jokingly ask her how she put up with Michael's totalitarian ways. And she would smile in her shy way and tell them that she loved him and that he had given her a life she could have never imagined. They would laugh through large puffs of smoke and ruddied cheeks and nudge Michael, telling him that 'he had a good one here'. He would glance at her, a contrived smile briefly crossing his face, before turning away and throwing his mouth wide, laughing instantaneously at the next mildly amusing comment to be made.

It was true that Margaret did feel grateful for the life she had been given. There were so many positive experiences and elements that, at times, she had cursed herself for allowing feelings of ungratefulness to creep in. She knew her role and she played it to perfection. Never cracking. Never removing the mask. But she knew, as the laughter increased and the next bottle of Martinborough Pinot Noir arrived, that slowly she was beginning to disappear.

The shop was extremely busy that morning. It seemed like every tourist in the quaint market town decided to come in that day. The cold air outside and the shop's peculiar exterior acted as a magnet. Martha enjoyed her morning of treasure hunts, spending time conversing with the clientele. With typical thespian aplomb she would exclaim loudly how she loved one lady's hat or 'simply must have a pair of those boots'. Her exuberance served to whip up a bustling trade, and Jane stood scanning book after book through the till. She would then carefully post each purchase into a thin pink paper bag which was sealed with a *Les Celestins* sticker. Martha had visited *Les Celestins* numerous times, stating more than once that the world-famous French theatre was 'the eighth wonder of the world'. She had celebrated her love for the theatre by having a simple line drawing of the exterior printed on every sticker giving each customer a reminder of their visit.

Jane swayed slightly from side to side; her legs were beginning to ache.

Suddenly, a clap of hands rang out across the shop.

"Okay, everyone," said Martha, "it's been a busy morning and my assistant, Jane, and I are tired."

The five or so customers that were left looked blankly at her.

She continued, "So we're sure you'll appreciate that our little feet need a rest."

Jane smirked; this wasn't unusual.

"So…" She stretched out her hands and then brought them together in a prayer-like way in front of her enormous bosom. "I am locking the door for half an hour. If you want to buy something then please, darlings, do it now. If you want to leave, do so now. If you want to stay and browse then do. But please don't bother us for a little while."

A man in his sixties, looking slightly fearful, motioned that he'd like to leave.

"Come on then, you," Martha said, leading him quickly by the elbow. She deposited him on the pavement and turned the big brass handle to lock the door. Flipping the window sign to display 'Open' to those who remained, she turned and flopped dramatically onto the high-backed leather chair by the doorway.

"Earl Grey, I think, Jane!"

The remaining customers stood, mouths open.

Jane went into the back of the shop to the kitchenette. The room was small and quite dark. To her left was a small sink and sideboard. Boxes of various Twining teas were strewn across the work surface. Some were empty and had been for some time. There was a cafetière which hadn't been cleaned since their first drink of the day. A sludge of coffee sat in the bottom. Somewhere in the corner there was a microwave but this had long since been obscured by the piles of books which surrounded it. On the back of the door were two hooks. One held Martha's long squirrel-fur coat, the other Jane's brown fitted duffel.

It was the first time that her father had entered her thoughts since she arrived at work and she reached into her coat pocket to retrieve her phone.

No messages.

No missed calls.

She hadn't liked how the telephone conversation had ended that morning and decided that she would call him. She scrolled to her call register and tapped her father's number. After six rings, the answer machine sprang to life at the other end.

"This is Michael Sewell. Leave a message. I'll get back to you."

Jane paused. Did she need to leave a message? Perhaps not, but she knew that on seeing a missed call, her father would contact her again. Probably at a time convenient only to him. And if that time wasn't convenient to her, for whatever reason, she would get his usual disappointed tone at the other on her voicemail. And then the balance of power would be back with him. She would feel the overwhelming urge to apologetically explain the reason she missed his call and assure him that she wasn't in the throes of anything that was more important than him.

"Hi, Dad." A bright, jaunty tone had possessed her voice. "Just to say that I hope your day is going well, and it's nice and warm…" She was rambling. "…and, well, everything is, er, okay. I mean, er, as good as it can be…and, er, I hope to speak to you soon."

She cursed herself for ringing and switched the kettle on.

Michael dabbed the corners of his mouth with a paper napkin from a metal dispenser on the table. He signalled that he wanted the bill by using his hand to write invisibly in the air in front of him. The proprietor pressed his half-smoked cigarette into the ash tray in front of him and went inside.

He brought over a small metal plate to which the receipt was neatly clipped and tossed it onto the table where Michael was sitting. He immediately turned away.

"Agua?" said Michael.

The proprietor nodded, and returned a few seconds later with a warm bottle of water, which he rolled across the table. Michael reacted quickly and caught the bottle before it hit the ground. A sharp pain shot up to his wrist. He looked down at his finger, where the pain had begun. A tiny piece of wood was clearly visible under his skin. The area around it was beginning to slightly swell and the skin had turned a scarlet colour.

The proprietor amended the bill, untidily scrawling the cost of the water on the bottom. He walked away.

Michael liked the man. He did what was asked of him without exception. He used no unnecessary words. He didn't try to befriend Michael. He didn't try to force a stilted conversation in pigeon-English and pigeon-Spanish. There were none of the embarrassed smiles and laughs as two people try to communicate in a language they don't know very well. Michael hated such conversations. Why spend time finding out how many children a stranger had? Or which football team they supported? You would never see one another again. Nobody gained anything from that conversation. In Michael's opinion the chat was just a means for the waiter to get larger tips. Why it was that customers in restaurants around the world played along with this charade of responding to a waiter's inane questions he couldn't fathom. It was so obvious: the waiter wanted to maximise income and was quite prepared to conversationally prostitute himself to do so. The customer joining in made no sense, unless the customer was stupid. Michael had concluded long ago that most people were.

The bill came to six euros. Michael left ten. The proprietor should be rewarded for keeping out of his life.

He picked up the water and left, following the dust track on. The proprietor didn't look up. Michael didn't look back.

many years ago

nine

Michael Ernest Sewell had first met Margaret Seversby in 1977 at the offices of Milton, Knight and Haxby. On the seventh day of October, he had walked proudly into the quaint offices of his first employer. Having completed his degree and then his legal exams, he had been informed three weeks earlier by the principal, George Haxby, that he had been successful in his application as junior solicitor. The offices were housed in an average-sized Tudor building in a small market town just outside Oxford. The firm had been established by the great-grandfather of Alan Milton some hundred years earlier. Michael was the fourth qualified solicitor in the practice. The other three lawyers had their own names above the door at the eponymously named practice. From the moment Michael first stepped foot in the office that morning, he believed that one day 'Sewell' would be added to the sign. Accepting a job at this firm, which seemed not to have moved on very much since it first opened its doors, appeared the ideal opportunity for Michael to make his mark in the world. His parents (father: a miner; mother: a housewife) had assured him since he was very little that one day he would be someone known throughout the world. Without the distraction of siblings, he was continually reminded of their dreams for him throughout his childhood. And so a mixture of excitement and pressure overcame him as he pushed open the large panelled wooden door. There was, however, just a little tinge of regret that neither of his parents were alive to see this day.

He had been in the reception area once before when he attended his interview. The room was fairly large, lit by a single window which looked out onto the street outside. The dark oak panelling that covered the walls seemed to lean slightly, pulling the size of the room inwards. There were a number of chairs lined up in a row against the wall. After the last chair was a small table on which lay a scattering of leaflets and a spider plant, its long leaves reaching to the parquet floor below. Opposite were large carved wooden stairs, half-covered with a maroon carpet which ran up the middle. Michael had never been up the staircase and wondered whether that was where his office would be. He gazed around the room, allowing myriad dreams to enter his mind.

"Can I help you?" a voice asked.

Michael snapped back into the present.

Immediately behind him a woman appeared and wedged herself into a high-armed wooden chair behind a large desk. From the side where Michael stood, the woman's stockinged legs were framed in the exposed gap between the drawers. A telephone sat to the women's left, a typewriter just off-centre to her right. The woman smiled a chubby smile from below her enormous, round glasses.

"I'm..."

"Mr Sewell," said the woman.

Michael liked the ring of that.

"Yes."

"I remember you from your interview, Mr Sewell," she said.

"Oh yes, of course."

Michael felt extremely important. He had parted his sandy hair perfectly that morning in the mirror, and applied Falcon hairspray until his hair hardened, giving the appearance that it was black. His navy suit was had been pressed and, just as his mother would have insisted, he had starched his white shirt. He had knotted his tie over and over until he was pleased enough with its shape to attach his silver tie clip. He had then added his silver glasses to his perfectly shaven face. His long brown Mac completed the outfit. On the bus journey into work he had worried that he may not look like a solicitor. The way the woman had addressed him let him know that he most certainly did.

The woman picked up the phone and pressed the small transparent cube marked '1'.

"Hello, Mr Milton. Mr Sewell is in reception."

She replaced the receiver.

"He won't be a moment, Mr Sewell. Please take a seat."

Michael walked over to the chairs. This was the beginning of his new empire. He put down his black leather briefcase on the first chair and sat alongside it. Five minutes later the floorboards above him gave an audible creak, and moments later he heard soft, deliberate footsteps padding their way towards him to his left. From the corner of his eye, Michael saw a hand grip the large wooden ball which signified the end of the bannister. He turned his head.

"Mr Sewell, good morning," Mr Milton smiled. It was clear from the lines on his face that this wasn't something he did regularly.

Michael stood and reached out his right hand. Mr Milton stretched out his, and the two hands clasped one another for less than a second. Michael noticed once again that his firm, almost persuasive handshake contrasted noticeably with Mr Milton's effort. It was like gripping a toad. The human contact obviously made Mr Milton uncomfortable and he retracted the amphibian almost instantly. Michael enjoyed the exchange, immediately recognising his own superiority.

"Morning, Mr Milton."

"Well, we'd better get you to work."

"Of course."

Mr Milton turned and began the journey back up the stairs. Michael collected his briefcase and followed, keeping a few steps behind. As they walked in silence he considered Mr Milton's appearance. Grey hair unbrushed; messy. A shirt that had perhaps once been white; unironed. A gaudy maroon and blue paisley tie. Unpolished shoes. This one is here for the taking, Michael thought.

Michael finally made it to the top of the stairs. At the top was a large, open landing with a number of oak-panelled doors. Mr Milton took him to just inside the doorway of the offices of the other two partners in the firm, who momentarily looked up from their desks. They seemed subtly enthusiastic but mainly distracted about their working day ahead. They obviously had more pressing matters to deal with and, like Mr Milton, didn't waste time making small talk. Michael got the distinct impression that Mr Milton was simply unable to make small talk. He was awkward and introverted, certainly not someone you would expect to go out and charm clients. Haxby and Knight, on the other hand, seemed more dynamic. Both appeared to be keenly focused on the business and their clients. They didn't have time to waste making small talk, they had money to make. Michael admired their commitment, but he sensed immediately that they would be more difficult to dislodge in his climb to the top.

Mr Milton took Michael into a room which, the hand-painted door sign declared, was 'The Typing Pool'.

"This is Mr Sewell," Mr Milton said. "Introduce yourselves and show him to his office, would you?"

Mr Milton didn't wait for an answer but retreated quickly across the landing to his own office and closed the door.

In the typing pool, Michael met with the only other two employees in the firm. Lynne, a lady in her forties, had a shock of blond hair. She wore thick red lipstick which had the consistency of pâté. Her eyelids were painted a shiny light blue. Her fingernails, which extended claw-like, were painted to match her lips. She smiled in a way that suggested that any joy she experienced in life was categorically outside of the workplace.

"I'm Lynne," she said, "and this is Margaret."

On hearing her name Margaret looked up from beneath her long fringe. She had brown eyes which matched the colour of her hair and a small, childlike face. She was pretty in a plain, 'all her features were in the correct place and none were too big or too small to be noticeable' type of way. She smiled shyly.

"Hello," said Michael, addressing them both.

Lynne sighed, pushing herself back from her desk using the wheels of her chair.

"I'd better show you to your office."

Margaret had always treated Michael like royalty. Right from that first moment they met. He was a solicitor and she…well, she was simply a secretary. He was her superior and she knew the importance of treating all the solicitors at the firm with total subservient respect. They were, after all, the people who earned the income to provide her with her own. From the day he had walked into the typing pool she been transfixed by him. He wasn't overly attractive. He wasn't even instantly likeable. But she immediately recognised his authority, the way that he stood and oozed dominance in the room. She was sure that he was going to be successful. She could also tell from those first few words that he was driven, that he would ensure his own success. These were all traits that she didn't share with him and their presence excited her.

Margaret had always dreamed of writing books for a living. From a young age she had collected scraps of paper filled with thoughts and short stories which she dreamed she would one day transform into longer ones. Stories that would be available worldwide, that would be in every bookshop in every town. While others her age collected dolls and coins, she collected sentences. She would make detailed notes of things she heard people say, observations she made and thoughts she had. Because of this, Margaret was always just outside the circle of her school friends. She did something different to the things that they chose to do, and in her early teens this made her a slight outsider. In those days they called her a wallflower. And when she wrote, she felt perfectly blossomed. From time to time she would write a tale of some adventure, casting one of her friends in the main role. When she was satisfied with it she would sit and read it out loud. Her friends, in turn, would sit wide-eyed and listen to her, transfixed by her storytelling. After she wrote half a dozen stories for her close friends, word began to spread. Soon she would be approached by girls who hadn't ever spoken to her before. They wanted to be included in a story written by Margaret. They wanted to be cast as the heroine in a tale invented entirely in Margaret's bedroom after the school day. The requests became a constant, so much so that Margaret had to write a list of names to keep up with the demand. Regardless of how they projected themselves amongst their peers, each girl was silently captivated by Margaret's stories, utterly enchanted by her seemingly endless plot structures. But after many months of writing and then reading her stories, Margaret became tired of the same requests. Girls now invariably asked her to include not only themselves in the story but also a boy, and she had no desire to continually churn out the same message. She was tired of the formulaic structure. It went:

Introduction of friend (looks; hair; brief dislike/likes).

Friend enamoured of boy.

Boy doesn't know friend exists.

Friend and boy meet at a local dance.

Boy kisses friend.

Friend and boy live happily ever after.

And so, at around fourteen, Margaret's short-lived popularity disappeared at the moment she refused to write any more. From then on she spent the most of her time collecting and forming ever more intricate sentences in her room or, when she tired of writing, taking long walks alone, observing the beauty of the nature around her. She had become more and more shy and more and more introverted. She left school at sixteen with few grades aside from English, at which point her disappointed father called in a favour from an old friend and she started work at Milton, Knight and Haxby.

"It's unfortunate, Margaret…" said Michael, staring at a sheet of paper he held tautly in front of his face. He was sitting in his office, resting back in his brown leather chair. During a purposeful pause, he scraped the fingers of his right hand on the well-worn arm. A few fragments of leather descended to the floor.

Margaret stood in front of his desk, slightly cowering. The chair to her left remained vacant. Her fringe covered the top of her eyes.

"…it's unfortunate because in the six months I've been here I haven't noticed one mistake at all in your typing."

She didn't look up but could feel Michael's eyes burning through the paper.

He lowered the paper so he could see her. "So?" he said.

"I'm so sorry, Mr Sewell."

"Hmm. I expect you are," he continued, sliding the paper onto the surface of the chipped mahogany desk. "Take a seat."

Margaret sat down, using an inch or two of the area available. She was rigid.

"Tell me, are the letters R and F close to one another on a typewriter?"

Margaret instantly pictured the keyboard in her head.

"Next to each other, Mr Sewell."

"Right," he nodded, picking up the paper again.

Margaret waited, desperate to know the error that she had made.

"Deaf Mr Carruthers…" Michael read.

Margaret was mortified. She had typed the letter late the previous day and was aware that it had been sent in Michael's absence that same evening. She would not usually have considered sending it out, but in a telephone conversation with Michael he had clearly instructed her to on the basis that he was with clients and wouldn't be back in time to sign it. He had also instructed her to ask one of the partners in the firm to check it before it went. When she had tried to get approval, she had been waved away by Mr Haxby, who had said that he knew the quality of her work and "was sure it was fine". She had protested, but he was clearly in no mood to relent. She had gone in search of Mr Milton, but he was also out of the office. She was already aware that Mr Knight was, as usual, on holiday. In the end, left with little alternative, she had posted the letter.

She gulped.

"Didn't I ask you to get this checked?"

Margaret nodded.

"And?"

"I did try to get it checked, but…"

"But?"

Margaret felt her chest redden. It always did when she was nervous.

"But what, Margaret?"

"Well, I…"

"You didn't get it checked, did you?"

"No."

"Why?"

"Well…"

"I specifically asked you to do something and you failed to do it, Margaret. Isn't that the case?"

"Yes."

"So, you failed."

"Yes."

"Say it."

"Pardon?"

"Say you failed."

"I failed, Mr Sewell."

"I know you did. Don't let this happen again, Margaret."

"No, Mr Sewell."

"You can go now."

Margaret rose to leave. The redness from her chest now covered her neck and she felt like she was about to cry. She headed toward the door.

"Oh, and Margaret…"

She turned, looking up through her fringe.

"…although I doubt you meant it, it was marginally amusing."

His thin lips stretched slightly.

She turned and left.

It was the first time she had seen him smile.

about now

ten

Michael was not enjoying his walk. Being alone with his own thoughts only served to exacerbate a sudden feeling of tightness in his chest. The sun beat down relentlessly, the sweat causing his clothing to take on a much darker hue than when he left the hotel. He wasn't about to be overcome by the tight feeling and powered on forwards, directly into the sun. By his side he carried his water bottle and at times he thought about pausing for a drink. But he couldn't stop, because stopping and quenching the thirst would be failure.

The sweat continued to drip down his chest and face, into his eyes. He refused to wipe it away because that would be an admission that the heat from the sun was overpowering him. No, it was he against the sun. And he would win, because he wouldn't accept defeat. He walked on, the tightness in his chest accompanying each step.

Then a new sensation added to the pressure: a small area of his hand heating up more quickly than the rest of his body. After about an hour, the hot feeling subsided, replaced by a quick, pulsating throb. Like a tiny heartbeat. Beating in the palm of his hand.

He refused to inspect the area where this feeling was coming from. His focus remained on the sun. The sun, for its part, seemed to open its rays wider, welcoming him to come closer. It was bright and it hurt Michael's eyes to stare at it. His sunglasses hung neatly from his shirt, one arm posted between buttons to keep them in place. He refused to put them on to shield his eyes. He did not fear the sun; he could overpower it.

In the distance, he could see the silhouette of a small rising in the flat greyish-brown dust which surrounded him. He estimated that it was about two miles away. He decided that this was the place where he would rest.

He walked on, his mouth dry. The only sound came from his sandals scuffing the dust below his feet. Had he turned to look he would have seen the perfect prints from his soles left in the displaced surface. The surrounding area was desolate and it appeared that nobody had been along this route for some time. It was a route that was leading to nowhere. Except the sun. High above the mound, far in the distance, he could see the jagged grey outline of the mountains. Michael focused his gaze directly into the sun, staring intently at it as if to challenge its power.

His hand continued to throb.

He quickly rejected his mind's suggestion to stop or rest for a moment, a thought that flashed into his consciousness from time to time. He was getting tired, and had there been anybody watching his journey they would have readily observed his pace slowing, the distance between his footprints becoming ever closer, his tall, upright stance becoming ever more hunched as the sun forced endless rays upon him.

He would not stop until he reached his goal.

The sun's movement from ahead to directly overhead told him that he had been walking for close to three hours. His neck strained ever upwards, his eyes focused. The small droplets of water which surrounded the bottle when he began his journey had disappeared. The water inside was now warm.

The tightness in his chest continued, but he disregarded that. The small rising in the dust was getting near now, perhaps only fifteen minutes away. His mouth was so dry that he found it difficult to open, his lips glued together by dried saliva. Sweat followed the outline of his lips, teasing him to poke his tongue out to collect some. His eyes were blurred by the sweat which had collected there, but Michael resolutely refused to blink it away and break his stare.

He was almost there. Not far to go now.

A feeling of elation collided with the tightness, jockeying for position in his chest. He now stood more upright, straightening his back, and his scuffed footprints gave way to long, determined strides. It was nothing more than he'd expected from the moment he had started his walk.

He was going to beat the sun.

He was more powerful than it was.

He knew that.

Michael reached the rising and sat down. He surveyed the dusty landscape. Small trees with waxy green leaves peppered the area around him. The trees, withered from the heat, seemed to be crying out for water that never came. Michael could identify with the hardship they seemed to live each day of their life. From his position he could see the sea, blue and still in the distance. The fact that it was so close to the trees yet they could not access it seemed an ironic joke.

The sun, undeterred by its apparent defeat, continued to beat down intensely directly above Michael's forehead. In the time it had taken to walk to the rising, the sun had moved into a position from which it would welcome him on his return journey. He breathed quick, heavy breaths as he used the sleeve of his shirt to wipe away the sweat from his eyes. Reaching down, he removed his sunglasses from his shirt and placed them victoriously on the bridge of his thin nose. He then twisted off the white plastic lid of the bottle and drank down the water. He felt a sharp burst of pain as he twisted the cap back onto the bottle, which reminded him to inspect his hand. Having succeeded in his battle against the sun, he now allowed himself to do this.

He stretched the fingers of his right hand out as wide as they would go and held his palm in front of his face. The pain was coming from his second finger at the point where it met his palm. The area had risen slightly and was an angry red. On closer inspection he noticed a small piece of wood deep in his flesh. A yellow bubble had begun to form around it. Where the swelling reduced to meet the unaffected skin on his palm he noticed that the redness had begun to stray southwards in the general direction of his wrist. It was obviously infected, and the small line moving away from it meant that the infection was spreading.

Michael sighed. It would have to wait until he returned to his room. In his leather bag he carried a small multi-purpose pocket knife with enough useful tools to remove the wood and treat the infection.

He gulped back another glug of water. Feeling refreshed, he was ready to make the journey back to his hotel. He glanced at his watch and noted that it was just past one o'clock – he would be back for five.

He stood and looked in the direction of the sun. Although still intensely showering him in its heat, it now seemed to shy away from him slightly. There was to be no challenge on the way back. The sun appeared to move to one side to allow him his path back, gracious in its own defeat.

Michael had won.

Michael always won.

He stretched and then strode down the small hillside, aware of his own power, greatness and velocity.

eleven

"Glass of *Châteauneuf-du-Pape*?" asked Martha. She turned and for the fourth time that day she flipped the sign on the door from open to closed.

"Er, I'm not sure," said Jane, buttoning up her coat. She leaned idly against the door frame of the kitchenette.

"Oh, go on," chimed Martha. "It'll do you good."

Jane considered her options. There were two. She could either take up Martha on her offer or go home. The latter was her preferred option but she didn't want to be alone and she was unsure what time Matt would be returning from work. Over the last few months, he seemed to be returning home later and later. It was some project that he had explained to her but she hadn't really understood. Matt working late could mean him returning at any time from eight p.m. to not coming home at all. For a second, she considered ringing him to see whether he could give her an idea of when he may be home. At least then she could choose between a night alone or a night with company. However, recently Matt had become quite angry about being contacted at work, and more latterly chose not to answer her calls. She put it down to the pressure of work. If she went straight home there was a high possibility that she would be spending a solitary evening on the sofa. This was something she wanted to avoid. Being alone would just lead her to worry about her father being on holiday, himself alone for the first time. She would become overwhelmed by such thoughts, unable to control the feeling of responsibility she had for her father. Should Matt return whilst she was still awake, he would be able to sense that in her behaviour. He was good at that. She wouldn't be able to rest as she would feel him looking at her suspiciously, waiting for her to make the first move and tell him that something was bothering her. Usually, he would question her once or twice, urging her to tell him what was on her mind. But she would reply steadfastly that she was fine, even though she knew that he was aware she was lying. Matt had always offered to listen to any of her problems, reassuring her that it was better to share these things than to keep them inside, but still, after all these years, it didn't come easy to her. The worry and fear inside her would grow like an inflating balloon. She'd continue to let the rubber stretch and stretch, until Matt appeared with a question which acted like a pinprick, and she could let her feelings out. Somehow, she was just unable to apply the pinprick herself.

Jane found her relationship with her father extremely difficult to deal with. She had spoken endlessly to Matt about the subject for as long as she had known him and surely now, she thought, he couldn't have the patience to listen to it all *yet again*. One day, she feared, he would tire of the continuation of the same theme. One day, he wouldn't listen any more. And her biggest fear was that when that day came, the one where he left would follow soon after.

"Well, Janey? My treat…"

Jane needed no more time to consider the invitation. She did not want to be alone tonight.

"Yes, I think I will join you. Why not?"

"Right, I'll just check everything's off upstairs, and I'll be back in a jiff, darling."

Martha scurried past Jane, her shoes making a tip-tapping sound on the wooden stairs as her chubby hands worked repetitively in tandem on the oak banister, pulling her up as quickly as her physique would allow.

Jane flashed a slight smile and reached into her coat pocket. She pushed the button on the phone, and slid her finger down the screen to get to the notifications centre. No missed calls. One text from Matt. His early-morning prediction was right: he was going to be in late; something had happened at work. Jane wondered for a second why Matt had felt the need to tell her this information again. She put it down to Matt perhaps being unsure whether she had heard him in her early-morning slumber. Drinks with Martha was the right decision. She replaced the phone in her pocket.

"Are you checking your phone?" said a distant voice from the floor above.

Jane smiled again, shaking her head. "Yes," she replied in the manner of a child who's been caught out by her parents.

"Well, don't!"

For what seemed like the tenth time that day, Jane wondered whether her father was all right. She was upset that he hadn't returned her call, but was resigned to the fact that there was a distinct possibility that he was withholding a return call simply because he knew how worried she'd be. It was exactly the type of thing he'd do.

Martha returned down the stairs, smiling. "All done." She stroked Jane's face affectionately as she passed her. Then she put on her fur coat and took Jane by the hand. "Come on, Janey darling," she said, "the darkness of the night needs us to illuminate it!"

Jane twirled to follow Martha.

A glass of wine was a good idea.

Following his walk, Michael stopped at a small supermarket to collect a bottle of whisky so if he felt so inclined, as he expected he would, he could drink alone in his room. He was disappointed to find that the shop only stocked what he would regard as the usual substandard brands and he paid for a bottle of Johnnie Walker Black Label begrudgingly. I wouldn't drink this piss at home, he thought.

It was a short walk from the supermarket to the hotel and the sun continued its relentless distribution of heat which beat down onto the white tiled pavement on which he walked. The whisky swung in his right hand as he rounded the corner to the hotel. There was a narrow black path up to the small wooden gatehouse, which acted as checkpoint to ensure only confirmed guests were using the hotel facilities. Cacti lined the path on either side, surrounded by glistening white pebbles. Tall palm trees stood behind the cacti, casting long shadows across the path. As he approached, Michael realised his route was blocked by a scene which was developing twenty yards ahead, just outside the checkpoint. He slowed his walk slightly.

A small child, no more than four years old, was lying on the floor. Its skin was red from the sun and it was screaming and refusing to move. Michael couldn't tell whether it was male or female. It had long, blond, curly hair which was matted with sand and salt. It wore small striped swimming trunks and its podgy face was caked with chocolate. Its mother was desperately trying to persuade it to enter the hotel. It became clear to Michael that it had flatly refused. The child was quite adamant that it was staying still. The mother finally lost patience and began dragging the child, oblivious that its knees were being gently skinned against the warm tarmac below.

After a few moments observing, Michael tried to bypass the scene, but the mother and child, along with an empty pushchair, blocked his path.

"Excuse me," he said.

The mother looked up. Her face was also red. "Sorry."

She tried to move to the side, but the child desisted and Michael made a small dart forward to what seemed like a route through. The pathway then rapidly evaporated as the mother's leg shot out behind her whilst the child revolved in what looked very much like a miniature death roll. Michael stepped back again.

"For God's sake, Christie, get up!"

Michael was still unclear of its sex. He felt his body tense and he curled his fingers tightly into his palms.

The child continued to scream, refusing to do what its mother had asked. "Let go! Let go! Let go!" it repeated.

The mother kept a tight grip on its wrist to stop it from making a quick run for freedom.

Michael wiped his forehead and removed his glasses. He felt rigid and he could hear the blood pumping loudly in his temples. He slowly bent his legs, crouching down to the child's level.

"Listen," he said quietly.

The child stopped, intrigued at the intervention, and looked up.

"Move out. Of my fucking way. Now."

The child's bottom lip immediately began to quiver, its struggle now over. It allowed itself to be scooped into the comfort of its mother's arms.

Michael returned to a standing position. "Thank you," he said to the mother.

The child rotated its head into its mother's neck, averting its whole face away from Michael. Its shoulders moved upwards then down as its lungs filled and exhaled rapidly.

The mother didn't speak. She wasn't entirely sure what she had just witnessed, but she knew at that moment she didn't want to see Michael again.

Without breaking his eye contact with the mother, Michael replaced his glasses and slowly walked by. He shared a nod of recognition with the man at the checkpoint as he walked around the corner toward the hotel reception.

Michael was finally back in his room. He placed the whisky on the bed and unbuttoned his shirt until one solitary button near the middle kept it together. He would accept (but only to himself) that he was a little tired from his day in the sun. Nothing, however, was going to spoil his mood. Victory was once again his. He had won and he was elated. He sat on the edge of the bed and allowed himself a few moments to bask in his own greatness.

The coins in his pocket dug into the side of his thighs and he rose and emptied them onto the small coffee table. As he did so, his finger caught on the inside of his pocket and a sharp needle of pain went from his hand into his arm. He held his hand up in front of him and noted that the line of redness was now nearing his wrist. He would need to operate and remove the tiny piece of wood.

The room was dark. The maid who had cleaned earlier had kindly pulled across the curtains to ensure that the temperature inside the room would not be unbearable. Michael strode over to the curtains and pulled them apart, instantly causing his irises to expand and then retract to take in the brightness. He opened the patio doors, which blasted hot air at him from the world outside that had become a huge oven.

Michael walked back across the room and retrieved his leather bag from the wardrobe. He had carefully hidden it inside a carrier bag, which he had placed beneath his travelling clothes inside his suitcase, which he had zipped and locked. He collected a glass from the coffee table along with the bottle of whisky and strolled back outside to the balcony. He sat down at the table.

"Come on, Janey darling. We'll sit over here at my favourite table." Martha seemed to sing the words.

Jane followed Martha to the corner table and took off her coat.

"I love it here," said Martha, "it's secluded and dark and a little bit sexy." She winked mischievously as she left for the bar.

Jane placed her coat on the mock-zebra-skin velour seat which circled the table in the booth and shuffled herself along. Jane had been to the Thirty-Eight Steps Bar on countless occasions. It was a little theatrical for her taste, which since university had remained firmly rooted in a more grungy (dirty, as Martha called it) style. Martha's good friend Alfonso owned the bar, which he had named after the novel of a similar name. Alfonso had dropped the thirty-ninth step from the bar's title, declaring that the final step was the one to true love. Alfonso had decorated the bar to his own particular taste, creating a good proportion of the items in there himself. A Barbie doll body (its head replaced by a naked red light bulb) served as a lamp at the table Jane and Martha shared.

Martha arrived back from the bar with a silver wine bucket and two glasses and shuffled in next to Jane. She was followed by Farouk, Alfonso's 'house guest' who was thirty years his junior and of Moroccan descent. Farouk placed down a bottle of Cuervo Especial Gold and three shot glasses. Martha rubbed her eyes and announced that Alfonso was extremely unwell and 'couldn't possibly face work that day because of his sudden, unexpected illness'.

"It's just so sad, so sad," she repeated to Jane and Farouk with puppy dog eyes.

"Teq-eela. For Alfonso!" said Farouk in broken English. "For Alfonso. For heez health."

Jane hated tequila and certainly was in no mood to spend the entire evening throwing back shots. She felt too fragile for that. However, as Farouk poured the tequila into each of the glasses she felt that at least at this early stage she should join in with a toast to Martha's ailing friend.

"To Alfonso," said Martha, "a wonderful, wonderful man and friend. May he soon be rid of this hateful curse."

Farouk looked at Martha blankly.

"Alfonso!" repeated Jane. Martha and Jane picked up their glasses, threw their heads back and swallowed the tequila.

Farouk followed suit.

"Another," said Martha.

Farouk picked up the bottle.

"No, no, not yet," said Jane, covering the top of her glass with her hand.

"Later, darling," instructed Martha, whilst shooing Farouk away with her hand.

Farouk at least understood this gesture and began to walk away.

"Er…"

He turned and Martha nodded sternly for him to leave the tequila. He looked embarrassed and placed the bottle back down. She motioned for him to fill the glasses with wine, which he did before bowing an apology to her.

"Sorry, Miz Martha."

"Go now, Farouk, go," she sang in the same way one would shoo away a dog.

"So," said Jane, "I'm sorry to hear about Alfonso."

"Yes, as was I, darling."

"Will he be okay?"

"I hope so Janey, dear, I hope so." She took Jane's hand into hers and gripped it tightly, as if to summon up strength.

"Can I ask, Martha, what's the matter with him?"

"Oh, Jane…" she said, throwing her head upwards to look at the maroon ceiling. "It's not good. Not good at all."

"Oh dear."

"It started with a sore throat last week, and now, well, he has the full thing. The full thing, darling. The most terrible sweats, and pain. The most terrible pain."

Jane frowned. This didn't sound good.

"The doctor has confirmed it. It's influenza, darling. He could be out of action for another week. Maybe longer. Oh, I do feel for him."

"Oh no," said Jane, trying to contain a smile, "that's terrible."

Michael adjusted his chair to ensure he was sitting in the shade and poured a whisky. He retrieved his mobile phone from the main compartment of his bag.

A missed call from Jane.

Michael shrugged slightly – there was a voicemail – he pushed the red button and deleted it. He then zipped the phone back inside the same compartment and rotated the bag to get to the press-stud pocket on the side. He fingered the inside, removing first a screwed-up piece of paper and then the red Swiss army knife. Sipping at his whisky he used his long, clean fingernails to carefully pull open the smallest knife.

He lifted his hand into the small triangle of bright sunlight across the table to get a better look. He tautly stretched the infected finger out, which resulted in a shot of further pain into his arm. The wood was deep below the surface and surrounded by an angry lemon pus. He gulped back the remainder of the whisky and picked up the knife, moving its blade from side to side, deciding on the best angle of entry. A couple of millimetres away from the splinter he pushed the knife deep into his hand, causing a mixture of pus and blood to exit into the palm of his hand.

It hurt.

He picked up the piece of screwed-up paper from the table and gently wiped away the liquid, before pushing the knife deeper into his hand. He felt the knife make contact with the wood and he flicked at it with the tip of the blade in an attempt to dislodge it from the skin that surrounded it. He removed the knife and cut again, this time from above the splinter, forcing it out from a second angle. Again he used the paper to wipe away the escaping blood. The blade touched the wood again, flicking it up, and this time it revealed itself further. Michael carefully coaxed it until half of it was above the skin's surface. He then placed the knife down, poured another whisky and retrieved the tweezers which were handily stored at the top end of the knife. He carefully grasped the end of the wood with the tweezers and slowly pulled. The splinter moved, and as it slipped out he adjusted his grip, pinching the wood closer to the wound to ensure it didn't snap. After a matter of seconds, and accompanied by one final shock of pain, the splinter was out. He placed the tweezers down on the table and wondered how something no more than a centimetre and a half long and a millimetre or two wide could cause so much pain.

Michael left the table and went into the bathroom to clean up his wound. He was disappointed to find that in his array of toiletries he had nothing that remotely resembled antiseptic cream. If Margaret had been here, this wouldn't have happened. There would have been burn cream, cream for wasp stings, antiseptic cream, plasters, cotton wool, insect repellent, you name it. Margaret was always ready for any type of emergency, no matter how remote. Michael had chided her on numerous occasions about the number of items that she packed that were simply never used. Margaret would simply smile sheepishly and nod. She knew what the outcome would be if one day she failed to pack any snake bite serum and Michael was suddenly struck down by an unlikely cobra bite. She always believed that it was better to over-pack than face the unexpected consequences. Whatever they may be.

Michael held his hand under the tap to clean the wound. Blood combined with water momentarily before spinning around the sink and into the plug hole. The water ran clear now. He turned off the tap. As he watched the water flow away he felt a sudden empty feeling of loss, which he quickly dispelled. He wouldn't allow his brain to entertain the thought of Margaret's absence, not even for a moment. Blood had now gathered at the site of the wound and Michael turned on the tap. One final blast of water to displace it. Before it could reappear, he wrapped his wet hand in a small white hand-towel and proceeded back to the table outside.

twelve

Michael removed the towel from his hand and inspected the wound. It was no longer bleeding. He placed the towel against the opening of the whisky bottle and tipped the bottle, waiting until a perfect circle of the white towel turned a deep brown as the liquid soaked in. He then dabbed it in and around the wound, gritting his teeth slightly as the whisky met with his blood stream. Inspecting the wound again, he was satisfied with his medical work and as a reward poured himself a further whisky. He then replaced the tweezers in the knife and put the knife in the bag. The 'click' of the press-stud indicated that the knife was safely stowed and Michael sat back and stretched, taking in the clear blue sky that seemed to glimmer in the early-evening sun.

A light breeze somersaulted the screwed-up piece of paper across the table and Michael grabbed it just before it reached the edge of the table and fell to the floor. Placing his whisky down on the table, he unwrapped the paper and held out the diagonally opposite corners, restoring it to its original rectangular shape. The paper was a muddy cream colour, similar to that of a tea bag. The bottom right-hand corner was slightly wet, tarnished by the mix of red and yellow liquid from the surgical site. Centrally at the bottom of the page was the number 163. At the top, in bold capitals, the name DIRK HEILLE. Michael quickly recognised the paper as the page which had attached itself to him the day before at the swimming pool. It was from a novel. His eyes scanned the page, reading quickly with a half-interest in what tiny part of the unknown story had been randomly blown to him by the wind. As he reached the damp part towards the end of the first side, he sat up sharply. He quickly turned over the page and read on. His eyes jumped from word to word and his forehead furrowed further as he reached the end of each sentence.

He stopped reading and sat upright, rigid. He pulled his chair in closer to the table and, holding the page in his right hand, flattened it out in repetitive strokes. He then turned the page back over to where he first began on page 163 and started to read again, more slowly this time. It was difficult to be entirely sure, due to the fact that Michael did not know the background to the story, but the excerpt from the book seemed to describe the aftermath of an accident. The main character, who shared Michael's name, seemed to have survived the accident but his wife, Margaret, sadly had not. The novel, it seemed, was written in simplistic English, in small, sharp bursts of sentence, many of which were mono- or disyllabic. Based on the language used and the name of the author Michael suspected this novel had been translated from perhaps German or some Scandinavian tongue.

He continued to read slowly. The main character clearly blamed himself for the accident; he told his daughter that he 'should have driven more carefully that night'. The daughter, it seemed, didn't seem to agree that her father should take the blame. She clearly pointed out that 'it was raining that night'; that 'it was simply an accident'. The story continued over the page to a point where the lead character was leaving to go on holiday alone for the first time. 'A holiday', Michael read, which 'would end in grave consequences'. On that sentence the text abruptly stopped, about two thirds of the way down the page. All that was left was the number 164 sitting adrift and isolated, at the bottom.

Michael slowly turned the page back over again and gulped

down another whisky. He laughed quietly, before easing himself backwards in the chair and resting his glass on the white hair around his navel. The nature of the story was indeed coincidental given his own circumstances, but that was all it was, a coincidence. He cursed himself for even thinking that this could have anything to do with his own life. He quickly banished a tiny feeling of fear which he had allowed to spring uninvited into his thoughts. The fear retreated back to the place it had arrived from. A place in the cold darkness deep in the back of his mind. He carefully folded the page into quarters and placed it alongside his traveller's cheques in the main compartment of his bag.

thirteen

Michael dried himself off, having enjoyed a long, hot shower. The water had stung the back of his neck where the sun had left its mark. He felt slightly woozy from the afternoon's whisky consumption. He swayed slightly as he stood and eyed himself in the bathroom mirror. Tiny blood vessels formed crimson river deltas around his grey eyes. He didn't feel hungry, the alcohol seemingly numbing his need to eat and instead crying for him to drink. He decided that he would again head out of town towards a small, softly lit tapas bar that he had passed in the taxi the night before. Then, if he felt hungry, he could eat. If not, he could simply watch the sun set over the night-time pandemonium that existed where the ocean met the beach. He would be far away from the snivelling children and their sickeningly fake families. Far away from the music and noise and laughter.

He parted his hair, applied his deodorant and splashed on some Paco Rabanne XS, before getting dressed. Cream chinos and a mint short-sleeved shirt. He collected his black bag and locked his door behind him. He was relieved to find he was the only passenger in the lift, and a drunken finger managed to hit the button marked '1' as well as another marked 'G'.

"Shit," he said.

The lift opened at floor one, the doors barely having chance to retract as Michael held a heavy thumb on the button to close them again. The lift continued its descent, and once the doors opened Michael walked swiftly out and through the air-conditioned hotel reception towards the outdoor courtyard which led to the checkpoint. It may have been the slightly fuzzy feeling that stopped him a few yards short of the checkpoint and made him turn around; he wasn't sure. However, his feet clearly had different ideas regarding his route, and moments later he found himself heading down the steps toward the swimming pool. Fortunately, the pool area was mostly empty (the families no doubt already in some loud restaurant by the beach, the parents trying to give the appearance of enjoyment while the children moaned and screamed about anything that didn't suit them) save for a handful of people taking in the last rays of the day. Michael marched toward the roped-off pool area where he had been the day before. It was almost deserted. He ignored a nod from a man cleaning the pool and headed in the direction of his sunbed. When he arrived he sat on the edge of the bed and surveyed the scene around him. Then he stood and quickly set about looking in each of the tall metal bins dotted around the perimeter of the pool. The bins, each neatly enclosed in a cardigan of willow screening, had all been emptied. A shiny new bin bag in each. There had only been a slim possibility that any further pages from the book would have still been there anyway. Somehow, though, Michael's curiosity had led him there.

"You're a fucking idiot, Michael Sewell," he said quietly to himself, "a fucking idiot."

He turned and left.

He needed a drink.

A man on a sunbed across the pool lifted his sunglasses. His eyes met with those of a woman who sat upright on her sunbed a few metres away. The man raised his eyebrows. The woman smiled and then looked back down at the book she was holding. She began to write in it again.

Jane had spent the last two hours offloading her current worries to Martha who, it had to be said, was an extremely good listener. From time to time their conversation had been broken when one of Martha's many friends had appeared at the table with an offer of a drink and the usual dramatic greeting. The friends would stay for a matter of minutes before flouncing off elsewhere to 'show their faces' to the other patrons. But Martha had listened, and nodded and advised only when she thought it her place. The problem was that each time Jane delved deeper into her innermost thoughts, Martha felt it appropriate to pour another tequila. And Jane, feeling that with each shot her mind allowed her to escape a little more, drank each one down almost medicinally.

Through the alcoholic mist, for the first time she could remember, Jane shared her feelings about the sheer volume of loss she had felt over the last few months. She sniffed back tears on more than one occasion, denouncing her own actions as 'silly'. She talked about the horror of the accident; about learning from her father that her mother had died. She spoke about her deep feelings of responsibility for her father; how she now felt that she had to take care of him. To push her own bereavement aside. She spoke about how she felt unloved by and disassociated from her father. And she spoke about her fear of being alone, and her anger that Matt was rarely around both before and, even more so, after the accident. Not there to help her through. To listen to her problems and help her make sense of the jumbled thoughts that spilled over the top of the neat boxes in her mind. Like toys spilling over the side of an undersized toy box, her fears and memories fell over one another, and she had to battle constantly to stop them hitting the floor. She felt that over the years she had somehow overused Matt and he was now tired. He was spent from the years of self-analysis and late-night conversations; now he had little left to give. Interestingly, Martha had pointed out that perhaps he had never been there as much as Jane had perceived and perhaps the gap her mother's death had left had suddenly made this more evident. Jane hoped that this wasn't true. Martha told her to let her tears flow and pulled her close on several occasions, leaving the residue of Jane's tears on her enormous bosom. Jane was fully and deeply committed to telling her tale, and the extravagant characters that appeared at the table and left always gave a sympathetic backward glance to Martha, who nodded appreciatively. It was unlike Jane to share herself in this way, even more unlike her to do it in public. But the combination of wine, tequila and Martha had assisted her. She was unsure whether the release of the weight of her thoughts or the heavy effects of the alcohol were bringing any clarity, but for now as far as she was concerned it felt good.

"So, how many do you think, daaarling?" slurred Martha.

Jane snapped out of what had been a prolonged stare at a Red Bull fridge across the bar. The light which proudly displayed the energy drink logo had been flickering for some time. It had kept her attention.

"Huh?" Jane said, unable to fully focus on the question. She made a vain attempt to turn her head toward Martha, but her eyes remained transfixed by the fridge. She was waiting to see whether the count in her head matched exactly when the light came back on.

"Janey, I'm talking. How many do you think?"

The light came on.

"Er."

Jane's head lolled from side to side like a pendulum, gently slowing in pace until she was facing Martha. Her eyes, still fixed in the endless stare, refocused down the length of the table at Martha.

Due to the number of guests arriving and several necessary toilet visits they had changed seating positions numerous times. Their current position was Martha at the head of the horseshoe table, Jane perched at the end of the right heel.

Martha was playing with something just below the height of the table.

"How many do you think there are?"

Jane giggled. "Martha, I have no idea what you're talking about!"

Martha stopped playing, in sudden shock. "Oh my goodness! Does Alfonso even know?" she said, apparently talking to the seat to her right. She laughed.

"Pffffh," exhaled Jane, smiling. "Are you talking to a seat?"

"A what?"

It was getting noisier now, the beat-driven dance music signalling that the after-work drinkers had left and the bar was beginning to cater for the night clientele. The ones who had been sensible enough to go home, shower, eat and then change before coming out. For today, Jane and Martha didn't fall into that bracket.

"A seat! Are you talking to a seat?"

"No, darling, I am not."

Martha pointed to below the table level on her right, her left hand making a 'Shh' motion on her lips, as if there was a sleeping baby tiger cub that mustn't be disturbed next to her. Jane tried to stand to peer over the edge of the table, but drunkenness stopped her and she grabbed the table edge to steady herself before falling heavily back to where she started. Martha giggled, again repeating her quietening motion.

To see what Martha was referring to Jane would have to stand and approach the left side of the heel of the horseshoe. It was not going to be too difficult, but perhaps a shot would assist her.

Perhaps steady her. She reached across the table to pick up the bottle of tequila, which was now significantly lighter than a few hours earlier. She smiled at Martha, pouring two further shots, which left the tequila bottle quicker than she had expected, flooding onto the table. Martha reached across and grabbed her glass from the puddle where it lay. In unspoken unison they simultaneously drank them and clattered their glasses back onto the table. The tequila bottle was now empty.

Jane then hauled herself onto unsteady feet and, using both hands, began her navigation of the thirty-six inches or so of the wooden end of the table. She was slow and meticulous, fixing her eyes on Martha's as she moved along, inch by inch, unwittingly nudging the ice bucket along before her. Her feet shuffled silently under the table. As she approached the edge, Martha gave her a 'you can do it' smile and switched her 'Shh' hand signal to a jolly-looking thumbs up. As Jane grabbed the end of the table in her final movement she managed to sweep the bucket over the edge of the table, and dump its contents – slushy cold water – onto the baby tiger.

In a scene similar to Dracula awaking in his coffin, Farouk shot up from his position on Martha's lap directly into Jane's face and screamed camply, *"Hwini! Hwini!"*

Jane, utterly shocked to see the man appear from absolutely nowhere, screamed and then stumbled backward, falling onto the carpet below her.

"*Hwini!* It's cold. It's cold."

He began wiping his chest down with a handful of serviettes from the table. Jane lifted her head and stared up from the floor. She could vaguely make out his face. In the dim red light however, should could make out his chest and that is when she discovered that Farouk was a hairy man. An exceptionally hairy man.

Farouk began to untwist his shirt, which had escaped the majority of the liquid due to the fact that Martha had all but taken it off whilst he slept.

Martha laughed; she was enjoying the spectacle.

"Janey, are you all right?"

Jane nodded, before laying her head back down in the crook of her elbow. "I'm happy here," she said, smiling.

"So, how many do you think?" said Martha.

"How many what?" said Jane, without opening her eyes.

"How many hairs does Farouk have on his chest?"

Jane allowed one eye to open.

Farouk had managed to get one full arm back in the shirt. He was now attempting to get in the other.

"A lot," said Jane. "A lot."

fourteen

Michael finished the last of his fried chorizo in garlic and olive oil and wiped around his mouth carefully before throwing his napkin down. The napkin landed on the numerous terracotta dishes which were spread across the small oak table in front of him. The dropping of a handkerchief in medieval times would have signalled the beginning of something; in Michael's case his action meant quite clearly he had finished. He had forced down a meal of several small dishes simply to ensure that he could drink more that evening and the hangover which would invariably greet him the next day wouldn't be quite so bad.

After leaving the hotel earlier that evening, Michael had found a small local bar en route to the hills and had enjoyed a couple of glasses of cold Estrella. Following this, he had headed up the hillside to where he was now. It was only when he had been seated in the large, dimly lit back garden of the restaurant that he had really accelerated his drinking. He wasn't entirely sure how he had made it to this establishment.

He had started in the direction of the small place he had seen the night before. Whether the drink had been a contributing factor he didn't know, but he had found it near impossible to find the same place on foot. A number of bars he had found looked similar, but that being said, so did most places on the hillside. They were an array of dimly lit, 'candle burning at each table' restaurants with tables too close together and the feeling of intimacy shared with couples less than a foot away. He had strolled past one or two before settling on a larger, yet still quiet place where he could be alone without staring into the eyes of sickeningly happy couples whispering admissions of love through the warm Spanish air.

Eventually he had come across this restaurant and settled upon it because of the large, sparsely populated outdoor area. The main area of the restaurant was situated inside and had views directly looking toward the sea. Michael didn't care about the view; he simply wanted to be away from people. He made his way to the back of the restaurant where a large garden was split into numerous discreet seating areas. A small path wound its way to each before setting off again to the next. Each area was dressed simply with a couple of small sofas and a table. In the centre of each table was a large white candle enclosed in a smoked-glass lamp. Each area was hidden between a combination of huge Rhododendrons and twisted olive trees. Dotted in the foliage were small cacti and dark-leaved shrubs. Only the barely visible flickering lights in the night sky which emanated from candles on other tables gave away the secret that another area existed somewhere along the path. Michael could just hear muted classical Spanish guitar music from the main restaurant.

When he arrived he had ordered a bottle of white Rioja, which he finished in less than an hour. He ordered another immediately. He had then eaten.

He poured another glass of wine, the mouth of the bottle chinking rather too heavily against the rim of the glass. He placed the bottle on the table, sliding the tapas dishes to the side to accommodate it. He then sat back deep into the cream sofa and stared up at the sky. It was clear and black. It reminded him of the night he lost Margaret. Although on that night it was wet, from his position looking up at the side of the river, he couldn't feel the rain any more. He could just feel the blackness of the sky. The darkness of knowing that Margaret had now gone.

He unzipped his bag and pulled out the page and placed it on the table in front of him. For the third time that evening he telephoned Jane.

As before, no reply.

He wondered whether she was now ignoring his calls in an attempt to gain revenge in some kind of game of wills. Giving him the bitter pill of rejection that he had so happily supplied her with earlier that day. If she was, it would be the first time she had ever done so. He considered this and quickly concluded that she simply wouldn't dare. He was, however, suddenly annoyed that something could be more important than responding to him. He resolved to let her know that this was unacceptable and would not happen again. Ever.

He reread the first side of the page. Although he didn't believe in superstition, he couldn't help but think that there was some kind of message there for him. He wasn't religious or spiritual in any way. Sure, he had gone along with others when they needed to rely on their faith, but he knew it was all nonsense. At the funeral, so many had offered kind words: that God's omnipotence was all around them; that Margaret was in 'a better place' and that Michael would one day be reunited with her. He had just nodded along, managing a stretched half-smile to give the impression he appreciated the effort taken to make the statement. Inside he was unwavering. The whole God delusion was based on manufactured half-truths and mythology. Born of fear to control the weak. Put simply, total bollocks. There was no God, there was no fate, there was no redemption. One life, so fucking well please yourself and make yourself happy. Fuck the rest.

He flipped over the page and again read down to the words 'grave consequences'. They were the words that he most objected to. The rest of the story did seem to describe his current circumstances quite specifically; however, there must be plenty of men called Michael who'd lost their wives in a car accident and gone on holiday alone for the first time. Christ, he thought, it's not as if his were unique circumstances. But still, he couldn't deny that the last two words slightly unnerved him.

The pickled anchovies were beginning to repeat on him and he took another large gulp from his wine. There was less than a glass left in the bottle. He tipped the bottle up, patiently allowing the remaining liquid to drip from height into his glass. He took another gulp. It'd be whisky next. His eyes reverted to the piece of paper on the table in front of him. He picked it up.

The scuffing of shoes broke his stare away from the page as a waiter arrived at his table. Following behind him was a tall, slim, attractive lady aged around fifty.

"Here, is okay?" said the waiter, motioning to the sofa opposite Michael.

The woman smiled sheepishly. Michael quickly realised that the waiter was suggesting she share the area with him. He sat up.

"Sir," said the waiter, "there are no more seats. Can the lady sit here?" He removed the napkin and began clearing the dishes from the table.

"It's okay if not," said the woman, embarrassed. Her accent had a lilt of both chocolate and velvet.

"Er, well…" Michael was caught off-guard. He hated it when this happened. Every second of his adult life had been regimentally organised. He was always ten minutes ahead of what was about to happen. Spontaneity did not figure in the way he lived. His life was his plan. No-one else's.

"If you want to finish your book, I'll be quiet…" The woman flashed a cheeky smile, nodding towards the page that Michael held.

He stretched his mouth wider, his face taking on a sarcastic, 'very funny' pose. He motioned with his right hand for her to sit. He finished his wine with his left. The woman sat down opposite.

"That's good. That's good. That's okay," said the waiter, seemingly approving of his customers' liaison. He collected the last of the dishes, leaving the table almost bare again. "And, er, more drinks?"

"Double whisky, dry ginger and ice," said Michael, not waiting his turn. It *was* his turn.

"For you?" said the waiter. The number of bowls, empty glasses and bottles he could carry was extremely impressive.

"Can you do a mojito?" she asked.

"Sure," the waiter nodded. He turned and headed down the path.

The woman looked up nervously.

It was impossible to miss how pretty she was and Michael hadn't. She had long dark-brown hair, straightened and parted to one side, which fell to breast level. A large, wide, white smile displayed her perfectly straight teeth. Her deep-brown eyes seemed to beckon those who saw them to dive in. A few dark-brown freckles peppered her forehead and the bridge of her nose. She wore a long, floaty summer dress patterned in paisley Technicolor, with two white straps contrasting with her caramel-coloured skin of her shoulders. A white sandal, visible from the leg she had crossed, allowed deep-green painted toenails to poke proudly through.

Michael allowed the corners of his mouth to jump up momentarily.

"What are you reading?"

Michael looked down at the page; he had forgotten he was still holding it. He looked back up and lifted the page slightly higher.

"Oh."

Michael folded the page carefully back into quarters, replaced it in his bag and zipping it tightly.

"So, do you like it here?"

Michael pointed down to the floor beneath him, using his finger as a question. His head was beginning to hurt slightly, the onset of a hangover that wasn't willing to wait until the morning. As he had got older this had happened more and more, and the only way to ward it off was to continue to drink. He was also concerned that he was beginning to feel sober again.

"Well, not necessarily here. I mean the resort really."

The waiter appeared with the drinks, helpfully placing them on small sun-shaped paper coasters.

Thank fuck, thought Michael, and removed his glass. He took an immediate drink.

"Not really, no. My daughter booked it. Wouldn't have come if I'd have known."

"I'm Claire, by the way." She offered her hand across the table.

Michael nodded; what he hoped came across as a disinterested nod.

"And you are?"

"Michael," he replied. He wasn't really in the mood for small talk; the story from the page kept reappearing in his thoughts.

"Are you here alone?"

"I am, yes."

"First time?"

"First time what?"

"First time on holiday alone?" Claire smiled. "It's okay, it's mine too."

"Okay."

Claire was strangely interested in the man opposite her. Not in a sexual way. Just interested. He had obviously been drinking; the empty wine bottles that were on the table when she arrived had confirmed that. No, it was something else, something that lay behind his piercing grey eyes. She didn't believe it was possible for someone all alone in a public space to be so disengaged. If the man opposite her was really only interested in himself and didn't want to communicate with anyone in the outside world, he wouldn't have come into the outside world. He would have stayed in the quiet seclusion of his balcony drinking alone, isolated from the world.

But he hadn't.

He was here, in public, which was a silent invitation for someone to communicate with him. To break through the hardened exterior that he portrayed to the world. His rudeness was simply a diversion from the truth. From his loneliness. She wasn't about to give up yet. She would persevere for at least the duration of her drink. And anyway, *she* needed someone to talk to. And to drink with.

"So, come on, Michael," she teased, "tell me something about yourself."

"Like what?"

"Like anything."

Claire sipped at her mojito, a tiny piece of mint leaf catching between her front teeth.

"My wife died three months ago. My daughter, Jane, thought a holiday would do me good."

"Sorry to hear that. How?"

"Car accident."

"Oh, I'm sorry to hear that."

"You?"

"My husband, Paul, died just over a year ago."

Michael nodded.

"Cancer," Claire continued.

"Right."

"Bowel. Awful."

"Hmm. I expect so."

Claire took a large drink. The crushed ice clattered against her top lip.

"Do you have any other children apart from your daughter?"

Michael felt his body tense. He quickly composed himself. "No. Just Jane."

"How old is she?"

"Er. About thirty."

"About?"

"Yes. About thirty."

"Married?"

"Yes."

"Any grandchildren yet?"

"No."

"Okay. I have two sons."

Claire unclipped her clutch bag and passed a well-worn photograph across.

"Neil and Daniel. That's Paul in the middle."

Michael nodded again. "They look like you." It was the only thing that he could think to say. He had no interest in the photograph.

"Yeah, happier times…"

"Another drink?" said Michael, noticing the waiter was heading down the path. He realised he was still holding the photograph, which made him feel immediately uncomfortable. He passed it back across the table.

"Why not?" she replied, placing the photograph back in her handbag. "I'm just going to nip to the ladies'."

"Same again?"

Claire nodded and rose from the table. She mouthed 'two mins' to Michael as she passed the waiter.

She was right.

He did want to talk.

And so did she.

fifteen

"When exactly were you going to tell me that I had mint leaves in my teeth?" said Claire. Dimples formed in her cheeks.

Michael managed a slight smile. It looked uncomfortable, and suggested he was holding a mouthful of vomit behind it.

"I didn't want embarrass you."

"I think I'd have been less embarrassed had you told me. Rather than looking in the bathroom mirror and realising I had walked through a busy restaurant with a plant in my mouth."

While Claire had been away, Michael had taken the opportunity to read the page again and telephone Jane, who to his frustration had again failed to answer. She would pay for this. Claire noticed his phone on the table, next to a bottle of Disaronno which had appeared at the same time as their fresh drinks.

"Are you trying to get me drunk?" she teased.

"Not at all," said Michael, unscrewing the cap of the bottle and raising his eyebrows to form the question 'Do you want one?'.

Claire nodded her approval and Michael poured the almond-flavoured liqueur into two chunky shot glasses. They looked like giant crystals with a cylindrical hole drilled neatly in the top. The light-brown liqueur changed the entire colour of the glass. He passed one to Claire.

"To those who aren't here," offered Claire.

Michael lifted his glass.

"Salut!" she said. The celebratory nature of the word was lost in a situation which dripped with regret.

Michael nodded and they clinked their glasses, drank and replaced them on the table. Over the next few hours they repeated the same process peppered with the usual staid exchanges about previous holidays, places they liked to visit and places they'd like to go in the future. The conversation floated buoyantly on the surface; neither wished to go to the depths below where they were swimming in the sea of the thing that united them. Their loss.

"So, what was that piece of paper you were reading?" Claire asked, the alcohol giving her that extra level of confidence.

Michael shrugged.

"The page that you were reading when I arrived?"

"Oh, just something from a book."

"Obviously. But why did you have it?"

"I found it yesterday."

"And you kept it?"

"Yeah."

"Why?"

"It's interesting."

"Because…"

Michael unzipped the bag and passed the page to Claire. She unfolded it and read it. She looked up.

"Spooky."

"Hmm," said Michael, reaching across and collecting it from her. He folded it neatly again and put it back in his bag.

The bottle was empty.

"Another?" said Claire.

Michael's chance to answer was lost as his telephone on the table in front of him began to buzz, the light from its screen reflecting against the glass of the empty bottle of liqueur.

He looked down at the phone. It was Jane. He glanced back at

Claire and then stared directly at the phone, in his mind commanding it to stop.

"Aren't you going to answer it?"

Michael said nothing and waited until the buzzing stopped and the screen went dark. He looked up slowly at Claire. The light from the candle caused dark shadows to appear around his eyes.

"No, she can fucking wait for me for a change."

The tone unnerved Claire.

There was nothing that she could say.

Instead, she finished what was left of her drink and faked a yawn. She looked at her watch; just after midnight. Perhaps it was time to go.

"Take care, Janey, darling. Safe journey. Text me!"

Martha waved from the door to the entrance of the bar. She watched as Farouk helped Jane into the taxi and shut the door behind her. Seconds earlier he had been half-cuddling half-carrying Jane across the pavement to the car. The taxi driver shook his head. Farouk leaned into the passenger side window and passed a small piece of paper bearing Jane's address to the taxi driver. Martha had thought this a wise move considering Jane's current state. Also, the taxi drivers around this area were no longer locals. They drove in from the outskirts of the poorer surrounding towns to make a living in the more affluent tourist areas. It was unlikely that most of them had even been in the country for more than a few years. They were no more likely to find Jane's house than she was at this stage. If Jane had forgotten where she lived, there was no way the taxi driver would know. Martha had drawn a simple map on the back for completeness.

"She'd better not be sick in here," said the taxi driver to Farouk.

Farouk smiled, showing his perfect white teeth, and nodded.

He had no idea what the taxi driver had said. He then took a step back from the car and gave a long, rigid wave as it reversed. The firmness of the wave seemed to wish the taxi driver 'good luck'. Martha waved too, but couldn't make out Jane's face in the darkness of the rear seats. She returned to the brightness of the bar. Her night wasn't over yet.

Jane rummaged in her bag and pulled out her phone. The taxi driver watched cautiously in the rear-view mirror. She pressed the one circular button on the front of the phone and the screen lit up. The message on the screen which required the user to 'slide to unlock' the phone had moved into a new and previously unencountered place. This was confusing. She slid from right to left (instead of the usual left to right). The keypad appeared, unusually, at the top of the screen. She stared at the keypad; the letters on each key didn't look quite right, either. This was strange; her phone had never done this to her before. She looked around for inspiration, catching the taxi driver's omniscient eye in the mirror. She looked back down at the phone and a broad grin crossed her face as she realised her error and rotated her phone one hundred and eighty degrees. Everything now made sense. The keypad returned to the bottom of the screen. The letters on each key were recognisable again.

Jane's phone displayed that she had three missed phone calls and one text. She opted for the text first. When she pushed the correct place on the screen the text appeared in its own white speech bubble, announcing that the sender would 'be later than expected'. There were two kisses after the message. It was from Matt.

"Jesus," said Jane, managing to focus enough to see that Matt's message was from five to nine and the time was now ten past ten.

"You all right, love?" asked the taxi driver in an English dialect that Jane hadn't heard before. In truth he was more concerned that the contents of Jane's stomach weren't about to leap onto his upholstery.

She nodded. His eyes left hers for a second, concentrating his line of sight back to the road. He immediately glanced back at her, and noticed she was again looking at her phone.

Jane attempted to reply to the text but it appeared that the alcohol she had consumed had made her fingers balloon to double the size. The characters her shaky finger was aiming for didn't appear to be translating to the text she was trying to type in her own green bubble. She deleted the mish-mash of random characters and sat forward, holding the phone tightly in her hand to steady it. She tried again. Once again, the characters that eagerly jumped into the bubble were not the ones that her mind had suggested to her fingertips.

"Nope, it's not gonna happen," she said, smiling. "Too pissed."

She sat back. Had she have been able to appreciate her surroundings she would have known that home was just ten minutes away.

The driver continued his stare. She caught his eye and smiled back at him, the corners of her eyes crinkling slightly. He looked away. In the darkness, the car continued on, the driver careful to round the necessary corners slowly.

Drifting slightly, Jane was awoken from a half-sleep by a buzzing in her hand. She opened her eyes and focused on the screen. It was her father. She pondered, her finger hovering over the 'red to ignore' and 'green to answer' keys. Her father made the decision for her and the buzzing stopped. A green square appeared on the screen, housing the white outline of a telephone receiver. It quietly announced it was her fourth missed call from him.

The taxi abruptly pulled to a halt.

"Here you go," said the driver, turning on the interior light.

"Thanks," said Jane, putting her phone back in her bag. "How much is it?"

"Let me see." He pressed a button on the console ahead of him. "Eight pounds."

"Okay."

She passed him a crumpled ten-pound note from her purse and collected the change before pushing the door open.

"Have a good one."

The driver nodded.

She looked at the house. It was in darkness. Matt wasn't home yet.

about three months earlier

sixteen

The car had left the road on a tight bend, near a small stone bridge. The rain had made visibility difficult. Michael's speed had made manoeuvrability near impossible. The car had clipped a small stone wall which ran the length of each side of the bridge. The wall was no more than a foot or two high down its length but had metre-high stone columns which seemed to guard the entrances to the bridge. Michael's front passenger-side wheel had hit one of the columns and headed across onto the wrong side of the road. The stone column punctured Margaret's window as the paintwork on her side screeched and scraped against the wall. Then a large jolt rolled the car spectacularly onto Michael's side, its windows shattering as they made contact with the trees and bracken on the riverside. Michael heard a scream and then a large thud, as the car lurched back over onto all four wheels and came to rest in the river.

Michael felt a tightness across his chest and around his shoulders. He wiped away the blood which trickled into his eye from a small wound on his forehead and removed his seatbelt. He was okay. He glanced to his left and noticed that the passenger door was open, its frame twisted, the hinge broken. Water gushed in through its openness. Margaret was no longer in the vehicle.

It was dark, the only light coming from the moon, the heavy broken cloud making its beams more subtle. The light was further dimmed by the thousands of pieces of now frosted glass which held themselves resolutely together on his right. He reached for the interior light and toggled the switch. Nothing. Blood covered its plastic casing.

He pulled at the handle for his door, which made the usual click. He pushed on the door, which moved momentarily before clicking back in place. The water continued to pour into the car, its current coming from his left. The rain water had swollen the river to a much higher level than Michael would have expected. He was lucky that his door wasn't pushing against the flow and he again pulled on the handle. Click. At that moment he forced his elbow against the car interior, using it as a lever to force the door open. A second click.

He rotated himself, lifting his legs from under the steering column, until his feet were pointing in the direction of the car door. The water lapped against the gear stick behind him, throwing icy water against the bottom of his back. Much like a sea wall. Michael pulled himself forward, gripping loosely at the handle with the tips of the fingers of his left hand whilst simultaneously kicking his legs forwards against the door. It sprang open, and the moonlight shone down onto the river which flowed under the car and beneath his feet. He moved right to the edge of the seat, his legs bent, his feet on the edge of the car trim. He steadied himself, using his left hand to hold the car door and wrapping the seatbelt around his right wrist.

He held that position, pausing to catch his breath and again wipe the blood from his eye. He couldn't believe that he had managed to come out the accident relatively unscathed. Now he needed to find Margaret.

He breathed long and steady breaths, filling his lungs as much as he could, trying to slow the beating of his heart. In his head, he counted down from three, and then he pushed himself forward. The immersion into the cold water instantly shocked him. It gushed between his legs just above knee height. Panting, he held tightly to the car door, gripping the seatbelt to steady himself. The rain continued to fire long glass straws from the sky which stung his face and neck as he tried desperately to make his way around the car door toward to the passenger side. He let go of the seatbelt, which untwisted itself and retracted back into place with a clunk.

The current immediately pulled him away from the car, and he clawed at branches which projected from beneath the water. The branches ripped against his palms, stripping layers of skin off. He yelped and let go. The current caused him to drift further from the car. He tried to wade forward up the river, the water bubbling and foaming around his groin. It was no use. He grabbed again. Grasses. Leaves. There was little in the way of resistance, and one by one they snapped in his hand. It was hopeless: he drifted further still.

He decided instead to aim for the riverbank, somewhere he could be safe. On solid ground he may be able to locate Margaret more easily. He waded with the torrent now, aiming to reach the nearest side, which was opposite to where the car had left the road. From there he could walk back toward the bridge and hopefully find help. He was cold and soaking wet. He moved quickly now, the water's current propelling him six or seven metres in less than a few seconds, and he came to rest against a large weeping willow solemnly guarding the riverside. He pulled himself backward up the riverbank, his fingers slipping through the mud and clay which led down a small incline to the river's edge. He lay on his back, resting for a moment.

Michael needed to find Margaret. It was essential. He had heard nothing from her in the five or so minutes since the car had hit the river. If she was unconscious, it was unlikely she'd survive for very long in the river. He pulled himself to his knees, his hands stinging as he grabbed at the foliage around to help him get to his feet. He retreated a few paces away from the river where the land was less slippery and walked slowly in the direction of the car. Blood continued to drip into his eye, diluted by the rain which continued down relentlessly.

He wandered along the river bank until he was opposite the car. Its front doors were spewed wide open so that it looked like a metal snow angel in the water. The water continued its flow, running directly through the car's interior, the current not quite strong enough to move or dislodge it. In the darkness he could just make out the windscreen. From the driver's side long, thick cracks wound their way from the corners toward the centre, like thunderbolts from a wizard's wand. Just off-centre on the passenger's side the window bulged forward in a mass of tiny fragments, giving the glass the appearance of being white. The bulge was about the size of a watermelon, and although Michael was unable to see from his position, on the inside the glass was covered in a thick maroon liquid.

Walking forwards a few more paces, Michael managed to locate his wife in the water. She was lying face down in the river, next to the passenger door. Her head was twisted to the side, her right cheek resting on the surface of the water. Her hair was sodden, matted untidily around her eyes. Her hands seemed to be clutching at her head. Her shoeless left leg was splayed out toward the centre of the river, her right inexplicably caught below the water against the twisted car door. From where he stood, Michael couldn't tell whether she was alive or dead. He had to get to her.

He already knew that crossing the river was far too difficult; instead he scrambled through the wet trees and bracken toward the roadside. Moments later he crossed the bridge and scrambled back down the other side to the water's edge, taking the wide path cleared by the car's spectacular descent into the river. Margaret hadn't moved. Her condition was no clearer from this side – the car had awkwardly come to rest almost exactly in the centre of the river.

Using his sleeve to wipe away the rain water from his eyes, he stepped back into the water, allowing the current to guide him towards his motionless wife. The water rotated him, choosing its own direction for him, which caused him to drift directly toward the inside of the car door. As the current pushed him, he grasped at the door, wrapping the crook of his elbow around the frame where the window used to be. The jolt was enough to dislodge Margaret's foot, which set her free, and the river slowly dragged her away. Michael pulled himself around to the outside of the car door as Margaret's stockinged foot drifted just out of reach. He leapt forward, headlong into the river, almost diving on top of her. His splash propelled her forward further, the velocity turning her to face in the opposite direction. Momentarily, Michael could see the blood which covered her entire face. Her arms moved down to her side, her feet seemingly trying to catch the surface of the river bed to slow her. Michael wasn't sure whether she was moving by her own volition or the water was giving the impression of life.

He had to get to her.

Now.

She was heading toward the weeping willow, and Michael followed her, a metre or so behind. Her face brushed the leaves which hung into the water. Michael reached out to grab her legs, the water carrying him under the giant parasol and into the darkness where the moonlight couldn't reach.

"Margaret?" he pleaded.

"Is that a car?"
A male voice came through the darkness.
"Where?"

"There in the river, see."

"Jesus, I think it is," replied a female.

"I told you I thought I saw something moving in the river back there."

"Better call the police and an ambulance, Lee. It looks serious."

about now

seventeen

Michael enjoyed his refreshing early-morning swim and he had left the pool long before any of the other hotel guests had arrived. Perhaps even woken. The swim had to some extent washed away the dirty feeling on his skin that the excesses of the previous night had caused. Alcohol always made his skin feel tighter and dirtier. It felt as though he had a coating all over his body. Half an hour alone in the cool water had, if only momentarily, removed that feeling. But, for perhaps the first time he could remember, he felt uneasy. Anxious almost. The feeling of foreboding had ambushed him as soon as he opened his eyes. It was as if it had lay dormant while he slept, planning and plotting its appearance for the following morning. And, planned to perfection, it appeared in his chest at the moment he woke. A slight fluttering to let him know that something was amiss. It wasn't the enormous butterfly feeling that you may get before giving a speech or getting married. No, it was a tiny feeling, not enough to cause sickness but enough to let Michael know it was there.

After the swim Michael returned to his room and dressed. He put the feeling down simply to alcohol excess and decided to try to walk it off. He collected his bag, and the feeling made itself more apparent. A quicker and slightly deeper flutter. A feeling that pushed itself further outwards in his chest. Michael grabbed the room key and left, allowing the door to slam behind him. He wouldn't be defeated; he would beat the feeling, whatever it took.

He left the hotel and headed away from the crowds.

Elsewhere in the town, Claire opened her eyes. The sun blazed into the room, warming the white cotton sheets where she lay. Her head hurt. Opening her eyes made it worse. She closed them again, pulling a pillow over her face. She had drunk a fair amount the previous night and an unexpected hangover had joined the sun in welcoming her into the new day. She was surprised by just how bad she felt; it was rare that alcohol affected the following morning these days. In her head she started an alcohol post-mortem, beginning with the first drink of the day before. If she could pinpoint the number of drinks she had consumed, she could perhaps calculate why she was feeling this way.

Since Paul died, she could easily consume a bottle of wine in an evening. Red or white, she was easy. She would perhaps finish the evening with a gin and tonic. Just as a nightcap. She felt that the bitter freshness of the tonic cleansed her mouth before bed, making the transition between wine and toothpaste much more pleasant.

The post-mortem was proving difficult. It wasn't easy to remember the drinks in any particular order. She knew that the previous day had started with an early-morning glass of bucks fizz. This was justifiable. She was on holiday, after all. Why not? The vast majority of the people in the resort, she deliberated, would be having orange juice with their breakfast. What was wrong with a little champagne to give it that extra sparkle? Yes, she had sat out on the balcony, reading and enjoying the heat and her book. She was in no rush. Her children had told her to go there and relax, and that's exactly what she was doing. The bucks fizz had gone down perfectly and she had telephoned room service for a large jug of orange juice. Less than ten minutes later it had arrived, the oranges freshly squeezed. The ice cubes had raced eagerly to the spout before realising they were too large to escape without Claire's permission. Claire allowed two to fall into the glass and they chinked on the bottom before the orange waterfall from above covered them. She retrieved the champagne bottle from the fridge and poured it over the top. Little orange bubbles fizzed and popped above the surface. "Why not?" she repeated to herself, this time out loud, and continued with her book.

A couple of hours later, it was the champagne that had run dry. Claire felt wonderful. So relaxed. So happy. She put her book down and moved from the chair to a long wooden sun lounger. She telephoned her eldest son, Neil. It went straight to voicemail. His work commitments were similar to those his father had, meaning that catching him during the day was rare. She left a message to say that she was thinking about him.

Next she called her youngest son, Daniel, for a catch-up. He answered after one ring and sounded tired. This was normal.

"Hello?"

"Hi, Daniel. It's Mum."

"Oh, hi, Mum. How are you?" There was a concerted injection of energy toward the end of his sentence.

"I'm fine, thanks. And you?"

"Oh, you know. Pretty tired." The energy injection had expired almost instantaneously.

"Oh dear."

"Yeah, Jacob." He was referring to his six-month-old son.

"Keeping you up, is he?"

"Yeah, you could say that."

"Is he okay, though?"

"Yeah, I suppose." He sounded resigned. "Doesn't sleep so much."

Claire considered suggesting that after her holiday she would come to help out for a week. It was difficult for Claire to offer 'I'll-take-him-off-your-hands-for-a-few hours' help due to distance. Daniel and his wife, Helen, lived more than three hundred miles away from Claire. She would have been more than willing to help out the family. Both Daniel and Helen had chosen careers in health care and their shift patterns rarely allowed them much time together. Claire didn't want to put any further strain on her son's marriage by being there when the couple did have a few hours alone. The main reason that Claire didn't offer help though was more the fact that Helen was extremely proud. She wanted, perhaps understandably, the feeling that she had done everything for Jacob without any external assistance. The few times that Claire had been to help out had led to uncomfortable friction, which had made Claire feel like her suggestions and assistance were better kept to herself.

"Oh well. It'll get better with time. How's Helen?"

"She's okay, I think. We're like ships in the night, though. She finishes her shift, gets home, I pass Jacob to her, I start my shift."

"Oh dear. It'll pick up, Daniel, I remember when I first had you…"

"Yeah. Listen, I'm gonna go. Jacob's having a nap and I'm going to try to get some sleep myself for a bit. I'm working tonight."

"That's fine. Just wanted to make sure you were all right."

"Yeah, yeah, we are." There was just enough energy in his voice to make it sound upbeat, although the end of the sentence seemed to drift, leaving the impression that Daniel would consider whether his statement was actually true at some point following the phone call.

"Good," said Claire, unconvinced but knowing better than to pry further.

"Right, Mum, I'll speak to you soon."

"Yes, nice to speak to you, Daniel. If you need any help…"

"Yeah, thanks."

"Okay, bye."

"Yeah, bye. Oh, er, Mum?"

"Yes?"

"Are you going on holiday soon?"

"I'm already here. I'm calling from Spain!"

"Oh right. How is it?"

"It's lovely."

"Good. Okay, speak soon. Bye."

"Bye."

Claire put the phone on the floor by her side and closed her eyes. She would have a little nap before facing the day properly.

Following her sleep, the rest of the day had been spent consuming drinks at the bar by the pool. That's where her memory began to fade. She couldn't remember exactly what drinks she had consumed, and in what measure. She knew she would have started with beer; the chrome pumps artificially dripping with ice-cold water always attracted her. However, she would have swiftly switched to cocktails as her taste buds signalled a desire to move away from the blandness of the standard Spanish beer. From here on in it was anybody's guess what she had drunk.

She abruptly stopped the post-mortem and faced the fact that, regardless of what she had drunk the previous day, she felt appalling now. She pulled the pillow away from her face, daring the light to enter. Her head hurt behind her eyes. A deep, stabbing pain. With both thumbs she pushed hard against her closed eyelids, willing the pain to stop. It didn't work. She removed her thumbs, and the sun momentarily provided a spectacular kaleidoscope of red and white circles as her eyes fought to regain focus behind her eyelids.

She opened her eyes again, reaching out her left arm to the bedside table. Her hand clutched blindly on the table as she tried to locate some painkillers. As she swept her hand from side to side, she caught a glass, which rocked slightly before spinning its way off the table and onto the floor. It shattered. "Jesus," she whispered, rolling onto her side. A thousand tiny square fragments littered the floor. Some were caught in the sunlight and lit up like diamonds.

Claire slumped onto her back. Seconds later she was caught in a moment of inspiration. She forcefully kicked away the cotton sheets which had mummified her legs during the night and sat up. It was time to start her day. There was no use in lying down moping about the fact that her head hurt. There was no point in trying to work out why she felt that way. She did, it was as simple as that, and trying to assess the pain behind her eyes was not going to make it go away. She needed to get up, start her day and basically get on with it.

She slid to the bottom of the bed and stood, using the chest of drawers to steady herself. A shot of pain tore from her eyes to her temples and back again. She sat back down, allowing herself time to breathe. Then she was up again, moving slowly along the front of the drawers toward the wardrobe. On top of the drawers, amongst jewellery, her purse and various coins and screwed-up notes, she located a packet of paracetamol. She popped them through the foil one by one onto the surface.

She then reached down under the table to her left and opened the fridge. The sudden movement made her feel dizzy. Ripples of nausea flowed through her chest. The fridge was almost empty. She pushed the bottles of Amstel to one side and reached to the back. Her hand clamped around a large bottle of sparkling water and dragged it forwards, skittling the beer bottles to the side. She stood again and swept the tablets from the top of the drawers before throwing all four in her mouth in one go. The familiar whoosh of pressure escaped from the bottle, followed by a metallic crack as the screw top detached. Claire gulped down a large, cold mouthful, washing away the tablets and the memories of the day before. Today was going to be like any other.

The feeling was proving hard to overcome. It had decided to follow Michael on his walk that morning. Wherever he went it followed, uninvited. Michael had considered stopping for a whisky to appease his visitor, but had concluded that would simply feed it further. Instead, he had decided to walk far along the coast, away from the people. It had taken around two hours before the body of holidaymakers had thinned to one or two dotted around the beach.

Michael spotted a small café, its outdoor terrace reaching out over the rocks beneath it. He imagined it was the type of place that got extremely busy in the evening; its views across the ocean directly where the sun finally set would be an attractive pull for its customers. That morning, however, it was all but deserted. Its distance from the packed beaches and high-rise hotels was enough to put off a family from making the walk. It was perfect for Michael. No children, no music, no laughter. And, aside from the lap of the sea, silence.

Michael climbed the wooden steps which led from the beach and made his way past the empty tables. He positioned himself at a shaded table at the front of the terrace, overlooking the sea. A moment or two later, he ordered a large coffee and sat back, alone aside from the feeling. The walk had to some extent kept the feeling at bay. It was still there but not as prevalent. This had been a short-lived cessation however, as it had simply waited for Michael to rest and now reappeared. This time with a new energy. Michael sat forward again, his heart beginning to race. He could feel each miniature beat in his chest repetitively jabbing at him from deep inside. This time it seemed to mean business. The beats continued, getting stronger and stronger. A sick feeling filled his throat, and he coughed nervously, as if to allow the feeling to escape. But the feeling seemed happy where it was. Relentlessly pounding him.

The waiter appeared.

"Coffee, sir?" he smiled.

The feeling subsided slightly, allowing the waiter to have his turn.

"Thank you."

"Anything else for you today?"

"No. No, thank you."

"Okay. Enjoy."

The waiter beamed a second smile and left.

The brief interruption served only to power the feeling, which leapt back instantaneously. Stronger now than before. Michael turned to catch the retreating waiter.

"Actually yes, I will. I'll have a whisky."

The waiter looked at his watch and raised his eyebrows in staged shock. "Single?"

"Double."

"Bourbon? Single malt? Blended?" The words sounded funny in a thick Spanish accent.

"Single malt. No ice."

"Okay, sir."

The waiter continued to the bar.

"Ey sir," the waiter called from behind the bar. "We have no single malt. Johnnie Walker Black Label okay?"

Michael nodded. "It'll have to fucking be," he muttered under his breath. Perhaps that shit would kill the feeling off, he thought.

Michael pulled his bag onto the table and retrieved his phone. The screen was black. He held down the power button, until the manufacturer's logo appeared on the screen to signify it was loading. He placed the phone on the glass table as the waiter reappeared with his drinks. The waiter took the coffee from a large black tray and put it down in front of Michael. He then placed a cream beermat with navy lettering on the table and put the whisky on top. Michael retrieved it and threw it back in one, hoping the heat of the alcohol would burn the feeling, which was still pounding at the bottom of his throat.

"Another?" said the waiter.

Michael nodded.

"Another." The waiter shook his head and walked back toward the bar. Behind it, a phone mounted on the wall was ringing.

A buzz from Michael's phone echoed on the glass beneath it. The screen lit up to alert Michael that it was eleven twenty and he had four messages. He could see without leaning forwards that they were all from Jane. He considered reading them but for now decided against. He had to focus on fighting the feeling within.

"Mind if I join you?"

Michael knew the voice. It was still as silky and smooth as the last time he heard it. A river of melted chocolate. He turned and motioned to the chair opposite him. Claire pulled it back and sat down. The waiter returned with the second whisky. This time Michael allowed it to rest on the beermat. Claire raised her eyebrows.

"Starting early, aren't we?"

Michael didn't care. He shrugged.

"For you, madam?"

"Just a glass of white Rioja, please."

Michael turned, giving her a pot-kettle-black look.

The waiter smiled wryly again and left for the bar.

Claire turned to Michael. "Are you stalking me?" she smiled.

Michael smiled briefly, his eyes still fixed on the horizon. The feeling getting ever stronger.

"Listen, if you want to be alone, it's fine. I did the same today. Just set off walking away from all the people and noise."

Michael let out a barely audible "Mmm" in agreement.

"Suppose we had the same thing in mind, eh?"

Michael stared at the ocean.

"Look, it was nice to meet you last nigh–"

"Can we just sit and not speak?" said Michael firmly.

Claire nodded. "Sorry."

It was only after Claire had finished her third glass of Rioja that she had the courage to break the silence and ask Michael about Margaret.

"Do you miss her?"

Michael continued to stare toward the sea, ignoring the question. The sea was a perfect blue. Completely calm.

"I'm sorry," Claire said. "I shouldn't have asked that."

"Do you miss him?" Michael shot back. His voice dripped with bitterness. His eyes fixed firmly on Claire's. The look made her feel uneasy.

Claire ignored his tone. "Of course I do," she said. "Of course I do."

many years ago

eighteen

Michael Sewell took pride in having a home in which everything had a place, and that 'everything' included all members of the household. The family lived in a typical 1970s' new-build semi-detached house on a leafy estate half an hour by car from the nearest town. The house was small, yet functional. A porch lined with neatly stacked shoes. A lounge with a huge wall-to-wall fireplace and a big, but not vulgarly big, television. Shelves in the hall bearing photographs of the family, collected by Margaret, and a large silver trophy presented to Michael for achieving the highest mark amongst his peers in his law degree (it should have been returned to the law school to be presented to the following year's high achiever; however, Michael didn't see why his efforts should not be celebrated permanently). A dining room so small the table would only seat four and two remaining chairs had been relegated to the garage. A poky kitchen rendered dark by the huge conifers that dulled the hum of the motorway that ran behind. Upstairs, four white doors guarded a small square of orangey-yellow patterned carpet. All four doors were exactly the same, and when closed none of them gave up the identity of the room which lay behind. There was a bathroom featuring a bath, toilet and sink in a mustard colour and three bedrooms, one of which, the master, Michael had claimed as his study. Only Michael was allowed inside that room. The door was always closed. It was his room, his quiet space to which he retreated from the distasteful noise and sights and demands of family. No matter that the bed he and Margaret shared was squeezed into a smaller bedroom. No matter that Jane was fast outgrowing the box room. No matter, even, that there was nowhere to put a crib.

Margaret knew how important it was that everything be in its place and everyone know their place. That was why, for example, she kept the wooden stairs in the house polished to perfection, just how Michael liked it, even though Jane, aged three, slipped about on the treads and Margaret had to shepherd her up and down while clinging hard to the bannister. That was also why, the day her second child was born, she did not tell Michael for some time that she was in labour.

It had been an uneventful pregnancy for Margaret, and she had got on with life in her usual unassuming, stoic way. Early labour was to be no different. She felt the first tightening at breakfast, while serving Michael his scrambled eggs, but said nothing. She felt the next as she handed Michael his briefcase and coat at the door, but said nothing. Michael was a busy man with an important job. Labour could take many hours, she knew.

Three hours later, with a heavy heart, Margaret had to concede that while labour could take many hours, it could also take only a few. Since dropping Jane off with a sympathetic neighbour, she had timed each contraction and noted both the regularity and the strength increasing as the morning slipped by. Then, as she was dusting skirting boards in the lounge, a startling pop followed by a gush of warm fluid confirmed that it was time.

Margaret allowed herself another twenty minutes to breathe through a contraction, change her outfit and thoroughly clean up the mess she had made, and then she rang Michael's office.

"Hello, Milton, Knight and Haxby. How can I be of assistance?"

Margaret recognised Lynne's voice from the time she had worked at the firm. A job she had abruptly quit after she and Michael married. Michael had informed her on their honeymoon that it was unacceptable for them to continue to work together. He told her that he had already hired her replacement and the matter was not up for discussion.

"Oh, er, hello, Lynne…"

"Margaret? It's not like you to ring…" Both Lynne and Margaret were clear that Michael wouldn't stand for any interruptions at work.

"No, I know," Margaret gasped. The pain was building again. "I wouldn't…usually ring…but…"

"Are you okay?"

"I'm…in…labour."

"Oh," said Lynne gravely. "I'll call Mr Sewell."

The line went silent.

Michael sat back in his brown leather chair. The legs creaked, groaning from years of use. He read the letter in his hand again and smiled. The writer was correct. He had indeed done a 'wonderful job for the family' and he wholeheartedly agreed that 'if it wasn't for his intervention, there may have been a very different outcome'. The writer had extended his praise further in the penultimate paragraph, before agreeing Michael's suggested fee of fifteen thousand pounds 'without hesitation' for the work performed. A fee of this size was ammunition to use in his continuing battle with the senior partners. It was clear to him that by now he should be made partner, something that the partners were resisting. He couldn't understand why he wasn't already sharing in the profits of the firm. The discord around the office was beginning to escalate. At that time, the market was packed with small-time legal practices all trying to outdo one another by reducing fees, but Michael knew he was the best in the area and so people should pay handsomely for his skill and expertise. He read the letter again, noticing at the same time that his fingernails looked perfect. The tip of each nail stretched out three or four millimetres, which allowed him to make a nice tapping sound on the desk in front of him. He rested his hands on the desk and, using each finger in turn, began to beat out a hypnotic rhythm. When his superiors returned to the office later that day he would demand a meeting – 'fifteen thousand pounds, *without hesitation,*' he would tell them. His thoughts were interrupted by the phone ringing.

"Michael Sewell," he said authoritatively.

"Oh, Mr Sewell, it's Marg…er, Mrs Sewell on line two. It's –"

"I haven't time."

"Mr Sewell, I do think you'd better speak to her."

"Excuse me? I've just told you, I haven't time."

"She's in labour, Mr Sewell."

Labour. The last time, Michael remembered, had ended in utter disappointment. The unnecessary, if not gratuitous, screaming and panting seemed to go on for hours. He'd checked his watch on numerous occasions, wondering when this ridiculous theatrical show would finish. He had remained seated at the far end of the room for just under three painful hours until it was finally over and the grunting stopped. A smell of urine filled the air. The baby was placed on Margaret's naked chest and she smiled at Michael through sweat-matted hair. The purple creature which she held closely was covered in blood and mucus. It was disgusting. He had collected his coat and left the room in search of a glass of water for his dry throat. He would return when the baby was clean and his wife was bathed and more suitably dressed. When the blood had been wiped away.

Lynne was unsure whether Michael's silence meant he hadn't heard her. The old phone lines did from time to time have a tendency to crackle or fizz, or simply go dead. She decided to repeat herself.

"Mr Sewell, she's in labour."

"Tell her I'm too busy. In a meeting. Whatever. I'll call the hospital later."

Michael replaced the receiver and resumed his rhythmic tap.

When Michael arrived at the hospital later that evening, to his relief there was no panting or grunting or howling or screaming. Margaret lay in bed in her private room. She was a little pale and her cardigan was buttoned unevenly, but at least she was clean this time. And quiet. Aside from her bed and a chair, the only other object in the room was a crudely moulded plastic cot. In it was a blue blanket. Thank God, he thought. A boy.

"I'm sorry, held up at work."

He sat on the chair beside the bed and the empty cot. At this distance he saw that Margaret's eyes were red and puffy. They reminded him of a half-inflated dinghy. The corners of her mouth turned downwards and the tears which had fallen intermittently that afternoon began again. For a moment the room was silent.

"I couldn't get away. New client."

The slight smell of whisky followed his words.

Margaret bowed her head, shaking it slowly from side to side. Michael noticed she hadn't brushed her hair at the back. A tangled clump was bunched at her crown. It looked untidy.

"He's not well," she sobbed, "not well at all."

Michael frowned.

"Where is he?"

"Tests," Margaret said without looking up.

"What kind of tests?"

"I don't know. Tests." She didn't feel like expanding any further at that stage. She didn't feel like saying anything at all, she was utterly consumed by guilt.

It was her fault. It was all her fault. She should not have stayed at home. She should not have waited for Michael.

Margaret had realised her mistake while waiting for the ambulance. Angry with herself for the disappointment that had gripped her at facing the birth alone – she had been foolish to have expected more of Michael – she had attempted to occupy her mind by checking her overnight bag. She took the items out one by one, placing them on the lounge floor. A towel, pyjamas, a dressing gown, slippers, her address book, her purse and her wash bag. Inside that, a small plastic container of Mum roll-on deodorant, a toothbrush and paste, a small vial of perfume, a compact mirror –

A strong pain shot from just below her ribs, directly through her bump. She gasped, unable to breathe for a second. Another contraction was at least five minutes away. That hadn't been a contraction. Odd.

Ten or so breaths later, she regained her rhythmic breathing and leaned down once again to her bag. She removed an eye-shadow set and opened it. The four colours – silver, blue, jade and gold – were split neatly into four equal squares. A brush separated the aqueous colours from their metallic counterparts. The black plastic base was visible beneath the blue and jade, the colours cowering in the corners, seemingly fearful of the return of the brush. The gold and silver, on the other hand, were largely untouched; only a few tell-tale brush marks told of previous use. Margaret remembered she had tried those colours before, but Michael had not approved. He had said –

A second pain shot through her, hot and sharp. The pain ran directly down her large bump, like a scalpel slicing her from the inside. She held her bump, her hands pulling tightly against herself, holding the sharpness inside until the pain finally waned.

Anxiety gave way to fear, and she set about scooping up the items from the floor and shoving them into the bag. Whatever she could grab went in: toothpaste thrown in with her slippers; her towel shoved in with her dressing gown. She strained to pull the large zipper across the top of the overnight bag; the teeth of the zip did not wish to meet. She had it halfway across when the next contraction came, but this time there was no time to breathe into it, no slow build to the crest of the wave of pain, because the sharp pain was there, slicing her open, driving the contraction to new heights. She screamed out with the shock and the terror and the agonising knowledge that something was very wrong.

It was dark when Margaret awoke. She felt groggy. She lifted her arm to move the hair from her eyes to get a better look. Her hand was abruptly stopped by a plastic tube which was stretched to its limit. The pulling nipped her hand and she ceased, her eyes tracing the path of the tube from the cannula taped to her hand to the drip stand on her left. The wheels on its metal frame squeaked slightly. Using her other hand, she swept her hair out of her eyes. She was in a small room, its walls yellowed by the artificial light. It was a hospital room. She was alone. Her hand flew to her bump. It was gone.

She tried to sit up, but pain in her abdomen quickly pushed her head back into the plastic-covered pillow. Her eyes darted around for an alarm, something to press to attract attention. She arched her head backwards to see the red button she needed to press was hooked high above her on the wall. There was no way she could reach it, but she tried anyway, until her cry of pain brought a nurse into the room. She was older than Margaret, around fifty. Her hair was pulled tightly in a bun on the top of her head, the tightness pulling her eyes upwards with it. The end of her nose curled upwards slightly too, in a show of allegiance. She smiled, a quick flash, before sitting on the bed beside Margaret.

"I'm Joanne," she said quietly.

Margaret smiled as best she could. "Where's my baby?"

"He's with the doctors."

Margaret tried to sit up again.

"Rest," the nurse said, stroking Margaret's arm.

"Is he okay?"

"I'll get the doctor."

The nurse stood and made her way to the door.

"Is he okay?"

The nurse turned. "I'll be two minutes."

She returned a minute later with a tall grey-haired man with thick black-rimmed glasses; every television doctor of that era was surely based on his appearance. He strode over to Margaret, his brow slightly furrowed. The nurse resumed her position on the bed. The doctor pulled across a weathered armchair, its navy plastic fabric picked away at the arms by the boredom of previous visitors. The doctor placed the chair so it faced the pillow where Margaret lay. The ceremony suggested that this wasn't likely to be good news.

"Mrs Sewell," said the doctor, fixing his stare on Margaret. It was somewhere between a question and a confirming statement.

Margaret nodded. "Where's my baby?" she whispered.

"Yes, Mrs Sewell. Your baby. Your son is having tests at the moment." His tone was calming.

"Why?" managed Margaret. "What for?"

The nurse glanced at the doctor. The doctor remained focused on Margaret.

"There are problems, Mrs Sewell."

"Is he okay?"

The doctor gently explained that Margaret had undergone an emergency caesarean section to deliver her baby. Her son. He had been unresponsive initially and they were concerned about a growth 'about the size of a small orange' which began above his right cheek, covered his eye and stretched around his temple, finishing just above his right ear. It was also clear that his palette hadn't formed correctly, causing a gap 'wide enough to fit your little finger through' in his upper lip.

"My fault..." breathed Margaret.

"No," said the nurse.

"I should have telephoned earlier..."

"No, Mrs Sewell. That wouldn't have made any difference at all."

"If I had telephoned sooner then perhaps my son –"

"No," said the doctor. "That wouldn't have mattered, Mrs Sewell. The problems your son has developed whilst inside your womb. The birth itself did not materially affect what we now have to deal with."

"And what exactly do we have to deal with?"

"I don't want to speculate, Mrs Sewell. That's why we're doing the tests. I assure you I'll let you know as soon we know anything."

The doctor tapped Margaret's shoulder twice as he rose from the chair. "I'll leave you with the nurse," he said. He walked away from the bed and the door clicked quietly behind him.

Margaret turned to the nurse. "Will he be all right?"

She smiled sympathetically. "They're doing everything they can."

nineteen

Michael remained at the hospital with Margaret in near silence for more than three hours. It was now just into the early hours of the next day. Occasionally, the door would open and a nurse would enter to ask whether Margaret needed anything. Each time, the light from the corridor brought new hope, which was extinguished by the lack of accompanying news. Margaret managed short bursts of sleep. Michael positioned himself in the chair next to the bed. He attempted to stroke Margaret's hair, but she turned her head away. A clear indication of her mood. The cot remained empty alongside the bed.

Initially, Michael had broken the silence with questions: "Do you need anything?" "How are you feeling?" "What exactly did the doctor say?" Margaret had listened to the questions, the very sound of Michael's voice just about stripping the skin from her ear drum. His questions were shrill and piercing; tortuous. She wanted to scream that had he been here earlier he would have heard what the doctors had said and he would know the answers, but she didn't. Michael had demanded that she answer him. That it was his son and he deserved to know. Never before had he seen the look that Margaret fired in his direction. A look that said, 'Don't you fucking dare.' Michael had chosen, for the time being at least, to let Margaret have her way. There would be time to correct this when they were back home.

Another hour passed. Michael considered whether his presence was absolutely necessary at this stage. The tests could go on through the night and he may be better heading home to get some sleep. He would be able to deal with things much better after a good night's sleep. Also, he (very briefly) considered, Margaret may be able to get a better night's sleep without him being there. In addition, the chair was becoming increasingly uncomfortable. The plastic material was stretched past its recommended elasticity and he could feel the wooden frame pushing into his back. He was about to suggest his plan to Margaret when the door opened again.

The doctor walked into the room. Behind him was the nurse. In her arms she carried a baby.

"You must be Mr Sewell," stated the doctor.

Michael rose to shake the doctor's hand, but the doctor signalled with a horizontal wave of his right hand that Michael should remain seated. Michael took an instant dislike to him.

The nurse carried the baby over and sat on the bed. "Your son," she whispered, laying the baby in Margaret's arms.

Margaret looked down for the first glimpse at her son. He was wrapped from head to toe in a chewing-gum-white hospital-issue blanket that continued beyond his feet into a tapered triangle which made him look much longer than he was. Using a crooked finger, she gingerly pulled the blanket down so she could see her son's face more clearly. His harelip exposed soft, wet gum. His right eye was swollen and bulged into a red, puffy mass. The expansion was convex to the same extent that his left eye was convex. The bulge continued around the side of his head, stretching his tiny ear outwards. The area was bruised and pulsated a little. His left eye flickered open and then closed again. Margaret smiled. He was beautiful.

Michael's view was blocked by Margaret's arm, so he lifted himself slightly from the chair. He looked at his son momentarily and then sat back down sharply. The doctor watched him, and then moved to stand alongside Margaret, and when he spoke he addressed her.

"We have performed as many tests as we can at this stage. It appears that your son has a tumour in the frontal part of his brain."

"Okay…" Margaret whispered, urging the doctor to continue.

"We believe that it's operable. However, we can't tell at this stage what potential damage that operation may do. We've run tests with regard to your son's hearing, eyesight…"

The baby let out a short, loud squawk. Margaret smiled and stroked his cheek.

"Now we need to run more tests. These will let us know what type of tumour your son has. Due to the seriousness of his condition, we're rushing these through. We hope to know something more later today."

"Will he be all right?" said Michael.

The doctor turned to Michael "It's too early to give a long-term prognosis, Mr Sewell. Far too early."

"I think a man in your position must know something more, Doctor."

"I can't say any more at this stage, Mr Sewell. I'm sorry."

Michael raised his eyebrows.

The doctor turned back to Margaret and smiled. "I'll leave you here with the nurse for a few more moments and then we'll take your son back to the neonatal ward for the night."

The doctor tapped Margaret's shoulder and turned to leave.

"He's called Thomas," she said. "Thomas Charles Stuart Sewell."

"Thomas," confirmed the doctor. "A good name, Mrs Sewell."

Michael would have argued that a firstborn son should take his father's name. But not this son.

Margaret was already awake when the door was pushed open again. The sun was just rising and bright light was piercing through the translucent white curtains. The fact was that she hadn't been asleep at all. The doctor walked briskly in and over to the bed.

"Good morning, Mrs Sewell." The doctor glanced to his right. "Mr Sewell."

Michael had been sleeping in the chair. His legs were stretched out in front of him, his hands clasped across his belt line, his spine rigid, almost horizontal. His eyes snapped open, and he quickly adjusted his position to sitting.

"How is Thomas, Doctor?" Margaret asked.

Michael rubbed his eyes.

The doctor sat on the bed. "Thomas is doing well. We've monitored him all night, and although he needed a little help with his breathing at one point, he generally seems in good shape, considering his condition."

"Good," said Margaret quietly.

The doctor opened the folder he was holding. Margaret followed his eyes as they in turn followed the words concealed on the paper within. He read for a moment, and then closed it.

"Mrs Sewell…"

Michael cleared his throat. The doctor turned his head.

"Mr Sewell. The results have come back regarding your son's tumour. I have good news. It's benign. This means it's not cancerous."

Margaret gasped, and a slight smile began to appear on her face. Michael reached to hold his wife's hand. Margaret didn't move, and Michael had to settle for cupping his hand around her balled fist.

"Having said that, we now feel that the position of the tumour could…" The doctor lengthened the final word, considering his next words carefully. "…cause extremely serious problems for Thomas at this time."

Margaret's smile slipped.

Michael pushed himself more upright in the chair. "And, Doctor…?" he encouraged, his tone suggesting that he felt himself on a professional level with this man. "What does that mean exactly?"

The doctor rose to the challenge in Michael's tone, and proceeded to explain carefully and thoroughly the details of Thomas's condition, and the treatment plan.

"So you see," he finished, "we really have little choice but to operate on Thomas. The tumour is causing a high level of intracranial pressure."

"That may be the case, Doctor," said Michael. "I do feel, however, that my wife and I should consider all the possibilities before we make that decision."

Michael looked at Margaret. She pulled her fist away from his hand.

"Doctor, without surgery what will happen to Thomas?" she asked quietly.

"It's hard to say, Mrs Sewell. The risk of permanent brain damage is high. Or…"

"Then that's what we'll do." Margaret sounded resolute. "Thomas will have the surgery."

"Now, Margaret. Let's not be so hasty."

She turned head slowly toward Michael, making eye contact with him for the first time that morning. She propped herself up on one elbow, ensuring that none of her skin was touching his.

"Michael. Thomas is having the operation."

Michael did not recognise this tone from his wife. It was the first time she had used it. And it was making him look stupid in front of the doctor. Not just stupid. Weak. He felt his toes curl inwardly inside his shoes and a tight pulling across his chest. He looked back at her. He had never seen this expression before either. She looked strong and powerful. Resolute. Immoveable.

"I just think…"

"No. No, Michael. I don't care what you think. Thomas is having the operation. Today."

Michael stored everything he had experienced in the last few moments away in the back of his mind. He wouldn't forget this humiliation. Not ever. He turned to the doctor.

"Your son's welfare is my only concern, Mr Sewell. I strongly suggest that we operate…"

"Go ahead."

It had been Michael's decision after all.

The doctor stood. "I'll go and get the preparations underway for surgery immediately," he said.

As he reached the door he turned and smiled at Margaret. She thought she saw pity in his eyes.

"Can I see Thomas?"

"You can, Mrs Sewell. I'll have the nurse bring him through for a few moments."

twenty

Thomas recovered from the surgery to remove the tumour extremely well. The doctors were very pleased with his progress, and after four weeks he was discharged and Margaret took him home. Aside from the obvious physical signs of surgery, a five-inch scar from just above his right eye to the top of his right ear and a line from his upper lip to his nose, he was much like Jane had been at his age. Margaret placed his cot alongside her bed so she could monitor him every night. Michael bought a single bed for his study, so whilst Thomas was young he could get the rest he needed, he said, to do his difficult job.

Jane, who had been largely excluded in the early weeks, quickly began to warm to her little brother. She had been told that he was very special and was hugely protective of him. Helping her mother at bath-time and popping the press-studs on his blue babygros were amongst her favourite tasks.

Life fell into a pattern for Margaret over the next months and then years. She rose to feed Thomas around five in the morning, said goodbye to Michael as he left for work an hour later, then woke, fed and dressed Jane. Another feed for Thomas would follow mid-morning, whilst Jane would, in her own motherly way, 'tidy' around. Thomas would sleep again following the feed, which then left a couple of hours for lunch and time alone with Jane. Reading, painting, playing and laughing were then abruptly interrupted by Thomas. Jane would again 'tidy' up whilst Margaret fed her son. Then, whilst Thomas napped in the late afternoon,

Margaret would prepare the evening meal. After a further short playtime, she would read Jane a story and tuck her up in bed, and then give Thomas his final feed before placing him down to sleep.

In the early days, Margaret would wait to have her meal with Michael after the children were in bed, but many nights ended in her sitting at the table alone, watching the clock. It quickly became apparent that his firm had too much work on, and so her evenings were invariably spent alone on the sofa with a book. She would be in bed by the time she heard Michael putting his key into the front door, but he rarely came straight up, and by the time he did come to bed, Margaret would be sound asleep.

Fridays were different, however. On that day, Michael would likely be home from work around five. He would wash, shave and change, and they would all sit and have their evening meal together. Michael would give Margaret an update on the cases that he was currently working on, and if there was time, Margaret would update Michael on the family's achievements: a smile Thomas had flashed; how Jane could now successfully recite the alphabet. At six thirty precisely the meal would be abruptly interrupted by the sound of a car horn, and Michael would kiss the top of his wife's head before departing for his evening at the pub with his friends. 'His only outlet', he called it. The smell of Brut would hang heavy in the room for a good hour after he left. Margaret would continue her routine, and come back to clear the table and wash up once Jane was in bed.

The weekly routine was repetitive but Margaret loved it. It was true that she sometimes wished for more company when the long days were over and her children were settled, fast asleep, upstairs. But she reminded herself that she was very fortunate to have the life that she had. Yes, her husband worked long hours and spent the weekends playing golf or locked away in his study, but he was providing for them, ensuring financial stability. And her time with the children each day was what she had always wanted. It was tiring and admittedly sometimes monotonous, but she wouldn't change it for anything.

What she would change, though, if she could was the hardships her son faced. Eight operations over half as many years had rectified Thomas's health issues as far as was possible within the medical limitations of the time. But he had been left profoundly deaf in his right ear and his vision on the same side was limited to what doctors believed was no more than a blur. The removal of the tumour had left his forehead misshapen with a prominent lump, though it was covered by blond-brown curls which bounced as he marauded around the house, destroying much of what was in his path. The tumour had left him with a weakness in the left side of his body which slightly affected his balance. Thus it was common for Thomas to storm off toward an object which caught his eye, only to veer off to the left and fall – his body unable to perform the commands his brain had intended. This led to numerous cuts, bruises and bangs, which put Margaret on round-the-clock watch so as to avert any possible accident before it happened. The doctors had informed her that bumps for Thomas would be no worse than for a normal child, but she didn't want to take the risk. In addition, Margaret was acutely aware that Michael would berate her for any cuts and bruises that Thomas had suffered when the family gathered for their Friday night meal. It was so rare that they did anything as a family; she didn't want the time they had spoiled by accusations that she wasn't taking care of Thomas properly.

Beyond the physical issues Thomas faced, the tumour had left mental scars. He was a lovely boy – capable of great gentleness and extremely playful, especially fond of hiding and popping up out of a laundry basket, from behind the sofa, from out of a wardrobe.

But Thomas would become quickly frustrated and argumentative, rewarding any perceived misdeed or rebuke with a barrage of toys launched at the accuser. He was prone to tantrums and shouting and did not like to be told what to do. He would scream at Margaret, his face red, an inch away from hers, for minutes at a time. This capacity for noisy emotion within meant Margaret had to tread very, very carefully when Michael was home. Michael did not like outbursts. Not at all.

Take Saturday mornings. After his Friday evening out at the pub with friends, Michael liked to sleep until late the next day. Margaret would do anything to keep her two children entertained and quiet, which usually meant whispered jigsaws and monitored colouring of a jumbo-sized colouring book. Margaret would sit and watch meticulously, marking each pen stroke within the lines with a celebratory smile. This was to ensure there was no scribbling; Margaret was fearful the sound of scratched felt against paper would be enough to wake her husband.

Michael would usually rise around lunchtime and enter the dining room (where the family would invariably be sitting) in his bottle-green dressing gown. His paisley pyjama bottoms would be visible from the thigh down, blue velour slippers keeping his feet warm. Unlike any other time of week, his sandy hair would not be perfectly parted. Instead it would sit messily on top of his head, reminiscent of a piece of turf hacked out of the ground by a bad golfer.

Their father's appearance was the cue for all silence to stop, as screams of "Daddy!" would fill the air, both children scrambling down from their chairs just in time grab the back of their father's legs. Margaret hated this part. Michael would stop in his tracks, aware that if he continued into the kitchen, he would lose his pyjama bottoms or one of the children would fall. He would rotate instead, the children now positioned in front of him, arms gripped tightly around his thighs, eyes looking eagerly upwards.

"Enough."

Margaret would intervene: "Jane. Thomas. Let Daddy into the kitchen. He'll be thirsty."

The children would loosen their grip and Margaret would coax them back to the table. Michael would continue into the kitchen, grumpily muttering "So bloody noisy" or "For Christ's sake, can't I have a minute?" on his way to the fridge. Margaret would invariably hear the comments, but history had taught her to ignore them.

After a large glass of water and a few minutes preparing a coffee for himself, Michael would make his way back through the dining room into the lounge. He would sit in his favourite chair, holding the coffee in one hand, the other resting on the chair arm. Then he would stare silently through the window, from time to time lifting his mug and taking a drink. The children and Margaret had learned that these moments were to be silent and they continued their colouring peacefully. The whole silent staring routine would last about ten minutes. At the end of it, Michael would place his mug on the floor next to him and release a loud, discontented sigh. He would then stand and make his way upstairs, the wooden stairs squeaking as the rubber sole of each slipper made contact. Once Margaret heard the sound of the bathroom door clicking, she would let out a relieved sigh which would signal that the children could talk at their own volume.

Occasionally, though, the morning didn't go smoothly. These were the times that Margaret feared the most. One such morning stuck in her mind. And it would stay with her daughter for a lifetime.

When Margaret first woke the red digital clock displayed 5:05, a little dot alongside the time somewhat pointlessly indicating that it was 'AM'. Margaret lay on her side next to Michael, careful not to move an inch. She stared across the room at the curtains until the light slowly began to seep in. She listened to Michael's long snores, which whistled like a small kettle in his nose. Just over an hour passed, then she heard a small bump, its impact muted by the carpet. Thomas was awake. She slid out of the bed, expertly ensuring that no cold air rushed under the duvet to disturb Michael. She was greeted on the landing by both Jane and Thomas. Jane had invariably awoken as Thomas got off the bunk bed in their tiny room. Margaret lifted one finger to her mouth and used her other hand to point to the top of the stairs. Jane rubbed her eyes and silently made her way to the top, dragging her favourite grey rabbit alongside her. Thomas stretched out both his arms and Margaret collected him up, shushing in his ear as she carried him. Four feet gingerly made their way down the wooden stairs, ignoring the coldness beneath them.

When they arrived in the lounge, Margaret put Thomas on the floor and pulled both children toward her. "Good morning, beautiful children," she whispered. They both smiled and she pulled them in for a tighter squeeze. "Let's all get a drink."

They both nodded and the three walked through the half-light of the lounge into the kitchen. It was there that Margaret was confident enough to turn on the first light of the day, and their whispers could be replaced by ever-so-slightly louder talk.

"Did you both sleep well?" she asked, opening the fridge.

Thomas nodded. He still looked tired.

"I did, Mummy," said Jane.

"And did you dream, sweetheart?"

"Er…" Jane looked to the ceiling. "I don't know."

"Oh."

"Did you, Mummy?"

Margaret had dreamed. It had unnerved her.

"No. Not last night, sweetheart. Milk or juice?"

Both children selected milk. Margaret wanted tea, but the noise from the kettle excluded this as an option. She opted for milk as well. They made their way through to the dining room and sat at the table.

"Jigsaws?"

"No. Not jigsaws," said Thomas resolutely, pushing the box away. A film of milk covered his top lip.

"Okay. Colouring?"

Jane nodded and retrieved a pencil case and two large colouring books from the chair beside her.

"Not colouring," said Thomas, his voice slightly raised.

Margaret put her hand over his, fearing he may bang it on the table. Jane flicked through the book to find her page and took a pink felt-tip from the case.

"What would you like –"

"TV," Thomas said firmly.

"Well, Daddy is in bed…"

"TV," he repeated, much louder than a whisper.

Jane looked up from her book. "Shoosh," she said, pointing toward the ceiling.

"TV! TV! TV!"

"Thomas, stop it," said Margaret.

Thomas struggled to release his right hand. "No. TV!"

"Thomas, I mean it. Please be quiet."

"TV! TV!" he shouted. He picked up the pencil case with his left hand and threw it across the table. Pens flew in all directions and the half-empty pencil case hit Jane squarely in the face. She immediately began to cry. Margaret turned to Jane, allowing Thomas to wriggle his hand free.

"Sweetheart, are you okay?" She turned back to Thomas, who had now climbed down from his chair and was continuing his chanting. "Thomas, for goodness sake, be quiet!"

Margaret kissed the top of Jane's head repeatedly as she continued to cry loudly. Thomas made his way into the lounge, shouting for the television. He was unsure how to turn it on. He crawled onto the sofa and then leapt back onto the floor, shouting all the while. He was slightly out of Margaret's line of vision and she decided that her shouting to the other room would just add to the current pandemonium. Jane's crying subsided to a pant as Margaret calmed her. She kissed Jane's head one last time, saying "I'll not be a minute, sweetheart" as she stepped into the lounge.

"Thomas!" she said firmly, but still not allowing herself to shout.

"TV!" he repeated, pointing to the television.

"No," said Margaret.

A movement in her peripheral vision caught her eye. She turned slowly. Michael was coming down the stairs.

"Thomas! Come here," she said in a different tone, her voice slightly louder, slightly wavering.

Thomas looked at her and then behind him. He walked toward his mother.

"What the *fuck* is going on?" said Michael as he reached the last step.

Margaret picked up her son, her eyes wide, fixed on Michael. He strode toward them. Margaret backed up slightly.

"Come on," she said, tapping Thomas's bottom in encouragement. "Let's get back to colouring, Thomas."

Thomas pushed his head into Margaret's chest. She walked backwards through the arch into the dining room. Jane stared through the arch, her cheeks red from crying.

"I said," Michael repeated, this time more slowly, "what the *fuck* is going on?"

Margaret rounded the edge of table, ever closer to Jane. Michael stood at the opposite end. His frame looked enormous. His hand clasped the edge of the table, his back arched. He stared down the table at each of them. Thomas kept his head tight against Margaret. She lowered herself and put her right arm around Jane.

The room was silent for several long moments.

Michael eventually broke the silence: "Listen, I work hard all week. For you all. I bring home money. I feed you. All I want is the chance to get some rest when I'm not working. Okay?"

Margaret nodded in agreement. Thomas turned his head slightly. His father's low, calm tone had diffused some fear.

"And I do not appreciate being woken" – Michael's voice became louder on each word – "on the one day that I don't have to *fucking* work."

He leaned forward and swept a long arm across the table, shattering a half-empty glass of milk against the wall.

"Is it so *fucking* hard to understand," he spat through gritted teeth, "that *I* might need some *fucking* rest when I've been working all week to feed you three?"

Jane began to cry and she stood on her chair, pushing her face into Margaret's neck. Margaret wrapped her arm tightly around Jane's waist.

"Well, is it? And you, you can stop crying, that's all I could *fucking* hear upstairs," he roared. "You and that *fucking* idiot shouting."

Michael grabbed the jigsaw box from the table and threw it at the huddled three, who cringed as one. The box hit the patio doors behind Margaret and exploded open, the wooden pieces making a tiny 'plink' noise as they impacted on the glass.

"And as for you," Michael leered, making eye contact with the only person who was looking at him, "call yourself a mother? You can't bloody control them, can you? You can't do the one thing I ask of you."

Margaret was glad the table separated them. She continued to look at him, holding the children close, unsure what he would do next.

"All I want, Margaret," he said quietly, "is some *fucking* sleep. Okay?"

She nodded repeatedly.

Michael picked up an empty glass from the table and squeezed it tightly for a few seconds, his arm shaking. His stare never left Margaret. Then he banged the glass down on the table and turned to leave the room.

"Some *fucking* sleep," he muttered as he strode across the lounge toward the stairs.

Margaret held Jane and Thomas.

"It's okay," she whispered. "Daddy's just really tired today. It's okay."

Michael was back in the room.

"What did you fucking say?"

"I said, you were just really tired today, that's all."

"It's not tiredness, Margaret. It's you. All of you. That little idiot shouting all the time. Her scratching away with her pens. Fucking colouring. Is that all you can do, Jane? Colour?"

Jane didn't look up.

"Well, is it? Colouring? Great. It's about all you're good for. You'll never amount to anything more than that."

Margaret continued to hold the children. Her shaking was more visible now.

"And you, Margaret. Mother to these two. Well done. You must be really proud. Really fucking proud."

He wiped the spit from his upper lip and walked out of the room. The three listened to his feet stomp up the stairs, one by one. Then the bedroom door clicked shut.

A few moments passed in silence before Margaret released the children, wiping the tears from her eyes before they noticed.

twenty-one

Three months passed and there were no repeat incidents. Michael had briefly witnessed a few of Thomas' tantrums but had simply remained quiet and left the room. But one particular Saturday morning, however, there was a good reason for noise.

Margaret lay in bed, awake as usual, awaiting the signal to start the day. The clock made its way past seven o'clock and there was still no noise. No early-morning thud as feet met carpet. Aside from the heavy snoring and occasional effluvium of gas, the first sound of the morning was the slight creaking of a bedroom door. Little, light footsteps made their way across the landing and then stopped. After a short while, the footsteps began again, padding softly on the wood below them. It was unlike Thomas not to rise first. It was also unlike Jane to make her way downstairs alone.

Margaret waited a short while. There were no further sounds. She crept out of the bedroom and swiftly made her way onto the landing. Crouching on the third step down, she peered between the stairs and saw the glow of light coming from the dining room. She hadn't even heard Jane press the light switch. Bless her, she thought.

She made her way back up the stairs and quietly pushed open the door to the children's bedroom. She could make out the figure on the bottom bunk, wrapped warmly up beneath his Action Man duvet. His left leg was the only part of him uncovered. He faced away from her, toward the wall. The only light came from outside, the blackout blind shutting out all but two thin lines of light to each side and a thicker line of light across the bottom. She watched for a moment and then closed the door.

She paused on the landing, considering whether to wake Thomas. If she went downstairs now, it was likely he would wake shortly and he could then in turn wake Michael. Conversely, if Jane was left unmonitored for too long, she could accidentally drop or break something from the fridge, which could wake Michael. Then again, it seemed a shame to wake Thomas while he was sleeping so soundly. This was an unprecedented situation, and she was unsure what to do. She took a step toward the top of the stairs, paused, thought for a while longer and then went back into the children's room.

She approached the bed and peered over the duvet which half-covered her son's face. "Time to wake up, sweetheart," she whispered close to his ear. She moved his hair away from his eyes and used the crook of her first finger to stroke his cheek. It was cold.

"Wakey wakey, Thomas – it's a new day…" she half-sung. "Come on, little man, wakey wakey…"

She stroked his forehead. It was cold as well. Something wasn't right.

She pulled the duvet back and shook his shoulder. No response.

She reached down to his arm. It too was cold.

She pulled him from his side onto his back. His body flopped over. His eyes stared at her, unseeing.

Loud, wrenching screams filled the house.

twenty-two

For the five years following Thomas's death, life for Michael at Milton, Knight and Haxby just got better and better. His reputation grew in the locality, and in some cases much further afield, and it seemed that he could do no wrong. He made partner at the firm and it wouldn't be long, he half-joked, until the firm would be renamed Milton, Knight, Haxby and Sewell. Whilst Margaret and Jane struggled desperately to continue the same routine each day, now one less in number, Michael spent more and more time working or following work-related pursuits. Now Margaret seldom saw her husband for more than a quarter of an hour each day: a quick change after work into a lounge suit or, more frequently, a tuxedo, and then the sound of a car horn outside would signal his lift to whatever function or dinner he was attending.

Such was Michael's rise through the business community that he was frequently asked to be the main speaker at numerous events, which invariably involved overnight stays. His candid and humorous speeches became folklore, displaying a personality which was achingly vacant in his family life. When he wasn't speaking or attending dinners with the professional community, he was instead dining out with clients. Ensuring they were happy with the work he was doing for them. Ensuring he kept them close. The dinners became more lavish and the clients were at times in awe of the lengths he went to, and more so the quality of the wine he purchased at such events. All on expenses, of course.

And this presented a new problem. His clients and

professional colleagues were not averse to letting their wives share in these evenings. In fact, many clients insisted that their spouses should meet Michael. He was regularly introduced as 'the man who ensures we continue to live in the style to which we've become accustomed' or 'the man who's saved us a fortune'. Whilst Michael drank up the accolades, people were beginning to ask less about their business affairs and more about his family life. It was true that Michael had shared details of his family, and indeed professionally it had sometimes played into his hands that he could announce sombrely that he had lost a son. However, as the trust the clients had for him grew, they accepted his keen legal decisions almost without question and instead wanted to know what the Michael Sewell they knew did outside of work. The questions continued until it became a standing joke that perhaps Michael didn't even have a wife. Or daughter. Perhaps he didn't even have a home, they laughed, just a bed in his office.

And so this forced Michael's hand and he reluctantly invited Margaret to selected events. The ones that Michael deemed appropriate. It had taken an enormous amount of effort to force the actual words out the very first time he asked her.

"Margaret, a moment please."

Michael spat the words loudly into the centre of the room from where he was sitting on the sofa reading the Sunday paper.

Margaret scurried in from the kitchen and stood beneath the archway, eyes willing. "Yes, Michael?"

She was used to this routine, although she wasn't used to the politeness this time in Michael's instruction. Usually, she would hear a shout of "Salt!" or "Tea!" and quickly rummage through the cupboards to take the salt through for him to shake on his dinner or flick on the kettle with one hand and grab a mug from the cupboard with the other. Indeed, after many years of responding to such demands, she had compiled a mental list of the most regularly demanded items and she kept them to hand at the front of the cupboard. Her willingness to please him instantly was always met with silence and never with recognition.

Michael looked at her. "Get yourself a dress. We're meeting Peter Gledhow and his wife on Saturday night."

Margaret stared at him.

"What?" he snapped.

"Do you want me to come?"

"Yes."

"What about Jane? Who'll look after her?"

"I don't know. Your mother? You sort it."

And that was it. That was the first invite that Margaret received.

That Saturday night was to be like every one of the many hundreds of functions they attended together over the many years ahead.

Margaret spent three hours bathing and preparing herself for the evening. She neatly styled her brown hair, adding half a can of hairspray to ensure that each hair lay (and remained) exactly where she wanted it. Next she sat in front of the mirror in her bedroom and carefully applied her make-up, applying and reapplying different eye-shadows until satisfied that she looked the best she could. And then, the dress. She had spent many hours trawling around the local town centre until she found something that she thought suitable. Michael had not been forthcoming as to the type of evening to expect and so she was forced to shop blind. She selected something she felt glamorous enough yet somehow understated just in case. She put on the dress and attached small pearl earrings and a matching necklace, then stood in front of the mirror. She smiled at the beautiful woman who smiled back at her and concluded that she couldn't have done any better. She had not felt like this since her wedding day.

A car horn sounded outside and she heard Michael grunt "Taxi" from the lounge below. Excitedly, she walked slowly down the wooden stairs ready to exhibit herself to her husband. She wished that Jane had been there to see her; however, she had arranged for her to sleep at her mother's that night. As she reached the bottom of the stairs, she noticed the front door was already open with the keys inserted in the outside. She could see the open door of the taxi on the street outside. The interior light lit Michael's face; he was scowling and pointing to his watch. She closed the front door and locked it behind her.

"So you do exist!" said the smiling, large man who stood before her. His cheeks were the same colour red as his favourite wine. He bent and kissed her hand.

"Hello."

"This is my wife, Margaret. Margaret, this is Mr Peter Gledhow."

"She knows who I am, old chap. I've just kissed her hand."

"And, I'm Julia," said the extremely pretty dark-haired lady standing alongside. She smiled widely. Margaret sensed immediately that it was genuine.

"Hello, Julia," said Margaret, offering a hand to greet her. Julia shook it gently.

"How are you, Michael?" she said.

"Very well, Julia, very well. Shall we?"

Michael nodded to their usual table in the corner by the window. This time it was set for four. The evening was largely convivial. Michael and Peter traded self-compliments about Peter's recent business ventures and Michael's growing case list whilst the women listened intently. Wine flowed, each glass topping up the crimson glow in Peter's cheeks. Margaret noticed that Michael was a good host, always filling his guests' glasses just that little bit more than his own. The main course was served and Peter tucked greedily into his, sharing loud stories of travel and holidays between open mouthfuls of beef. Michael carefully waited for the prompt before laughing along with his client at just the right time. He also strategically avoided questions about his own travels, instead conceding that work was a little too busy for them to consider anything other than a week holidaying by the coast.

As dessert was served, the conversation turned to family. It was Margaret and Julia's turn to talk and they traded stories of their daughters. It turned out Julia had two daughters, one a similar age to Jane, the other five years younger. Julia spoke at length about her eldest's love of the clarinet and how she was soon to be representing her county in cross-country running. Her youngest, it seemed, had an early talent for piano. Margaret spoke about Jane and her love of art. About how her teachers had picked her out as a child with exceptional artistic talent (a fact that Michael had been unaware of until this point. He made a mental note to store it for use on other evenings out). The women spoke happily together, laughing and smiling. Michael and Peter raised their eyebrows at one another. A look to signify that perhaps the women were getting a little carried away.

"Another drink, Julia?" asked Michael.

Julia broke off her conversation with Margaret. "A coffee, please."

Michael nodded at Margaret, the movement of his head asking her the same question.

"Yes, please. The same."

Julia turned back to Margaret and the women instantly continued their conversation.

Michael ordered four coffees, two with whisky. The conversation lowered whilst they drank the final drinks of the evening. The men, looking slightly worse for wear, dabbed the corners of their mouths with the crumpled white napkins from their knees.

"Well, I guess we'd better call it a night," slurred Peter, his extra share of wine now beginning to show.

Michael nodded in agreement. He was getting tired. He called the waiter over and settled the bill.

The foursome retrieved their coats and stood in the restaurant foyer awaiting the taxis that the waiter had kindly arranged. Julia pulled Margaret close, squeezing her hand.

"It has been wonderful to meet you," she said.

"And you," said Margaret, the slight fuzz of wine warming her cheeks.

"We must get the girls together. I'm sure that Harriet would love to see Jane's art."

"Absolutely," smiled Margaret.

"You'll have to bring her again!" chortled Peter, nudging Michael and then steadying himself against Michael's arm.

Michael smiled. Margaret caught the look. It was anything but genuine.

The taxis arrived and the two couples separated, saying their goodbyes in the same way that they had greeted four hours earlier. Margaret linked arms with Michael and strode through the darkness to their taxi. She waved over her shoulder to Julia. The taxi door slammed shut behind them and Michael told the driver their address. He then sat back in his seat alongside Margaret. Margaret turned to him.

"What a lovely couple."

Silence.

"I really like Julia; she's so friendly."

Michael turned to Margaret.

"It's not about who *you* liked Margaret. It's about business. Not about family or clarinets or fucking art. It's about business. So the next time you feel liked rattling on about all that shit. Don't."

Margaret turned and stared at the bright street lights as the shop-fronts of the city raced by.

And so life continued in this way for many years. An endless pattern of dinners, speaking engagements and social events. Of reluctant family holidays. Of work. Of keeping Michael happy. Of keeping family life balanced. Through Jane passing her exams and leaving for university. Through Jane getting her first home. Through Jane getting married. Life continued in this way, the early bond between mother and daughter always strong, always unbreakable. They shared unspoken feelings toward husband, toward father. More dinners. More social events. More humiliation. More feelings of worthlessness. More disappointment. Until one day, after many weeks of asking, the day arrived that Michael relented and allowed Margaret on his instruction, to 'book an appointment' with him.

And that appointment took place one dark, rainy night at a pub somewhere in the countryside.

about now

twenty-three

Michael rose from the table immediately. He pulled his wallet from his back pocket and threw down two twenty-euro notes. It would more than cover the bill.

"Michael, I'm sorry."

He slowly pushed the chair under the table where he had been sitting. His eyes focused on Claire's throughout. She looked back at him, trying to find something in him, some kind of understanding. But he no longer seemed to be behind his eyes, their steely-grey an impenetrable wall to pass through. There was nothing.

"Michael, please. I'm so sorry. I didn't mean to upset…"

Michael leaned down to her level, their noses no more than an inch apart. His eyes were still fixed on hers.

"Fuck. You."

Michael removed his sandals and slowly lay down on his bed. The sun had been relentless as usual. It wasn't the wisest of ideas to walk back during the hottest part of the day, but if he hadn't left when he did…well, he wasn't sure what he would have done. Who the fuck did she think she was? Questioning him about whether he missed Margaret. She had overstepped the mark. By a long way. The feeling that had haunted him all day had in that moment been replaced by rage. A rage that Michael had felt before. A rage that when at its most potent he found difficult to control. He had done the right thing by leaving when he did. She had better not cross his path again.

He stared at the ceiling, noticing for the first time a crack which strayed from the wall above him to the centre of the room. Its journey ended at a yellowed smoke alarm whose red light winked intermittently at him. The feeling inside him discreetly began to reappear from its slumber. The power of his rage had caused it to retreat for cover until it was safe to come out again. A little pulse beat in his chest in time with the light on the ceiling.

Jane woke. It was early. She could tell by the fact that the room was still dark. She hadn't yet opened her eyes, but she could sense the darkness. Her head hurt. She rolled over across the bed, gripping the underside of her pillow with one hand. A claw-like grip to ensure that she could roll straight back into position. Matt wasn't there. She rolled back over, resting on her right side. She opened her mouth and sucked in the air. After three large gulps, she rolled onto her back and slowly opened her eyes. It was dark. She felt sick.

She moved her tongue around the inside of her mouth; it stuck momentarily to the roof. The thin layers of tequila, wine and whatever else she had been drinking had now formed a putrid-tasting film on her tongue and the roof of her mouth. She stared at the ceiling, a solitary cobweb causing a brief distraction from the pounding in her head. She imagined that the beating inside her head was visible as little repetitive pulses bulging her temples on the outside. She pulled her hands up and, using the middle fingers on each hand, she pushed deeply into her temples, willing the pain to cease. The pushing caused further pain, but it was a different type of pain. A long, almost electric fizz that began at the temples and then moved around to the back of her head. It was a temporary release.

She struggled back onto her side and clumsily clawed her

watch over from the bedside table. She lifted it in front of her eyes and tried to read the face. It was too dark, and for a moment or two she angled the watch into different positions, sometimes getting sight of the one of the two hands. It was impossible to read and, defeated, she let her hands drop heavily onto the white duvet.

A second later she rolled over again and retrieved her phone from the same place. She clicked the button on the front and the screen lit up. Christ, she thought. It was early. Half-past-five early. She slid her finger across the screen to open the main menu. The screen instructed her to enter her passcode. She tapped at the screen, her lack of focus made it impossible for her to hit the circular numbers she desired. Each incorrect tap caused the phone to release a quick vibration and the screen reset. The phone now warned her that it was her last attempt prior to it locking.

Jane rested the phone on the duvet and pulled herself up. A feeling of sickness rushed up her throat. Her head spun. She closed her eyes and shook her head slightly, trying to shake away the feeling. She then opened her eyes again and picked up the phone. She craned over it, bringing it in her left hand to within six inches of her face. With her right hand she carefully entered the numbers one after the other: 3-9-6-3. To her relief, the passcode screen whizzed to the left and the home screen appeared. Jane let her head drop back down onto the pillow.

The green speech bubble at the bottom of the screen indicated that there were no new messages. She tapped through to piece together where her husband may be. His last message stated he would be 'later than expected', she vaguely remembered that. She also noticed that she had attempted a reply which she had obviously aborted, due to the fact that Matt was unlikely to know what 'KO sdrd yiu' meant. There was no further indication as to Matt's movements after that. Jane returned to the main menu and checked the messages marked 'Dad'. She'd received no new messages. The four previous ones which Jane had sent sat neatly on top of one another to the right of the screen. There were four missed calls, however. All from her father.

Jane put the phone back on the duvet and resumed her 'stare at the ceiling' pose. Her head continued to throb, reminding her why she rarely drank. She pondered the events of the night before. Had she spoken out of turn? No, she didn't think so. She couldn't remember any dispute or argument. And anyway, aside from one or two isolated incidents, being argumentative was not in her character, sober or otherwise. Had she done something stupid? Well, she remembered the incident with Farouk, but that was just a bit of fun. Nothing sinister there. How had she got home? She thought for a while before remembering the taxi ride. Where was Matt? This she didn't know. She had no idea what time she had arrived home. She remembered that the house was dark and Matt wasn't yet home, but after that…well, it was impossible to recall. Her memory seemed to stop there. And now it was quarter to six in the morning, and Matt wasn't there.

A sudden rush of nausea hit her. She realised that she wasn't going to be able to stop it. She froze momentarily before swinging her legs over the side of the bed and pulling herself up. The vomit shot from her stomach into her mouth, burning her throat. She felt her way around the end of the bed, breathing quickly and heavily through her nose. The vomit swilled in her mouth, filling her cheeks. She stumbled from the end of the bed to the small en-suite. She threw herself forward, opening her mouth as she fell toward the toilet. The vomit splashed forward, covering the lower part of the lifted toilet seat and the inside of the pan. More came, forcing itself up from her stomach and out through her mouth. By this time, Jane was cradling the toilet and her aim improved.

The vomit gathered like a putrid oil slick on the surface of the water. A few small pieces of perhaps vegetable attached themselves to her dark hair, which hung down into the toilet like long brown vines. Another retch, and then she discharged more, her whole body lifting slightly as each movement came. Small bubbles of vomit appeared and then popped from her nostrils. She reached up toward the sink, her right hand fumbling in the dark for the tap. She found the lever and pulled it upwards. Water rushed from the tap and she filled her hand as best she could before pulling it back toward her and wiping around her mouth. She pinched the middle of her nose and blew heavily. The air forced more small pieces of solid out of her nose; they flew like small darts into the toilet, sticking to the sides. She cupped another handful of water and repeated the blow, clearing the acidic liquid from her nose. She retched again. And again. Nothing came. Her stomach was empty. She breathed quickly out through her mouth, back in through her mouth. The worst was over.

A few minutes passed. Jane pulled herself up from the toilet onto the sink. She tilted her head and leaned under the tap until her mouth caught the ice-cold running water. She splashed her face, rubbing the water into her eyes. The pain had moved from her temples to across her forehead. If it was possible, it was a nicer pain. A long, continuous buzz; no accompanying throb or beat.

She took a step backwards and reached around the door frame for the light switch, which was situated inside the bedroom. The room lit up and she looked in the mirror. Her eyes had sunken and dark rings surrounded them. Her hair was matted into small wet rats' tails, the vomit still visible. If her dad could see her now, she thought. He'd be disgusted. Disgusted that his daughter – 'at her age' – could get herself into such a state.

She blew her nose under the tap, clearing it fully for the first time. Using her fingers, she pulled her hands through the strands of hair from around halfway to the tip, loosening the vomit, which plopped into the sink before being swept away by the water. While she was doing so, she noticed the smell in the bathroom. Through the strong, pungent odour of bile and undigested food she could clearly smell Matt's aftershave. She reached over and flushed the toilet, closing the lid as she did so. She sucked in another mouthful of water and switched off the tap. Yes, the distinct smell of Matt's Hugo Boss aftershave was still in the air. Matt must have been home, she thought, and not too long ago.

She put down the toilet seat and sat, wiping her face with a towel. A small orange fragment left her hair and landed on her bare foot. She rested for a few minutes longer and then decided to get on with the day. She was due in work that morning and a shower would hopefully be step toward feeling better.

"Matt?"

"Hi," said Matt. His tone was low and sharp. The number of rings it had taken for him to pick up indicated that he had considered ignoring the call.

Jane had expected this. After all, it was entirely her fault that she hadn't seen him the night before. She pulled a brush through her wet hair, the water dripping on her white robe, a little on the kitchen work surface.

"Are you okay?" she chirped, suspecting he would see through the faked jauntiness. Her headache now rested behind her eyes.

He did. "Not really, no. You?"

"Yeah, I'm fine, thanks. Bit of a headache, y'know, but…" She wasn't sure what belonged after the 'but'. It could have been a pathetic "I'm surviving" or an equally pitiful "it's no less than expected", which was why she stopped herself. Matt hated babbling.

"You were pissed last night, Jane." It was Matt's turn to pause.

"I wasn't that bad," said Jane, dragging the 'that' out in what she hoped would come across in a slightly flirty way.

"You were battered. I found you fully dressed on the bed. Took me fucking ages to get your clothes off and get you into bed."

Jane stopped, the brush seemingly frozen in time at the side of her head. She had no recollection of this.

"You were fucking kicking out at me and moaning."

"Sorry," she said, putting the brush down.

"Listen, I don't mind you going out. You can do what the fuck you want, you know that. But you said to me that you weren't going to get that pissed again. You know, after last time."

Jane clearly remembered last time. It wasn't pretty. There was swearing and screaming and pushing. All by her. Matt had tried to calm her, but the sound of his voice had irritated her further, each word driving a rage inside her. She had shoved him backwards when he had tried to hug her. And she had screamed at him. Inches from his face. The next day, she had regretted everything. She had never, never been that way before. The anger hadn't been aimed at him; he had done nothing wrong. She had vowed not to drink as much after that.

"I'm sorry. Really I am."

The apology was sincere. Unfortunately, with no recollection of the previous night's events, she was unclear what she was apologising for.

"I slept on the sofa. You were too pissed. Spread-eagled across the bed."

"I'm so sorry. What time did you get in?"

"About midnight."

"How come?"

"Couldn't get the servers running properly. We had to stay back."

"What time did you leave this morning?"

"About five. Had a shower and then set off back here." His tone had mellowed.

"God, that's early." Jane fingered the rim of her coffee cup. It was warm.

"I know. I'm knackered."

"I bet you are, sweetheart."

Matt yawned. Jane wasn't sure whether it was real or not. It was perhaps just an oral prop to give Matt's statement more veracity.

"Yeah, might be the same hours again tonight as well. Depends if we can get it running?"

"Oh no, really? I was hoping we could curl up and watch a film together."

There was a crackle on the line, then what sounded to Jane like a muffled giggle.

"Sorry?" said Matt.

"I said I was hoping we could watch a film together tonight. Aren't you listening?"

"Sorry, I got distracted. No, think I'll be working late again tonight. We'll have to do it some other time. There's meant to be four of us doing this project; turns out there's just us two."

"Okay," said Jane, slightly defeated. She gulped back a mouthful of coffee. The movement of her head caused her to feel temporarily dizzy. It was going to be a long day.

"Sorry, nothing I can do about it. You working today?"

"Sure am." She glanced at the digital clock on the cooker. "Start in a couple of hours."

The phone crackled again; it sounded like someone was

screwing up crêpe paper at the other end. The definite sound of a giggle followed it.

"Listen, I've got to go, Jane. I'll call you later, yeah?"

"Yeah, er, fine." Jane raised her eyebrows and shook her head slightly, persuading herself it was.

"Okay, have a good day at work."

"You too. I'm really sorry about last night."

"It's okay. Listen, I've really got to go."

"Okay. I love you."

"You too."

Jane tapped the screen to end the call and replaced the phone on the kitchen worktop. She picked up the brush and began to pull it through her hair slowly, trying to ignore the pain in her head. It was going to be a *very* long day.

A dull, long buzz broke the repetitive dance between the smoke alarm light and the feeling in Michael's chest. He realised that his phone was ringing. He sat up and unzipped the black bag to retrieve it. It was Jane. He paused for a moment, considering whether he wanted to take the call, and then pressed the green button when he decided he did.

"Hi, Dad?" Jane asked, her tone suggesting she was unsure whether it was Michael who had picked up.

"Hello, Jane."

"Hi, Dad. Where have you been? I've been worrying –"

"Jane, I'm fine," he interrupted.

"I've texted and called numerous times, but not heard a thing…" Jane decided that she didn't need to pursue this line any further and quickly changed tack. "How's the, er, weather?"

"It's very hot."

"Are you enjoying yourself?"

"Not really, Jane."

"Oh. Is there much to do there?"

"No."

Michael's unenthusiastic, monotonous responses were making a conversation extremely difficult.

"Oh, well, I was worried about you so I thought I'd ring. I'm on my lunch break at work, and I thought it may be a good time to ring." Jane knew she was babbling; her head still ached.

The line went quiet.

Michael was pondering whether to embark down the path that his next sentence may lead.

"Dad?"

His journey began.

"Jane?"

"Yes?"

"Did you say you were at work at the moment?" He spoke slowly with a slightly inquisitive tone.

"Yes, Dad."

"I wonder, could you check something out for me, please?"

"Uh-huh."

"Can you search your database, or system or whatever, for any book?"

This was the first time Michael had ever asked anything about Jane's job. In fact, she couldn't remember him even referring to it before, aside from the time he told her that he knew she'd never make anything of herself and he 'had known since she was little that she'd end up in a dead-end job in a shop or something similar'. Her mother had lowered both her eyebrows and smiled briefly at her, ensuring that Michael didn't catch her expression when he turned around to ask whether she agreed. She had, as usual, expertly managed to avoid the question without indicating she agreed or otherwise.

"Yes, I can, Dad." An excited inflection that she couldn't control found its way into Jane's voice. She could be of use to Michael. "What is it you want?"

The feeling suddenly began to beat more quickly in Michael's chest. An ever louder rhythm building up to his next sentence. He swallowed.

"I'm after some information about an author…" He was unsure whether to proceed. The beating continued.

"Yes? Who is it?" The words skipped from Jane's mouth.

"Well, he's not very well known. I don't think."

"Okay."

"He's called Dirk Heille." Boom. Boom. Boom.

"Dirk Hi-lah? Just give me a second."

Jane left the small kitchenette and returned to the shop floor. A customer smiled, her head moving to the side to signal she wanted assistance. Jane smiled back indicating with her fingers that she would be two minutes, and the customer nodded her understanding. With her phone in one hand, Jane tapped the screen in front of her, which led her directly to the intranet site of JayListBooks, a book distributor and wholesaler that supplied Martha with new releases. The login screen claimed that their database had worldwide details of every IBSN, the unique international book code that helps a reader to identify a title. After two failed attempts to log in, a sentence appeared informing Jane that the site was currently offline. Jane balanced the phone under her ear and grabbed a piece of paper and a pen. Martha, eager to learn the source of the sudden excitement, appeared alongside Jane at the till and helpfully held the paper still so Jane could take control of the phone again.

"Okay, Dad. The website doesn't seem to be working right now. Can you spell the name out and I'll check later?"

Michael sighed and wearily spelled out each letter. Jane repeated the name back to him. Martha beamed and set off to a small bookcase no more than ten metres away.

"Yes, that's right."

"Okay, I'll look as soon as it's working again and ring you back."

"Useless. Well, don't be long," said Michael, ensuring that Jane could hear his disappointment.

"As soon as I can, Dad. I promise."

At that moment Martha hurried toward Jane. She was holding a book in her right hand.

"Er, wait a second, Dad."

"What now?"

Martha held the book aloft as she reached Jane. She bore a passing resemblance to an overweight statue of liberty, albeit this one had replaced the torch with a tatty-looking novel. "Dirk Heille," she panted.

"Martha has his book, Dad." Martha passed the book to Jane. "We have it here."

Michael swallowed hard. His heart was pounding.

"Really?"

"Yes, *Picnic at Breeze Knoll* by Dirk Heille."

"Excellent. What does the back cover say?"

Jane read the blurb on the back cover to her father. It was the story of two German sisters who were separated during World War I. One was sent to America whilst the other remained in Germany. It was a love story and apparently, if the cover was to be believed, a beautiful story of hope and forgiveness.

Michael fumbled for his bag, unclipped the press-stud on the side and pulled out the page. This didn't sound right.

"What does page one hundred and sixty-three say?"

"Sorry?"

"Page one hundred and sixty-three," he said impatiently. "What does it say?"

Sensing her father's temper rising, Jane put her phone down and flicked through the book. Martha stood close by, trying to catch Jane's eye with a variation of puzzled and confused looks. A small queue began to form at the till. Jane scanned the page and retrieved her phone.

"Well, er, it talks about a girl called Olga who's painting a watercolour in her garden, and the colours of the trees in the wood behind her house, and –"

"No," interrupted Michael, "that's the wrong one."

"Pardon?"

"It's the wrong fucking book, Jane."

"..."

"Has he written any others?"

"What, er?"

"Flick to the front, Jane – it's not bloody hard. Has. He. Written. Any. Others?"

Jane flicked frantically to the front, holding the inside of the cover down with her elbow so she could see the list of other works by the author.

"Yes, Dad. He's written about thirty. Maybe more."

"Jesus."

Jane waited.

"Listen, Jane. You get on that computer as soon as it's working, okay? I want to know the names of them all and where I can get them."

Michael clicked the button on his phone to end the call.

Jane's eyes welled up. She looked at Martha.

Martha squeezed her arm and clapped her hands together.

"We've got customers to serve," she said. She scrunched up her face and nodded to suggest that they would discuss the strange call later. Jane swallowed noting that she hadn't once questioned her father why he suddenly needed to know this information. She turned to face the line of people in front of her.

"Who's next, please?" she asked.

Michael flattened out the creases from the page as best he could and laid it on the bed alongside him. He focused on the words, looking for some kind of further meaning. He read and reread it again. 'Grave consequences' – he just didn't like the sound of that at all. For a moment, he considered pouring himself a whisky from the half-empty bottle on the cabinet across the room. Instead, he grabbed the bottle, unscrewed its cap, made his way to the bathroom and emptied its contents into the sink. He turned on the taps and washed the remainder of the bottle down the plughole, letting the taps run long after the golden residue had been washed away. He then switched off the taps, satisfied that the strong smell had now gone. He put the empty bottle in the small metal bin under the sink. No more alcohol from now on; he needed his mind to be completely clear. He needed to think. It was paramount.

He stood, resting on the sink, for a moment, sure that if he removed his shirt he would be able to see his heart beating its way out of his chest.

twenty-four

When the day's final customer had left, Jane flipped the closed sign and sighed deeply. Her prediction was right; it had been an incredibly long day. She turned and made her way across the shop to collect her coat. She was exhausted and ready for home. Martha stopped her on her way out of the small kitchenette.

"Are you going home already?" she asked.

"I am, yes," Jane said, fearing another invitation for drinks.

"Are you sure you don't want a quick coffee?"

"Well –"

"Let's have a quick coffee together, Janey," Martha interrupted, "and you can let me know what your father wanted."

Jane retrieved her phone from her coat pocket. Two missed calls since their conversation earlier. She spun the screen around to show Martha.

"Whatever he wanted, he's keen! Listen, I'll pop the kettle on. Take your coat off and we'll have a quick drink."

Jane did as she was told. A drink now seemed like a good idea. There was no rush to get home anyway; it was unlikely she would see Matt. She removed her coat and folded it neatly into a square on the floor. Then she sat on the chaise-longue and retrieved her voicemail messages. Both were from her father. Both demanded she rang back immediately. Both enquired as to whether the '[insert expletive] computer' was working. This wasn't something she wanted to deal with now. She switched off her phone and gently dropped it down onto the cushioning of her coat.

Martha rounded the corner, carrying two large cups of coffee.

"Thanks," said Jane, taking her cup from Martha.

"How are you feeling, Janey?"

"Oh, not so bad now."

"Not felt your best today, have you?"

"Not at all," Jane said, her eyebrows furrowing.

"A few too many last night, darling? Not to worry."

Jane smiled.

"So, what was all the fuss with your father earlier? Never known him to ring you at work."

Jane paused. She wondered whether Martha was hinting that she shouldn't have taken her phone with her to the till. In fact, she wasn't sure why she had; it wasn't something she had ever done before. She blamed it on the fog of the day.

"I know. Sorry."

"It's not a problem, Janey. I'm more interested in the mystery of one Dirk Heille. So what, did you father want to know?"

"I don't really know," Jane replied honestly. "He just telephoned and asked me about him, completely out of the blue."

"Did he say why?"

"No. He just asked me about him. You brought over the book. I read a bit to him, and then he…well, you know the rest."

"How very peculiar. Why did he ask you to read from it?"

"I don't know that either." Jane realised that she had no explanation for the whole incident.

"Did he say, darling?"

"No. He just asked me to turn to page one hundred and sixty-three and read it. When I did, he told me it was the wrong effing book and basically hung up."

It was Martha's turn to furrow her brow.

"Well, that's strange. The book I brought over, *Picnic at Breezy Wotnot.*"

"Breeze Knoll."

"Yes, darling, *Picnic at Breeze Knoll.* That book's been in this shop for years and years. In fact it was probably here when my father was alive. I don't remember it coming in since I was here."

This was almost unquestionably true. Martha had an encyclopaedic knowledge of all the books in the shop, despite the topsy-turvy way they were sorted.

"Do we have any more by him?"

"No. Definitely not. I would know if we had."

Martha stood and took a couple of paces to the counter. She retrieved the book and plonked herself back down next to Jane, wheezing slightly as she did.

"Let's have a better look, shall we?"

Jane hunched over to see.

The book had seen better days. The spine itself was in good condition, still eagerly clutching the pages. Each of the two corners opposite, however, was curled back towards the spine, causing the book to slightly fan open. The cover itself was a mishmash of what was supposed to a beautiful sunrise contrasted with the dark silhouettes of soldiers in trenches toward the bottom. Across the middle was a crudely drawn picture of two women hugging one another. The book's title was printed across the top of the cover, bursting out of the sunrise in black scroll-type writing. Across the bottom, in bold white letters, the words 'DIRK HEILLE' punched through the black silhouettes of the soldiers. The original art, it appeared, was painted in oil. Remnants of various sticker adhesives were still visible when the book caught the right light.

Inside, the pages were yellowed. The print was small and tightly spaced, making reading difficult. This was perhaps why the spine was pretty much untouched. Martha flicked through the book, right to the end.

"Ugly-looking thing, isn't it?" she smiled.

Jane giggled.

"Ah, here we go, Janey."

Martha read from the penultimate page.

"'Dirk Heille was born in nineteen-oh-eight in Dresden, where he lives to this day. He has written more than thirty novels that have been translated into sixteen languages. He is married with two children.'"

Jane nodded her understanding.

"So your father is interested in the books of a German-born author."

"Weird, isn't it?"

Martha closed the book and turned it over. She began to read.

"It's a wartime love story…" Jane said.

Martha held up a finger. It signified silence. She continued to read the blurb to the end.

"Hmm," she said, looking up. "So your father is interested in the books of a German-born wartime romantic novelist!"

Jane laughed again. "I know. Bizarre!"

"But," said Martha, suddenly taking on a more serious and inquisitive tone, "this is not actually the book your father is after, is it?"

Jane shook her head, eyes wide.

"So what's the name of the one he wants?"

"I don't know," said Jane. "He didn't say."

Martha opened the book again and flicked a few pages in from the front. She stopped on the page which listed the author's other books.

"Well, there's a few to go at here."

"I know."

"It'd be helpful to know what your father's after and then we could try to get hold of them, Janey." She put her hand on Jane's knee and tapped lightly.

"I just have no clue why he's suddenly so interested. He doesn't really read that much anyway. Certainly not German love stories."

"Darling," said Martha excitedly. Her finger had stopped beneath one of the titles. "I think – sorry, I *know* we have this one."

"Really? Which one?" Jane asked eagerly.

"This one right here: *The Return of Mr Trenton*."

She stood up.

"But the one we have is not by Dirk Heille," she said, hurrying toward the back of the shop. Jane turned to watch. It was an odd sight, watching Martha get anywhere at pace. Her entire frame wasn't really built for speed. Her feet spilled out of the top of her bottle-green patent stilettos, making her walk more of a concerted waddle, and her wide backside swung from side to side rhythmically with each step. She reached the section marked 'T' and eagerly scanned the shelves. Her eyes darted from left to right until they came across what she was looking for. Fortunately for her, it was at shoulder height, and she coaxed the top of it out with her chubby finger. When she had squeezed enough of it out, she grabbed it and held it aloft in excitement.

"*The Return of Mr Trenton!* I told you, Janey!"

"Who's it by?"

"Er, let me see. It's by Ed Drewhorn."

"Who?"

"Ed Drewhorn," she repeated. Martha waddled back toward where Jane was sitting. "Look," she said, holding the book out to Jane. Her cheeks were red. She was out of breath.

Jane went to take the book, but Martha inched it back toward herself, the movement making it clear that she wanted to play the role of lead detective. They both scanned the cover. It wasn't dissimilar to the artwork of the previous book. Again, it was dark and crudely painted in oil. This time the face of a fedora-wearing, moustachioed male entered from the right, taking up around a third of the cover. Facing him was a small property, high up on a hillside. There was a light on inside. The book's title appeared across the top. The same font from the other book displayed the author's name across the bottom. The book was in a much better condition than the previous, the C-shaped curve of the spine suggesting it had been read at least once.

"Mr Trenton?" said Martha, prodding the man's face.

"Maybe."

Martha turned the book over and moved it slightly closer to Jane so they could both read. She kept a tight grip.

"Another love story," said Jane.

Martha opened the book at the back and flicked through a few pages. Jane couldn't see.

"Here we are," she said and then, "Ah-ha! Got it! 'Ed Drewhorn was born in Germany in 1908'…blah, blah, blah…'he also writes under the name of…'"

"Dirk Heille?"

"Dirk Heille," said Martha, pretending not to hear Jane. "It's the same author, Janey!"

"Wow!" said Jane. She wasn't entirely sure what this discovery meant, but it sounded exciting.

Martha was now hurriedly flicked through the book. "What page was it, Janey? What page?"

"Er, one hundred and sixty-three."

"Right, darling, one-six-three."

She flicked to right page and scanned the first few paragraphs. She looked up.

"And what was it supposed to say, Janey?"

"I don't know," said Jane. "He didn't tell me."

The bubble of excitement immediately burst.

"Oh. So how do we know whether it's the right book or not?" Martha sounded deflated.

"Well," said Jane, "it's probably not that one."

"Why?"

"Well Dad's book was by Dirk Heille. This is by Ed Drewhorn."

"But it could be this one. It could have been translated into English, and maybe the publisher changed his name to make it more appealing to overseas markets. You know, so people from English-speaking countries wouldn't be put off by his Germanic name, darling."

Jane wasn't sure whether Martha had a point or not. She sipped her coffee. "Maybe," seemed the most sensible answer.

"You'll have to ask your father exactly what he's looking for on the mysterious page one-six-three." Martha dragged out the word 'mysterious' for extra effect.

"I will," said Jane, knowing that she wouldn't do it that day. She couldn't take another rejection from him should it be the wrong book again.

"Ring him and ask, darling," said Martha eagerly. She was enjoying this game.

"I can't," Jane lied. "His last message said he wasn't available for the rest of the day."

"Oh, that's a shame."

"I know."

Martha flicked through to the front to find a bibliography

which stretched from the top of the page almost to the bottom. "There's a lot of books here to find, Janey."

Jane nodded. "One last look," she said, rising.

She made her way around to the till and tapped the JayList logo on the screen. Again, she was greeted with the message that they were 'experiencing difficulties' and the 'website was currently down'. She sighed.

"Still no go?" asked Martha.

"Unfortunately, yes."

"Oh dear, darling. Well, you can always pop in tomorrow and check, can't you?"

"Yeah, thanks, I will."

Jane made her way around the till and picked up her coat. "Time for home?"

"I'm meeting an old friend for a glass of wine first," said Martha mischievously. "Care to join?"

"No, thanks. Last night was enough for me. It'll be a few months before I drink again." She put on her coat and buttoned the front.

"Wait a moment, before you go."

Martha went behind the counter and opened the cupboard where the printer was situated. She opened the books and laid them flat on the glass screen and pressed a button on the top. The printer came to life, spewing out copies of the bibliographies and the author's biography from each book. Martha also copied page 163 of *The Return of Mr Trenton* and then rustled through various papers and unopened envelopes until she found an empty folder. She put the copies in and passed the folder to Jane.

"Here you go. Just in case you want to do any research tonight."

"Thanks," said Jane, trying to sound enthusiastic. For the first time since her mother had died she was considering painting that evening. The awful book covers had momentarily persuaded her that she did have a talent after all.

They hugged in a theatrical way and Jane made her way to the door.

"Janey. Let me know if you find anything, won't you?" Martha clasped her hands together with excitement.

"I will," Jane smiled, and closed the door behind her.

"It's so exciting," said Martha to no-one in particular.

The bus slowly pulled in at the side of the road. Jane thanked the driver, unsure whether he heard her over the whooshing sound the doors made. She stepped off the bus and turned left toward her home. Under her arm she carried the grey cardboard folder which Martha had prepared for her. The headache that had dogged her most of the day had finally subsided around four p.m. and she was now left with an empty feeling. Oh, and the same taste in her mouth. She found it incredible that, despite drinking tea, coffee, Coca-Cola, water and some still drink called Vitamin Water that Martha had sworn would get rid of her hangover, the same taste that had greeted her on waking still remained. The food she had forced down had not made a blind bit of difference either.

Martha had been her usual bouncy self throughout the day, showing no signs of suffering from the previous night's excesses. In fact, she had proudly told Jane, she had still been drinking at one a.m., when Farouk finally asked her and an old actor friend she had bumped into to leave. Jane, on the other hand, had felt dreadful. She privately guessed that Martha's lack of ill effects was likely down to how regularly she partook in *those* type of nights.

She rounded the corner, passing an old-fashioned red letterbox which, with the help of a permanent marker, had been converted into a crude penis. It was a mild evening, a light breeze shooshing the large trees that lined the street. She liked the area; it was always so quiet. So…well, normal. All the houses were similar, a typical white-clad repetition of 1960s'-style semi-detached houses. The pavement ran in front of the houses, separated from the road by rectangles of grass. Every fifteen or so paces the grass ended to allow entrance to each house's driveway. Trees reached up into the sky from every other patch.

Jane continued along the road, clutching the folder to her side. She really hadn't intended on looking any further into the background of the German author. Although her headache had disappeared, she felt physically and mentally drained. She just wanted to get home and spend an hour relaxing in the bath. The half hour bus journey had tired her further, and all thoughts of spending the evening painting had been dispelled. Her inspiration had quickly drained away. She would pick up her brush again one day. But not just yet.

She rounded the last corner of her journey. She could see her house getting ever closer. Again, it was dark. She remembered that Matt wouldn't be home until late that night. She considered whether this was good or bad thing. If he hadn't been working late, she could snuggle down alongside him on the sofa and watch mindless TV for a few hours. Feel the comfort and warmth of his arm around her waist as he lay behind her, his closeness making her feel safe. But, the fact was that he wasn't going to be home any time soon and frankly, she wasn't in the mood for talking. In fact, she wasn't really in the mood for any human interaction. She just wanted a bath, with candles and silence. She couldn't be bothered to talk about her day; what she had for lunch; whether it had been busy; what she had been doing. Certainly, after the earlier call with Matt, it was likely that any conversation they had would be strained anyway, and she simply didn't have the energy for it. Arriving home and going straight upstairs and into the solitude of the bathroom would likely make the atmosphere worse. It was likely in this frame of mind she would agree with him to keep him quiet. Agree with his points that were quite possibly the opposite of how she felt. Anyway, it didn't matter. Matt was coming home late, and so she could decide just how she would spend her night.

Jane reached the house. She unlocked the door, locked it behind her, threw her keys onto the sofa and removed her coat. She hung it on the pegs behind her and switched on the lights.

twenty-five

The sunshine and distant, excited chatter signified it was morning. Late morning. Michael rolled over to his side. He had been in the same place since six o'clock the previous night. On his bed. He had retreated to his room early needing some time from the outside world to think and to control his rage. There he had remained throughout the night until the morning light had awoken him. Then, he had whiled away well over an hour simply staring at the smoke alarm, disallowing any thoughts. A knock on the door had distracted him.

He bolted upright, his hands taking the weight of his body behind his back. Her stared at the back of the wooden door. The only sound was his own breathing, which was quick and shallow. He focused on taking longer breaths. Thoughts flew into his mind as to who could be on the other side. It could be any number of people. He knew that he didn't want to communicate with anybody. He also knew he wasn't going to answer the knock. He continued to listen. Continued to stare at the door, following the lines which ran vertically down it where each piece of wood slotted into the next. It was silent. Perhaps whoever had arrived had now departed. He hadn't heard them walk away from the door, however; therefore they may still be there. That being said, he considered, neither had he heard them approach in the first place. He breathed through his nose, long and slow, until he felt his lungs were filled to capacity. He then let out the air again through his tightly pursed lips, directing it toward his chin through the small opening. He listened for another ten long seconds and concluded there was no-one there; they had definitely gone. He allowed his hands to slide down the sheets, so his elbows now took his weight. He lowered his head back toward the pillow.

And there it was again. The knock at the door. Four swift taps on the outside. Michael slid up the bed into a sitting position, pulling his knees up to his chest. The knocks were gentle but determined. They were not bangs on the door, made with the soft part of a clenched fist; they were more coaxing, the first finger enquiring as to whether anyone was in the room. Taps designed not to wake or startle Michael, but simply let him know that someone was outside. They were almost apologetic in their nature.

Michael's breathing quickened again, and he fought to bring it under control. He focused on who could be on the outside. The type of knock suggested that it may be a member of the hotel staff, perhaps housekeeping or similar. Perhaps it was maintenance wishing to access the room to service something or other. In that circumstance, his refusal to answer was likely to lead to somebody entering the room anyway. He considered whether to shout some instruction through the door to ask them to leave, but experience told him that should they be a member of hotel staff, the language barrier may preclude their understanding of his instruction and this would lead them to enter anyway. He focused on the lock of the door, expecting the metallic clunk of a key any second. If he did shout and it wasn't a member of staff at the door, he would have given away, all too easily in his mind, the fact that he was in the room. He decided to sit tight, say nothing and wait for them to enter. It was extremely quiet.

Aside from hotel staff, there were few people it could actually be. He was alone in a foreign country and knew nobody here. Nobody. Therefore, whoever had come to the door had come looking for him. For a fleeting moment he imagined Jane on the other side of the door, having made the decision that she would come over to surprise him. She knew he was having a shit time. He had made that more than clear. He wouldn't put it past her to arrive in a misguided attempt to make things better for him. Not that her appearance would. It would just confirm what he already knew: that she would make nothing of herself, and that she was attaching herself to him now her mother, from whom she'd been inseparable, was gone. 'Making sure he was okay.' It was all so self-serving: she wasn't contacting him to make sure he was okay; she was doing it for herself. A purely selfish act to make her feel better about the fact that she and her mother had been so close. And it was all fuelled by guilt. Guilt that she had spent so many hours with her mother: shopping, chatting, spa weekends at hotels, walks in the countryside, card making, whatever. Guilt that she had never thought to spend any time with him for all those years. And now her mother was gone, she just felt she could pick him up and use him as her surrogate? That she could suddenly replace her mother with him instead and he would fill her time? I don't fucking think so, he thought. The years of feeling excluded in his own family wouldn't allow this. It was weak. And the scars of rejection ran way too deep.

Michael's thoughts were interrupted as for a third time by a light tapping on the door. Just two this time. A sort of signing-off by the visitor who had concluded there would be no answer. Still taking his bodyweight on his elbows, Michael continued his stare toward the door. Then he heard a kind of shuffling noise outside the door, before a squeak and then the clack-clack of sandals lifting and then hitting the tiled surface below. A second or so later they were gone. Michael instantly relaxed and laid his head back down on the pillow. He let out a long sigh. His heart continued to pump. A little too rapidly.

Jane made her way upstairs to her bedroom. She couldn't wait to get out of her clothes and into her pyjamas. In the few moments she had been the house, she had already decided that she didn't want a bath. It would be too quiet. She had also decided that mindless television didn't appeal either. This feeling of indecision didn't happen very often, but when it did it really frustrated her. She could easily walk from room to room, trying decide what it was she wanted to do with her time. She could make a decision to watch a film and spend up to an hour procrastinating over which one it would be. Once she had decided, she would begin to watch it and then decide that she had chosen unwisely. She would begin another. The same thing would happen. Eventually, frustrated with herself, she would simply turn off the television and stare at the blank screen or the ceiling, her evening completely gone, with nothing to show for it. A waste of her time.

No, she would get straight into her pyjamas. This was a ritual. A trigger which signified to her that she was now moving into relaxation mode. It also signified that now she was home, she had absolutely no intention of leaving the house again that day. It was her commitment to relaxation. She unbuttoned her blouse and tossed it into the wicker wash-basket in the corner. Then she relaxed back onto the bed, clawing at her jeans until they passed her thighs, before kicking her legs like a scuba diver until they slid into a heap on the floor. She sat up and reached around to remove her bra, and from across the room landed it directly on top of the blouse. She stood and collected the jeans from the floor before hanging them back in the wardrobe. They had another day left in them at least. She walked across the bedroom to the drawers, sliding them open to retrieve her nightwear.

As she turned she caught a glimpse of herself in the full-length mirror. She stopped and stared. In the brief struggle to remove her jeans, her bottom had partially swallowed her pants and she hooked a finger around them to cover her buttock. She smiled at herself. Her reflection followed suit. She wasn't sure exactly why she was smiling, and she raised her eyebrows in an 'I don't know' type of way at the mirror. She went closer to mirror, still holding her pyjamas. She wanted to look more closely at herself, at her face. She approached and smiled again. A big, beaming smile. Then she forced it wider, exposing her teeth more, the kind of exaggerated smile that a toddler gives when instructed for a photograph. Wide, almost manic.

Then her face cracked. Her bottom lip lowered slightly and the corners of her mouth turned down. Her eyes, bright moments earlier, seemed to immediately lose their sheen. The handful of light wrinkles which surrounded them quickly changed their direction from pointing upwards to downwards as the muscles relaxed. And now she couldn't control it. Her forehead capitulated, furrowing with gravity downward. Her eyes screwed up, tight, closer together. The tears didn't have time to well; they flooded down her cheeks. Dripped from the end of her nose. Her reflection showed her for the first time exactly how she felt inside.

She wailed loudly, elastic spit joining her top and bottom teeth before breaking and reforming. She sank to her knees and then into a sitting position, sideways to the mirror. The tears continued to fall, dragging mascara down her cheeks. A few black spots made their way off her chin and dripped onto her small breasts. Snot gathered and then slowly streamed onto her top lip. The noise was loud and deep; it sounded like she was in pain.

And she was. She was injured – not physically, but inside. This was worse than a splitting headache or a dental filling. Worse than a broken bone. No, *this* was worse than a stab wound or a gunshot wound. Worse than childbirth. This feeling was almost indescribable. It was real and it was the most intense pain she had ever felt.

Jane stared at the blurred image which used to look like her. The tears rushed down her face, and she gulped for air. She tried to level her breathing, to gain composure. Snot now gathered in a small off-white reservoir on her upper lip which, once full, flowed over her lip and inside her mouth. Beneath her eyes similar areas of black hung from below her eyes like dripped candle wax. Three or four black lines formed a delta which met to form one long river beneath each eye. Her mouth ached.

Still clutching her pyjamas, she refused to wipe her face. She wanted the picture of the pain she was feeling to stay in front of her. She wanted to remember this moment, because this was how she had felt every day since the accident that took her mother, her best friend, away. Even at the funeral, where people expected her to cry, it had been difficult; almost unnatural. Of course, she had been incapable of holding back the tears as the thick velvet curtains finally surrounded her mother's coffin; her last glimpse before her mother's body was taken to the flames. When the tears came she had wiped them away quickly, urging her tear ducts to suck the saline back inside. And she had been largely successful, allowing a few tears and a sniffle before steadying herself and pulling herself back from the brink. She knew she *could* let it go; she was, after all, surrounded by caring relatives and loving friends she had known all of her life. She was at the one place where people were going to understand her tears. She knew there would be no questions on that day, just constant embraces and helpless looks. But she couldn't let it go. Her father was always close by, and her tears would only show the kind of weakness he despised.

Today – this moment – was how she had felt on that day and every day since. And she wanted to capture it, because this was the first time she had really let everything out. She wanted to see, in the only visible way possible, what her mother's death had done to her, deep within her body and in the chasms of her mind. And not just her mother's death, but the years and years and years before that. The reflection was not just showing the last three months; it was showing the last thirty or so years.

She lay down in front of the mirror, unclenching her hand to release the pyjamas. Then she curled her head in, grasping her knees with each hand, and pulled herself into a tight ball. The tears had stopped and she pushed little bubbles of air through the spit and snot in a quiet repetitive 'fuh-fuh-fuh-fuh-fuh' sound not unlike a tiny steam train.

She remained in this position for several minutes until she had taken control of her breathing. Physically drained she stayed still for several minutes until she felt able to move. Then she released her knees slowly and lay on her side before rolling onto her front. With her hands under her chin, she looked at her reflection again. The black rivers had burst their banks and were smudged across her cheeks. The snot, still runny, had spread itself across one corner of her mouth. She shook her head slightly, a knowing, 'what the hell just happened to you?' kind of look, before closing the experience where it began. With a smile. This time the smile presented back to her looked different; it was a smile dripping with understanding. She pushed herself up, noticing that random black smudges of mascara covered her breasts and shoulders. She was reminded of a Dalmatian and she allowed herself another quick smile. She pulled herself to her feet and decided she would shower before changing.

About a thousand miles away, Michael turned onto his side. He reached down to the floor for his black bag. It was slightly out of reach and he had to quickly balance his weight to stop himself falling out of bed. He hooked the leather carry handle with his finger and dragged the bag closer. He then pulled the bag up onto the bed and rolled onto his back. He unclipped the press-stud of the side pocket and again retrieved the page. Reaching to the bedside table, he picked up his silver glasses, and put them on. He then neatly unfolded the page and held it up in front of him. His eyes scanned the words quickly and eagerly. Looking for clues. Looking for some kind of insight that he had not had before. He had read the page numerous times now and knew the small portion of the story off by heart. What he certainly didn't know was the huge volume of words which surrounded pages 163 and 164. This was something he could only speculate on. And since finding the page his mind had become a jumbled cat's cradle of thoughts as to what secrets the story held. What was clear was that it was vital he now uncovered the secret, if for no other reason than to untangle his woolly mind. He read it again, this time more slowly. This time out loud. On a number of occasions he had considered screwing the page up and simply disposing of it. But he knew that wouldn't work. Since the page had fallen into his possession it had become indelibly stamped on his mind. Simply throwing it away didn't mean that it didn't exist. He was not capable of just forgetting. It was too important.

He finished reading and laid the piece of paper down by his side on the sheet. His heart began to jump again, random leaps which seemed to push a different area of his chest out with each beat. When he was able to think logically he could conclude that it was just a stupid coincidence that he had ever seen the page. It had simply been a gust of wind which had randomly spilled pages into the blue sky and across the swimming pool. A gust that had delivered that particular one onto his chest. The content of the page was an issue, though. Yes, Michael and Margaret were fairly common names. Yes, car crashes did happen fairly regularly and had surely been written about hundreds, no, thousands of times over the years. But the chances of him receiving a random page which contained such specific references to his own circumstances so soon after Margaret's tragic death? Well, this seemed more than unlikely.

What further concerned him was that, assuming he put himself in the position of the Michael in the story, he didn't have the information available to him to find out what happened next. Without the rest of the novel, he wasn't able to find out Michael's fate. It was true that Margaret's life had been cruelly taken away from her. This was fact. Margaret in the story was dead. Margaret in real life was dead. Therefore, for the purposes of logical thinking at least, Margaret was irrelevant. She was dead either way. For Michael, it was a completely different story. He had survived both in reality and in the novel. And he still lived, now, in the present. And he had to go on without his wife. Therefore, for the sake of closure, he absolutely needed to know what happened next. Especially as the novel predicted – no, overtly stated – that there would be *grave consequences*.

As he lay in the bed, Michael's heartbeat continued to beat an irregular rhythm, chipping away at his brain's logical thought process. What concerned Michael the most was his current state of mind. It was an alien feeling, a feeling difficult for him to process. The butterflies. The heartbeat. The muddiness of his thoughts. Although he did not want to admit it to himself, he recognised that he suddenly felt afraid. This was more than unusual. He couldn't easily recall a time where he felt afraid or worried about *anything*. Thinking back into the past he truly believed that he had always been confident and resolute in his decisions. True, in his early days in business there were times when he had clashed with the other partners of Milton, Knight and Haxby about a particular decision regarding the future of the firm. And true, he had sometimes been overruled and outvoted. However, in those cases, he felt confident that the majority decision was made against his better judgement. And was incorrect. He was correct; he always had been. He thought back to his family life. To when the children were younger. Though he tried he couldn't bring to mind an event when he felt he had made an error of judgement. It seemed to come naturally to him to be correct. At all times. Of course, in the past he and Margaret had disagreed, but she had always quickly seen that she was incorrect and soon backed down. After a while she did not even question Michael, obviously in the knowledge that there was no point. His decisions were correct. He had no doubt she loved and respected him more so for that. It had got to a stage where instead of questioning him she would be happy to follow his choices. And when that happened Michael would smile, internally congratulating himself on the fact that he had made her life so much easier by taking the strain of decision-making away from her.

For the last few days, though, he had felt exposed. No, dare he think it, vulnerable. For the first time since Margaret's death he had let his guard down slightly and allowed these negative feelings to flood in. He drew on memory after memory reminding himself of the countless occasions where he had been correct. But following each memory he recalled, a tiny niggling doubt crept in from a corner of his mind. Perhaps this time he was wrong. He knew that his thoughts and fears regarding the page were illogical. But no matter how he tried to overcome his feelings by congratulating himself on his own successes, the tiny spark lit in his mind and reminded him perhaps he *had* made a wrong decision. And because of this, something that was now completely out of his control was just around the corner.

His heartbeat quickened again and the spark reignited. Michael rolled onto his front, covering his eyes with his hands. He could feel the pulse in his temples beating against his thumbs. His forehead was wet. Sweat. He screwed his eyes up tightly and clenched his teeth. He was not going to allow this negativity to seep in any further. He had made it through the last three months since the accident. That had been the most difficult part of his life. He had overcome the recent challenges he had faced and had done it unscathed, untouched. Just like in every other part of his life, he had been challenged and he had won. Regardless of the feelings he was now experiencing, he wasn't going to be ruled by a fucking piece of paper. This feeling had to stop. And it had to stop now. He would overpower it like he had everything else. He felt around on the bedclothes, grasped the piece of paper, pulled its corners toward its centre and wrapped his hand around it tightly until it was no more than a tiny ball.

After showering, Jane dried herself off and finally got into her pyjamas. She checked the clock. It had taken longer than she had expected to get comfortable. But then she hadn't accounted for the outpouring of emotion, which had snuck up unexpectedly and relentlessly catapulted itself out. She checked in the mirror to ensure that her face was completely clean. Her eyes were slightly bloodshot but she blamed this on shampoo and not tears. Her cheeks were also a little red, her smooth skin warmed by the water's heat. She slipped her feet into her pink slippers and switched the bedroom light off behind her. It was getting dark outside and the landing was dimly lit.

She heard a car arrive and walked into her studio to look out of the window. It was too early for Matt to be arriving home. She could see her next-door neighbour reaching into the car. After struggling for a moment, the neighbour stepped backwards holding her three-month-old baby with one arm, a nappy bag with the other. Jane smiled to herself. The baby, unexpectedly awoken, screamed grumpily before bursting into a loud cry. The neighbour kissed the child's forehead whilst using her hip to close the car door behind her. She shuffled toward the front door, the nappy bag slipping from her shoulder and trailing on the floor behind her. She was then out of view. Jane smiled again. Her smile quickly dropped as a small pang of self-doubt leapt into her mind. She recalled her agreement with Matt before their wedding that she too never wanted to have children of her own. The decision didn't seem quite so clear as the years passed.

Jane twisted the wooden pole, closing the blinds, and the room suddenly matched the colour of her thoughts. She walked over from the window and switched on the light. She perched on the edge of her painting stool. It was about the height of a bar stool with three long legs, each about the width of a broom handle. The stool had been with her since her university days and the numerous flecks of paint which covered it suggested it had seen a lot of use. Jane had found it one day outside an old junk store. At that time, it was already well used and covered in splashes of paint. She had fallen in love with it immediately, captivated by a daydream that some renowned painter may have used it before her. She had paid five pounds for it and carried it more than two miles back to her hall of residence.

She sat for a moment, her eyes scanning the walls around her, studying her own work. She was pleased with some of her earlier pieces; her brush strokes were neat and well defined. The more recent pieces were not so good. Her strokes had become larger and more haphazard. The fine detailing she had utilised so well previously had been replaced by a more reckless approach. It had been a few years since she had last lifted her brush, but now all of sudden she felt the urge to do so again. She was unsure what she wanted to paint – in some ways it didn't matter; she just wanted to paint. She wanted to replace the ugly horror of her most recent pieces with something newer. Something brighter. Shinier. More defined. More her.

She left the stool and crouched in the corner of the room, where she had thrown loose paints and brushes on top of various-sized artist boxes. She removed the loose items, placing them on the floor beside her. In total, there were six boxes stacked on top of one another. The top three were cheap plastic boxes in grey, brown and red, the type that fishermen used for tackle and seamstresses for buttons. She began to lift them, one by one. The plastic clasp on the front of the red box gave way, causing her to quickly push the top and bottom together to avert the contents spilling everywhere. She placed it by her side, and carefully moved the other two boxes alongside. She got onto her knees.

The three remaining boxes were all wooden and were all of a similar size. Each measured around two feet in length by a foot in width. The width matched the height. The corners had been carefully crafted to dovetail where the long side met the shorter end. There was a lid which opened a couple of inches from the top, held down at the front by two brass clasps. The lid opened upwards, joined to the box by one long, continuous hinge across the back.

Jane removed the top box, lifting its weight carefully with two hands. It was the second one that she was interested in. This one was a slightly darker wood than the other two and had numerous scratches across it. There were some deeper, more purposeful scratches where she had chipped through the varnish to scratch her name or the name of a band she had liked at the time. The top surface displayed her own name and Matt's. A crude heart shape was etched next to them. She smiled and traced the heart with her middle finger. She unclipped the clasps and opened the box. The hinge creaked slightly as she did so. She rummaged around inside the box, displacing half-used tubes of paint, various brushes and discarded cloths. At one end, standing neatly in a line, was a number of photographs. She pulled them from the box and flicked through. The pictures were curled and bent. A couple were simple pictures of her easel standing in the corner of a room. The wallpaper in the background bubbled and peeled from a wall which she instantly recognised as part of her room in her final year at university. The next was a Polaroid picture of her and Matt kissing. The initial vivid colours had now faded into varying shades of orange, giving the picture an autumnal feel. Matt's hand was on her cheek, pulling her closer. Her eyes were closed; she was lost in the moment. She loved that photograph, it epitomised quite simply the feeling of true love. She couldn't recall who had taken it. The final photograph was of her mother and father. Her mother beamed radiantly. Her left arm was linked through her father's, her hand tightly gripping his forearm to keep him close to her. Her father stood rigidly alongside, his stance giving the appearance that he wanted to be further away. She got the feeling that had the photo been taken numerous times in quick succession each shot would show her father edging to his left until he disappeared entirely. His eyes stared into the camera; empty. His face was expressionless.

Jane smiled at her mother, reached into the box and pulled out a large black bulldog clip. She held on to the photo of her parents and threw the others back in the box. She then closed the lid, and stood and walked over to where her last project stood grimly on the easel. She lifted the picture down from the easel and placed it on the floor alongside. It would be disposed of later. Squeezing the bulldog clip open, she attached the photograph to the frame of the easel. She would not paint tonight, but this was a start. She allowed the clip to close, ensuring that its jaws were firmly over her father. Her mother's smile seemed a little stronger.

Jane went downstairs into the kitchen. She opened the fridge door and was greeted by near darkness. Her eyes fixed on a half-full tin of beans. Matt must have put it there earlier; she certainly didn't remember from the day before. It had been placed in such a way as to obscure the interior light, and Jane slid it backwards to illuminate the rest of the fridge. As usual the fridge was packed with vegetables of all kinds. Normally, Jane would fix something for Matt to eat when he returned from work, but as he was working late again tonight she would simply cater for herself. She rummaged around the various brown bags which contained cuts of meat from the local farm shop. She was hungry but lacked the necessary motivation to prepare something from scratch. Her hands wandered the glass shelves, pushing items from side to side to see what lay behind. Cheese, a bag of muddied shitake mushrooms, celery, a cut of rump steak. It wasn't very inspiring. Eventually, she settled on a carton of strawberry and banana smoothie in the fridge door and removed it. The carton was half-empty and she emptied the remainder into a glass, squeezed the air out of the carton and replaced the plastic lid.

She bent down, closing the fridge door at the same time as she opened the freezer door. Her expectations were low; it was rare that the freezer contained much in the way of food. Generally, Jane insisted on preparing meals from scratch using fresh produce. It wasn't just the taste she enjoyed, it was the feeling of utter satisfaction when the meal was served. She also enjoyed the washing, the chopping, the boiling, the draining, the seasoning. She would plan the meal the night before from one of her many cookbooks which were packed together on the shelf above the back door. Then she would line up all the ingredients along the worktop and turn on the radio. The preparation then comprised a combination of singing, dancing and performance art along with actually getting the meal ready. If she had timed it correctly, the smell would greet Matt on his return from work and the meal would be ready to eat straight after his shower. Her favourite part was seeing the reaction in his eyes when she first served the meal. His initial comment following his first mouthful came a close second.

As expected, the freezer was near empty. The top drawer offered nothing more than three or four ice-cube trays, an almost-full bottle of Stolichnaya and two homemade frozen lasagnes which had been there for well over a year. She slid the drawer back in. An invisible layer of ice crunched, giving a little resistance as she slid the second drawer open. She was surprised to see a large tub of Häagen Dazs in the drawer, its only company a small packet of fish fingers. Jane knew immediately that she hadn't purchased the ice-cream. Much as she loved it, since Christmas time she had become extremely conscious of her weight. Ever since that time, seeing her reflection in the mirror had disallowed such treats. She picked up the tub and turned it toward her. Strawberry Cheesecake. Her absolute favourite. She stared at the tub for a few moments, trying to recall whether perhaps she had bought it. No, she concluded, she couldn't have. She had packed the freezer full for their New Year's Eve party and she clearly remembered there had certainly been no room for ice-cream. She removed the lid and looked inside. More than half of the contents were gone. A spoon remained, frozen into the pinkness. She reached up and placed the tub on the work surface. Then she slid in the drawer, closed the freezer door with her knee and stood up.

She stared at the tub again. She had definitely not bought it. Definitely. Which meant Matt must have. That was unusual for two reasons. The first was that she was left to do all the shopping. She couldn't remember a time when Matt had brought any food home. History had determined that both Jane and Matt preferred it that way. The second reason was that Matt's flavour of choice was Cookies and Cream. He had referred to Strawberry Cheesecake as merely 'tolerable' in the past. Jane rested her elbow on the work surface and scratched her forehead, staring at the grout between the black tiles for inspiration.

Her phone buzzed, and then again. She turned and retrieved the phone from the breakfast bar. The first message was from Matt, confirming again that 'he wouldn't be in until late' and that 'she needn't wait up'. He finished with a kiss. The second was from Ruby, a friend of Jane's from university, perhaps now her best friend. They had met on the same course all those years before. She was simply enquiring how things were going. She finished with eight kisses.

Ruby had worked in a gallery in New York for the best part of a decade but kept in touch when time permitted. It had been exactly three months since Jane had last seen Ruby. She had appeared for a few hours at the funeral, but then had to race back to catch her return flight; Ruby explained that the gallery had an important exhibition opening and a longer stay had just not been possible. Jane had hoped for a little longer with her friend. They had chatted briefly, but there were so many people that day that it was hopeless trying to steal more time. Jane had promised that one day she would visit Ruby in New York; an idea that Matt had seemed singularly unenthusiastic about. The few conversations in which Jane had attempted to turn the promise into reality had died almost before they began, Matt crushing the possibility by playing a 'lack of finances' card as the winning hand. Jane secretly believed that Matt's resistance to the trip was more likely that he didn't like Ruby. In fact, he didn't appear to like many of her friends. He never overtly stated as much; he simply avoided spending any time with them. Jane could have made the trip alone, but Matt didn't seem overly enamoured of that idea either. Instead, Jane had dropped the subject altogether. Although Ruby's visit was short, her effort to make the journey had not been lost on Jane. She missed Ruby. And she would visit her.

Jane put the phone back down. She would reply later.

twenty-six

"And has anyone asked you to carry anything?" said the girl, not bothering to look up. Her voice dripped with disinterest.

"No," said Claire.

"Okay." The girl signalled with a flippant shake of her finger toward the small conveyor belt alongside her.

Claire lifted her lime case onto the electronic scales next to the woman. A digital indicator raced up to forty-five kilograms before dropping rapidly back to eighteen and then settling on twenty-two. The conveyor shook momentarily and the case lurched forward. The woman removed a long white strip of paper and wrapped it around the handle of the case. The conveyor buzzed and the case moved forwards again, reaching a second conveyor which ran behind the woman. Almost in keeping with the woman's attitude, the case then flopped lifelessly on its side and disappeared along the conveyor belt behind a white screen.

"You can go," said the girl.

"How about have a nice flight?" Claire said under her breath, collecting her passport and boarding card from the high counter in front of her.

"I'm sorry?" said the woman, looking at Claire for the first time since she arrived.

"Nothing," said Claire, pushing the passport inside the large leather bag which was slung over her shoulder.

"You spoke?" said the woman, her tone slightly more aggressive.

"It doesn't matter."

Claire turned and walked away from the desk. She could do without another argument this holiday.

The airport was almost empty. She reached the departures screen and checked her watch. Her flight wasn't leaving for another hour and a half and the screen instructed her to 'Wait in Lounge'. It was too early to allocate her gate number. She pulled her bag up onto her shoulder and made her way over to a small coffee shop. She ordered a coffee, and the man behind the counter assured her that when it was ready the Barista would bring it over. She sat down at a table furthest from the counter, alongside a maroon rope which loosely separated the coffee shop from the airport. Moments later, a different man arrived with her coffee, accompanied by a beaming smile and the instruction that she should 'Have a nice day'. She resisted suggesting that she should introduce the Barista to the flight check-in girl and thanked him, smiling back.

Reaching down into her bag, she found her journal and pen. Perhaps today's experience in the airport was something that she would write about in the future. The journal was packed with various papers she had slipped inside: notes of conversations which had taken her interest, ideas and general observations. She began to unfold the papers on the table in front of her. Collecting her thoughts this way was usual. It was sometimes inconvenient to retrieve her journal when some incident of potential future importance took place. Instead she would write notes on whatever she could get her hands on: napkins, bus tickets, sweet wrappers, restaurant bills. She would later transpose these into her journal and discard the original notes. She hadn't updated her journal for the last couple of days and there were several papers to look through. She turned to the front page of the journal and the pages flipped through unassisted and helpfully settled on the next blank page. One by one she copied down the notes in her journal. Some of the notes were single words that she may or may not use in the future. She had the type of mind which if prompted by a single word could recall the exact circumstances, feelings, weather, conversation that had taken place. She could then use this material in the future if it seemed like an appropriate fit for something she was working on. Other notes were longer. A sentence or two which had popped into her mind that flowed beautifully like poetry. She continued to copy them down. The final item was a beermat. A single word, 'Ted's', was printed in dark-blue writing, the weight of the print punched into the cream-coloured card. Claire turned the beermat. There were five words hastily written in block capitals. They read: MICHAEL SEWELL DIRK HEILLE SOLICITOR.

Claire smiled slightly whilst transposing the words into her journal. She thought back to her two encounters with Michael. There was something about him which intrigued her. Something about him that didn't seem to fit. Something that worried her. And something, it appeared, that worried him more.

twenty-seven

Jane was sitting at the breakfast bar. In front of her was her open laptop. She had spent a moment or two prising the used spoon from the ice-cream and now the tub sat to her right, a fresh spoon protruding from the top. To her left lay her phone, playing music amplified by a small speaker that was plugged into the headphone socket. The house had been too quiet and she had scrolled through her music before settling on James's *Gold Mother* to provide some much-needed atmosphere.

She logged on and opened Google. Her fingers moved quickly and the enter key led her instantaneously to more than one hundred and sixty million hits. She scrolled down the screen, clicked a light-blue underlined sentence simply titled 'Bibliography' and was immediately transported to a black screen. In the top corner, in purple scroll text, were the words 'Dirks Wirks'. The rest of the website was unhelpfully coloured navy-blue, making the text difficult to read.

The screen displayed in chronological order all the books that Dirk Heille had written. Each was listed simply by title and year. There was no indication of what each book was about and no ISBN. Jane highlighted the screen with her mouse, instantly turning the black background to white and the blue text to yellow. This was no easier to read, so she copied the text into Microsoft Word and amended the font until it was a standard black on a white background.

The titles weren't numbered, so she scrolled slowly down the screen, counting each one by one. If the information on the website was to be believed, she could now be almost certain that Dirk Heille had written thirty-one novels; his apparent alter ego, Ed Drewhorn, a further twelve. Jane dug out another chunk of ice-cream and fed the spoon into her mouth. She opened the cardboard folder in front of her and began to tick off the titles on the photocopied bibliography against those on the screen. She hummed along to the music as she ticked each eagerly off her list. She giggled; it was a kind of 'book bingo'. Of the forty-three novels listed on screen, only seven were missing from her list. By deduction this would mean that *The Return of Mr Trenton* was one of the author's more recent titles. She proceeded to write the missing titles on the photocopy, and then leaned back on the high stool, raising her arms in the air and stretching all the way to her fingers. She took a celebratory scoop of ice-cream and lifted the bibliography in the air like a footballer lifting an end of season trophy.

She pushed the stool back, skipped over to the fridge and poured herself a glass of orange juice, singing as she did so in time with the song, "How was it for you? How was it for you indeed, Mr Heille?"

Jane sat back down at the breakfast bar. She realised that she hadn't actually achieved very much aside from completing the bibliography of the mysterious Mr Heille/Mr Drewhorn, but nevertheless it was a start. The next step was to locate the page that her father seemed so concerned about. She considered that it had not been in either book she and Martha had located earlier, and thus she had now narrowed down the search to a one in forty-one chance. Her father would be pleased about that, she had no doubt. She finished the ice-cream, admiring the detective work in front of her. She popped the spoon in the tub for the last time and unplugged the speakers from her phone.

The dial tone was long, the waiting laborious. Then, the tone ceased and the phone cut off. Jane dialled again. She heard the same tone but this time a click followed. There was no accompanying voice, so she pulled the phone away from her ear to view the screen. The call length timer was counting upwards, confirming she was connected. She put the phone back to her ear.

"Dad?"

No answer.

"Dad?"

Jane heard a deep nasal sigh.

"Dad? Are you there?"

"Hmm," a voice confirmed. He sounded like he had been sleeping.

"Oh, hi, Dad. I didn't wake you, did I?" Jane glanced at her watch. It was just before nine.

"Yes, Jane. You did."

"Oh. I'm sorry. I didn't realise you'd be –"

"What, Jane? What do you want?"

"I've been doing some research for you," she said, trying to retain some enthusiasm. "You know, about the book you were interested in."

"Right." He sounded neither interested nor otherwise. Simply matter-of-fact.

"I've been researching Dirk Heille. He's German; have I already mentioned that? Anyway, he writes under two names; the other is Ed Drewhorn." She read from the photocopied biography in front of her. "Like I said, he's German. 'He was born in nineteen-oh-eight.'"

"The point, Jane?" Michael interrupted.

Jane's eyes fell.

"Well, the point is, Dad, that I have his bibliography. You know, every book that he's –"

"I know what a fucking bibliography is, Jane."

She ignored the further interruption.

"He's written forty-three books in total, and –"

"Buy the fucking lot, Jane."

The line went dead.

Jane pulled the phone away from her ear. Although not necessary, she prodded the red button three times to hang up. "Well, fuck you then," she said.

Michael turned over, pushing his face back into the pillow. He was tired. Tired of all this thinking. Tired of this situation. Tired of everything. His heart began to race again and he screwed up his eyes, urging his brain to overpower the feeling in his chest. His left hand gripped his phone tightly; his right, a slightly damp, screwed-up piece of paper.

Jane closed the laptop lid. She didn't know why she even bothered. Her father had the ability to crush her mood in just a few words. It was him who had asked her to do the research into the mysterious and obscure writer. She could have refused to help him. She didn't *have* to spend her own time finding out this information for him. But she had, and this was because she loved him and she wanted to please him. And what did she receive in return? Nothing. Just a command barked down the phone in that superior tone. As if she were a child. An obedient little child who responded to his every demand. That is all she had ever done. And what made the situation even worse was that she had no idea why she was even doing the research. He hadn't told her the reason; he hadn't let her into that little secret. No. Instead, she had just carried out his orders without even questioning them. He had decided, after all, that for once in her life she was of some use to him, that for this short period of time she actually had some purpose, and so she had jumped at the attention. And then, as soon as she had reported her findings to him, he had just dropped her. Cut her off. But not before barking another order. An order to now locate all these books.

For reasons she didn't understand, Jane lifted the laptop screen again and logged back into Google. She picked the first book from her list and typed in the name, supported by the words 'Dirk Heille' and the year. The search led her to Amazon, which informed her the book was out of print. She repeated the same procedure with the second book on the list. Out of print. It was going to be a long night.

It would have been fantastically easy for Jane to let Matt return home later that night to find her asleep; her head crumpled into her arms, which still rested on the kitchen work surface; the breakfast bar chair slightly rocked forward so only its front two legs made contact with the tiled floor. He would notice this immediately, she imagined, and gently rock it backwards, instantly doubling its stability. He'd shake his head slightly and smile, wondering how she had managed not to fall from the chair. He'd stroke her hair slightly, running his hand back from the crown of her head to her shoulders, gently whispering her name and coaxing her slowly away from her dreams and back into reality. She would turn her head slightly and mutter something incomprehensible that made him delight in the spectacle. Eventually, she would realise that her husband was standing over her and she would smile through her half-sleep, knowing he was home and she was safe. Mechanically, she would edge to her feet, her husband stabilising her by putting a strong arm around her waist. Succumbing to the total trust that she felt for him, she would let him gently guide her through the lounge and up the stairs to the bedroom. There, he would sit her on the edge of the bed and in an instant she would turn and ball herself up on top of the duvet. He'd gently lift her head and squeeze a pillow beneath her long brown hair before brushing away the few strands that fell over her closed eyes. Then he'd laugh slightly to himself as he spent the next five or so minutes trying to extract the duvet from under her body. Initially, he would tease out small areas of the white embroidered cover from under her, trying not to wake her. But as he extracted each area, she would move a leg or an arm and trap another area beneath her. He'd again try to edge her out of the way whilst trying to cope with her somnolent manoeuvres. Eventually, after a few minutes of what was quickly becoming an impossible task, he would crumple to his knees and nuzzle his head into her chest, kissing her fondly through her checked pyjama top. Then, after a few more minutes' struggle, he would rise, give one great yank of the corner of the duvet, and catapult Jane across to the other side of the bed. She'd remain oblivious to his efforts, and he would try to stifle his laughter in the interests of not waking her. He would tug the duvet from beneath her body bit by bit until she was fully covered from above and her body finally rested on the sheets. Then he'd walk to the other side of the bed and slide the pillow under her head, again removing her hair from her face. At that stage, he could *finally* consider himself.

He'd slip off his tie and shirt and hang them over the edge of the slightly opened wardrobe door. Next he'd remove his shoes and socks. Then he'd undo his belt, take off his trousers, and hang them neatly on the hanger he'd removed them from that morning, which remained hooked over the top of the wardrobe door. Then, after brushing his teeth, he would climb into the bed alongside her and pull the duvet over himself. He would shuffle slightly up the bed to be closer to her. She would remain asleep, lying on her side facing away from him, her knees bent slightly. He would get closer, kissing the back of her neck as he did so. He would smell her skin, the scent of the day's perfume now almost indistinguishable. He would breathe deeply through his nose, retaining her smell for as long as it lasted. The smell that always made him smile. Then he would reach over her waist and nestle his hand between her tummy and the sheet. Finally, he would pull their bodies tightly into one another, solving the puzzle which only felt complete when they were together. Then he'd whisper that he loved her and after one final kiss, he'd lay his head on the pillow behind her and close his eyes.

This wasn't, however, how it happened.

The telephone call had all but crushed her spirit, but she felt compelled to continue searching. Though she couldn't remove the weight which hung inside her. A weight which reminded her that her father really did not deserve her spending this time on his behalf. She scrolled through the music on her phone, reconnected her speakers and her finger hovered over Guns 'N' Roses. The immediacy of the screaming guitar bursting through the speakers as the opening moments of 'Appetite for Destruction' played reflected her mood. She turned the volume up as high as it could go and typed in the words 'Dirk Heille' for what seemed like the hundredth time that day. She was directed to and redirected from website to website in search of his books, looking for places where she could buy copies. Invariably, a search would end in an unhelpful message telling her that the book she had selected was 'out of stock' or 'out of print'. Most websites would give her the option of registering with them, so she could be informed at some undetermined time in the future should the book ever come into stock. Due to the genre of books that Mr Heille appeared to have written, she passed up this opportunity, seeing it as nothing more than a way for the website to collect her details so it could bombard her with messages about other books 'she may be interested in'. By the time 'You're Crazy' burst into life, near-perforating the speakers, she'd had enough. She slammed the laptop lid down, and climbed down from the stool.

She collected her phone from the kitchen and slid her finger across the screen to check again for a message from Matt, which she knew hadn't arrived. A few moments passed until the chorus blared from the speakers, and she joined in loudly shouting the lyrics 'You're fucking crazy', whilst she smiled at the name 'Dad Mobile' on the list of those she had received messages from previously. She uncoupled the speakers from her phone and made her way upstairs.

She climbed into bed, her head sinking into the softness of the pillow. Almost instantly she was asleep. If the click of the front door had initially caused her to stir, it was the creak of the floorboard just outside her bedroom which woke her fully. The light from the moon made its way into the bedroom through a crack in the white curtains. She adjusted her head so she could see the door open. She watched through almost closed eyes as the bronze handle moved down slowly, precisely. Eventually, it reached its full distance and the door edged gently open. Matt moved into the room. She noticed that his shirt was already unbuttoned, the yellowed moonlight catching it flap as he moved. He removed the shirt quickly and pushed it deep into the wicker wash-basket, ensuring it didn't lie on the top. Off came his trousers which fell out of Jane's sight onto the floor beside the bed. He reached down and hooked a finger into his sock, pulling his foot out as he did so.

Then the other. And then he lifted the covers and slid into the bed, facing away from her.

"Hi," she whispered.

The break in the near-silence startled him.

"I didn't know you were awake," he said without turning. His tone was equally low, almost funereal.

"I wasn't."

"Good night?"

"Yeah, okay I suppose. You?"

"A long one." His words drifted. "Really long."

"Turn over, Matt. I want to see you."

Matt paused, and then arched his neck to look backwards over his right shoulder. It was a poor owl impression.

"No, properly. I want to see all of you."

Matt rotated his body. "I'm tired," he muttered.

Jane leaned in to kiss him. Matt adjusted his head, managing to catch her cheek with his return kiss. She could smell ethanol on his breath, with a light breeze of almond.

"Have you been drinking?"

Matt pushed his face down into the pillow, purposefully facing his mouth away from Jane's face.

"Yeah, had one after work."

"What time is it?"

"Dunno."

Jane rolled backwards and awkwardly felt for her watch at the side of the bed. She couldn't see the digital clock because of Matt's awkward position. Her hand staccatoed on the bedside table, falling on a book and then a box of paracetamol before finding her watch. She flopped onto her back and held it up in the near-darkness. It was hard to make out the hands in the light and she rotated it, trying to catch the moonlight more successfully. After several attempts, she gave in and switched the lamp on next to her. Matt burrowed his head further into the pillow, avoiding the light as if its rays were mortally harmful. Jane could see the face clearly now. She turned to Matt.

"Matt. It's four o'clock in the morning."

"Uh-hmm."

"What time did you leave work?"

Matt shrugged.

"Did you just shrug?"

No answer. Jane sat up in bed, staring straight down at the side of Matt's head, which remained half-buried in the pillow.

"Matt," she repeated, more loudly.

Again, no answer. If a medical scan were available at that time, it would have likely shown unprecedented activity in his brain.

Jane pushed at his shoulder in an attempt to roll him backwards so she could see his face.

"Matt!"

Matt turned his head, and immediately the almond scent got stronger.

"What?" His tone was that of a cornered child.

"Where have you been until four o'clock? What time did you finish work?"

"I dunno."

"You don't know? You don't know what time you finished work? And you don't know where you've been either?"

Matt closed his eyes tightly, feigning pain from the brightness of the lamp.

"And you can't even look at me, can you?"

"It's bright."

"Whatever, Matt. Look, I'm asking you a simple question. It's four o'clock in the morning, you've just come in, you've been drinking and I've basically heard nothing from you all evening. Where have you been?"

"I'm tired, Jane."

"I'm tired as well, Matt. You've just woken me up."

"Listen. I've been working all day and I've been out for one drink after work. I want to go to sleep now."

"So you expect me to believe that you finished work at three a.m. and then went for a drink before you came in. To unwind, no doubt?"

"Yes."

"And where 'round here is open until that time?"

"Jane. I'm tired. We'll talk about it tomorrow. Okay?"

The 'okay' wasn't really a question. It was a statement of simple finality. Jane had heard this tone too many times before. Defeated, she flopped down onto her back, her head deep in the pillow. She reached over and switched off the lamp and stared directly up at the blackness of the ceiling.

Matt turned away from her, his body seemingly lying on the last inch of mattress before the drop to the floor.

"Did you have ice-cream before your drinks?" Jane said quietly.

The words hung in the darkness long after they had both fallen asleep.

twenty-eight

It was time to leave.

Michael woke; his immediate feeling was that he was wet. He felt around the dampness in the bed and for a moment considered whether he had wet the bed. His hand moved to the front of his white cotton boxer shorts; they were equally damp. Surely he couldn't have? He nipped the front of his boxer shorts tightly between his thumb and first two fingers and rubbed the fabric together. He then pulled his hand from beneath the sheet to his nose and sniffed. The skin between his thin grey eyebrows gathered. No, it didn't seem to have any particular scent. He lifted the sheet and peered down his thin chest to see whether there was any discolouration. There didn't seem to be. He then climbed out of bed and kneeled prayer-like by the side of the bed. The bed was sodden, enough so that in places through the sheets he could make out the brand of mattress which was repeated in red diagonal text. He slowly moved his head toward the centre of the bed, his hands now clasped behind his back. At the wettest point the sheet clung to the mattress and the word 'FLEX' was clearly evident. He breathed in deeply as he got closer, smelling nothing but sweat and dampness. He moved closer again until his head was no more than a few inches away and breathed in. Nothing. Just sweat. His shoulders loosened and he rested his head on the sheet covering the red text. No urine. Just sweat. His position was similar to that of a man awaiting the removal of his head. The scene only needed a black-hooded man with an axe to complete it.

He lay for a second and thought about his night's sleep. It had been fractured to say the least. He had slept for some time before Jane had interrupted him with her pointless call. Why interrupt him with that information? She hadn't told him the name of the book he was looking for; she had simply stated that Dirk Heille had written lots of books. Some use that was. It was like him asking her to get him some potatoes and her ringing from the supermarket to tell him that there were lots of vegetables there. Fucking useless. But that was Jane. Always falling short.

Following Jane's call, he had managed to get back to sleep fairly quickly. But then the dream came. Simple, yet terrifying. It was one that had visited many times the month after Margaret died. It began with Michael lying by the side of a stream, his eyes closed. It was a warm autumnal day, and he could feel the sun gently draping a comforting shawl over his shoulders. His head was shaded by a tall oak tree, which crackled as the gentle breeze darted through its orange leaves, stripping off a handful each time. The stream rippled a tiny tune, giving off a slight coldness as it flowed by. It was quiet. There were no other sounds. Michael lay, silently enjoying his surroundings.

The shawl was pulled from his shoulders by a large gust of wind, which ripped alongside the river bank. He opened his eyes. The wind pulled leaves by their thousand from the tree, scattering them high up into the sky like ashes from a giant fire. The roots from the ground beneath him began to make their way up through the soil all around. They gripped and tugged at his trousers, rocking him slightly as they tore through the material to the flesh beneath. They began to climb over him, pulling his body from where they came. More roots came up around his shoulders, creeping quickly over his chest, pulling him further into the ground. The brown shoots twisted around his legs, holding him in place, meeting and wrapping around one another. As each took position, the roots hardened turning almost instantly to wood. For some reason, he didn't try to move but remained in place, letting the branches cover his arms, which lay slightly parted from his sides, the grass between his torso and arms creating large green triangles on either side. The grass cracked as more roots came through, holding him tightly in place. Taking position. Hardening. Now, with his body covered in soft, pale wood, he could only move his head.

There was a second gust of wind which pushed the leaves ever higher up into the sky, floating and twirling in the confusion of airflow and gravity. The air around him became still for a moment, and then the leaves began their descent, twisting faster and faster, grouping together into a mass that blackened the sky above. The first few landed upright and rigid in the grass around him. Then he felt a sharp pain as one hit the exposed skin on his arm and bedded into it. Blood flowed turning the end of the leaf from orange to a glossy red. There was a similar pain as one struck his chest. More and more fell, each landing with a small tapping sound as it lodged into the wood that surrounded his body. Another landed on his chest, causing him to shriek with pain. And another. He stared at the sky. There were thousands. All tearing toward him. Quicker, ever quicker. One twisted into his cheek, drilling through into his mouth. He tasted blood in the back of his throat and closed his eyes.

This nightmare had repeated through the night. Each time he closed his eyes in his dream, in reality his eyes had snapped open and he was back in his hotel bed, the distant sounds of music and the hum of people talking in the bars on the beachfront for once serving as a comfort.

He pushed himself up from the bed, for now avoiding the invisible executioner, and got to his feet. It was time to leave. He couldn't stay in this place for a moment longer. As he had predicted a few weeks earlier, the holiday had been a complete and utter waste of time. There was no need for him to have time away from home.

Yes, the car accident had changed everything for him. It was a moment of no return. After the accident, he had to face that his life had changed forever. But, he also accepted that what was done, was done and there was nothing that would reverse this. He consoled himself by considering the situation with Thomas. This too was a life changing experience. In some ways, more difficult. It had taken time, but he had overcome this. For a month or two he was forced to adapt, but he had eventually moved his own life forward. The shadow of Thomas, reappearing only briefly on scarce occasion. He cursed himself for letting Jane persuade him to take this holiday. It was unnecessary. A week in the sun wasn't going to change anything.

For the first month or so following the accident, he had generally been all right. Yes, there had been some sleepless nights, and some nights when the horrific dream would come. Of course there were. He had just lost his wife of over thirty years. He couldn't be expected to carry on as normal. The disturbed nights were not a sign of weakness; they were completely understandable. He had rationalised this in his mind some time ago.

The first month had been very different for other reasons too. The police had seen to it that the emptiness that Margaret had left behind was amply filled. From the day after the accident, Michael was required to attend numerous meetings with the police as they tried to get to the bottom of the accident. Drawing from his legal background, Michael knew that it was police procedure to investigate such incidents. After all, there was a fatality. The police were well within their rights to ask repeated questions about how fast he was going, whether he had been drinking, whether he had taken into consideration the weather and the nature of the roads. They were likely to check his past driving record (clean). They were likely to check the history of the vehicle (the tyres were legal and it had been recently serviced). They were likely to ask questions about what happened when the car hit the water, after the car hit the water, how he got out of the river. It was all procedural.

He had not expected quite so many questions about the nature of his relationship with Margaret, where they had been that night, what they had talked about. Similarly, he had not expected questions to be asked of his daughter or his work colleagues or his friends. This, he felt, was an invasion of his privacy. Yes, by all means investigate the accident, but the rest? Well, that was a little too much. He had just lost his wife, for fuck's sake, and he told them that.

The number of questions began to reduce in the weeks following the accident, and with that so did the sleepless nights and the nightmares. He was however aware that the police were still making enquiries; a fact that was confirmed by the presence of a plain clothes detective at the funeral. After that, on rare occasions the police still arrived at Michael's house unannounced, but their questions went unanswered: Michael refused to provide any further detail. He had told them enough times that he just wanted to be left alone to grieve.

Just to add to his overall annoyance, the police were still refusing to release his car to him, so he was unable to finalise his insurance claim. Jane had tearfully telephoned the police station twice to request the car's release, so she and her father could 'begin to move on'. On both occasions the sergeant helpfully promised he would locate the vehicle and make arrangements for its return, but that still hadn't transpired at the time Michael had left for his holiday.

Michael walked into the bathroom and looked at himself in the mirror. He smiled an ironic smile and rested his hands on the side of the sink. As he did a screwed-up ball of paper fell from his right hand. He knew what it was without even opening it, and dropped it in the wash bag which lay unzipped to his left. He ran the tap, filled his hands with water and threw it over his face and chest, splashing it on the floor.

He checked his watch: it was late – just past eleven. That ruled out any possibility of a morning swim. The pool area would be packed with people at this time. Snivelling children, crying, demanding, always needing something, always wanting. He couldn't bear that. In fact, he couldn't bear this country for one moment longer. He clawed at the various toiletries, picked them up and rammed them into his wash bag. It was definitely time to go. He was leaving.

He turned and pulled the chrome handle of the shower from twelve o'clock to three o'clock. Water cascaded down from above. He needed fresh water to wash away the water that had covered him through the night. He pulled the curtain across and removed his boxer shorts. He stepped over the side of the bath and into the shower, letting the water fall heavily onto him from above.

He would shower, pack up his belongings and then find the next available flight to get home. Jane was of no use. He would have to find the book himself.

twenty-nine

"Oh, you look tired, Janey," said Martha in a breathless whisper. She pulled both hands to her chest and dramatically crossed one over the other.

"I am. A little."

"Then why come here so early, Janey? Why not get more sleep?"

"I couldn't sleep."

"And neither could I, darling," Martha sang. "I've been here since seven."

This was extremely unusual for Martha. She would usually arrive at the shop fifteen minutes prior to the official opening time stated on the sign on the door. Of course, time didn't matter so much to Martha, and if there was a little gossip or a problem to be solved, she would be happy drinking coffee and chatting until such time as the issue was resolved. There were times when the shop hadn't opened until well past eleven.

Martha's choice of clothing was also extremely unusual. She had replaced flamboyancy with something much more sober today. Gone were the usual bright colours and feathers and sequins. Today, it seemed, was a day for tweed. Mustard tweed, checked in pale blue. She wore a fitted suit jacket which had it not have been for Martha's enormous bosom would have perhaps fitted. It certainly wouldn't fasten. Around her neck was a silver clasp which kept in place a matching cape, the bottom of which flowed just past her waistline. The outfit was finished with a bile yellow woollen dress and brown knee-length boots. Jane had to smile. Martha noticed.

"What is it, darling?"

"Oh, er, nothing."

"Is it this?" Martha removed her hands from her chest and stretched her arms slowly in front of her in one motion before she moved them out to her sides. She stood crucifix style.

Jane giggled. "Well, I'm just not used to seeing you dressed like this."

Martha beckoned Jane closer with a finger. Jane moved forwards. Martha stood on her tiptoes and whispered, "I'm a detective, you see."

"Oh," said Jane, raising her eyebrows knowingly.

Martha tapped her nose and winked.

"And what are you detecting, Martha?"

"Books, darling, books. Now follow me."

Martha walked over to the shop counter. Jane followed, removing her coat as she did so. Jane placed her coat over the back of the chaise-longue and Martha grabbed her hand.

"Come closer," she said.

The two huddled around the computer screen.

"Look!" said Martha, her chubby fingers gripping Jane's hand a little tighter.

The screen displayed a list of book names which Jane recognised.

"Dirk Heille, my darling, will soon be ours!"

Jane glanced at Martha. From that angle she could see about half of Martha's beaming smile which no doubt spread across her face. Jane looked at the screen again, unable to share in Martha's enthusiasm quite yet.

"Do you see?"

"I'm not really sure what I'm supposed to be looking at."

"The names of the books, darling. They're all Dirk Heille's novels."

"Yes…"

"Hmph," said Martha in mock disgust. She sounded like a disappointed teacher. "I thought you were at home studying this all night, Janey."

"Well, I was."

"*Well*, darling, these are some of his books."

"I know."

"And this morning, darling…I've bought them!"

Jane turned to Martha and gripped her hand. Jane had been determined to leave her father to sort out his own problems but Martha's enthusiasm was contagious.

"Yes," said Martha, pointing to the screen with the only free hand between them, "each and every one."

"No way," said Jane. "I looked last night and they were all out of print."

"I've been detecting," said Martha, smiling. "I've been searching through JayList and calling in a few favours from some friends in the book trade. I have contacts, you know."

"Wow. How many have you managed to find?"

"In the next day or so we'll have…" A chubby finger prodded the screen next to each title, causing the area around the text to distort slightly. "…exactly twenty-two of his novels."

"Thank you," said Jane squeezing tighter. She was extremely touched by the amount of effort that Martha had put on her behalf. The moment was altogether more poignant due to the fact that she had an ungrateful father who didn't deserve even one moment of time spending on him.

"And that's not all. We'll also have…" Her hand suffocated the mouse as she clicked on to the next page. "...one, two, three...er, twelve of Mr Drewhorn's books."

"That's absolutely fantastic! Thank you so much."

Martha released Jane's hand and hugged her, her head nestling into Jane's shoulder.

"It's my pleasure. I've not found them all yet, but I'm still detecting!"

The two parted.

"They must have cost a fortune to get hold of."

"Actually, they didn't. They were only a pound or two each. Seems that no-one except your father has any interest in him."

"Well, don't worry, I'll sort the money out for you."

"Don't be silly. As I said, it's my pleasure."

"Thank you. Thank you so much. Coffee?"

"Would love one, darling."

Jane returned a few minutes later with two mugs of steaming coffee. She held out the Monopoly mug to Martha, retaining the *Phantom of the Opera* one for herself. Martha's eyebrows furrowed and she nodded toward the other mug.

"Oooh, sorry," said Jane, switching the coffees.

Martha smiled broadly as she collected her drink. "So, you never said in all this excitement why you were here so early this morning, Janey?"

Martha remained behind the counter by the computer. She rested on her arms, not noticing that her bosom had hit the space bar, sending the cursor across the screen at breakneck speed. Jane rested on the arm of the chaise-longue.

"Couldn't sleep properly, so I thought I may as well get up and come in."

"Thinking about the books, no doubt, Janey."

"Er, yeah, that's right. The books."

"Well, that's one problem off your mind."

"It certainly is."

"'Cause that, my darling, is what friends are for."

thirty

It was three o'clock in the afternoon as Claire clicked her front door behind her. Her day, although extremely long, had gone without any hitch or complication at all. The early start at the hotel hadn't exactly been welcome, and the three-hour bus ride trailing in and out of every hotel en-route to the airport had added to the tedium. The time at the airport, however, had passed rapidly and she had spent the majority of the flight in a pleasant dream about her feet crunching through autumnal leaves. After the flight had landed, she had, for the first time ever, been the lucky winner at the baggage reclaim carousel, her bag appearing first through the plastic flaps. The short journey home from the airport had passed as a nothingness. Despite the travelling, she felt surprisingly alive.

She dumped her bags in the lounge and made her way through to the kitchen. On the kitchen work surface was her large grey bucket which she recognised from her back garden. From the doorway where she stood, the heads of three or four pink flowers were just visible. She smiled and walked over to inspect the contents of the bucket. Her eldest son, Neil, had obviously been around to the house in her absence. A scrawled note in Neil's almost illegible writing was trapped just under the bottom of the bucket. She could make out the words: 'Hope you've had a good time, Mum. Sure you'll be tired, so dinner at ours tomorrow 7 p.m. Neil x'.

Claire lifted the bucket into the sink and reached in to take out a lovely selection of English country flowers, mainly in pinks, yellows and whites. She placed them back into the bucket and ran a little more water in. She would display them later. She filled the kettle and plugged it into the wall. She flicked the switch and a fluorescent electric-blue glow light indicated it was about to start boiling. Whilst she waited she idly flicked through the small pile of post that had been neatly stacked next to the bucket. There was nothing of interest. A few bills, some junk mail offering her discounts on clothing and boots and an envelope displaying the name of a broadband provider addressed 'To the occupier' which she didn't even bother to open.

She fixed herself a black coffee and decided to unpack her suitcases. She wasn't tired so this was as good time as any to begin the usual repetitive task of loading and unloading the washer. She left her drink on the side, the steam swirling toward the ceiling. She collected the suitcase and laid it flat on the floor, unzipping it around the edge. Sorting the washing into piles, she was shocked to find that there were in fact only two loads of washing for her to do. This made her stop suddenly and steady herself against washing machine door. The large metal hinge creaked. The thought of her husband, Paul, was of course never far from her mind. However, it always had a great deal more impact when she was caught off-guard and a simple everyday task suddenly reminded her of what she had lost. She collected a pile of washing and pushed in into the machine. She clicked the door shut, took the box of washing powder from the adjacent cupboard and stood. She was shaking. She tried unsuccessfully to fill the drawer, and instead spilled the washing powder from the box over the sides. On the floor below a dark pile of clothes neatly awaiting its turn to be washed was partially covered like the base of an unused snow globe. Eventually she managed to get enough powder into the drawer and pushed it shut, hitting the green 'wash' button with the palm of her hand.

As the washing machine began its early churn, Claire went back into the kitchen. There, she lifted the flowers out of the bucket and laid them in a row on the kitchen side. Water dripped down from the stalks, landing in two large spots on the note which Neil had left. She scooped up the paper and dried it on her blouse. The water had smudged the ink, leaving two large blue sun shapes, their protruding rays going from dark to light blue. Claire swallowed hard and smiled. The scraggy note reminded her of what she still had. She laid it on the kitchen windowsill, the centre of the blue suns immediately attaching themselves to the tiled surface below.

After neatly arranging the flowers in a vase, she telephoned Neil to thank him. As usual there was no reply. It would take three or four missed calls for him to respond, and Claire considered that telephoning him more than once to simply thank him for the flowers may be a little excessive. She left a brief message and confirmed that she would be delighted to see him for dinner the next day.

She closed the utility room door to block out the sounds of washing machine and carried the flowers into the lounge. The centre of the windowsill was an ideal spot to display them; however she had found that flowers seemed to last three or four days longer out of direct sunlight. Instead, she placed them on the left-hand side of the marble mantelpiece, which from her usual place on the sofa would be directly in her line of vision.

She sat and reached down under the sofa to retrieve the laptop which was in its usual place just beneath her. The next job to cross off her list was checking her emails. This was something that she had made a concerted effort to do over the last year. It was also something that previously she had never taken any particular interest in. She had always been satisfied with Paul dealing with that side of things. Until his death, she was happy simply using Microsoft Word for her writing efforts, and the rest of the computer's capabilities were surplus to her requirements. Indeed, when the mood took her to write she would ask Paul to 'set her up', which effectively meant that he should open Word and bring up the last document she had edited. However, as Paul became more ill and the cancer began to spread, he had made time with her for basic computer lessons. Simple hour long sessions teaching her to send emails, access the internet, print documents, check utility bills, give meter readings online and that type of thing. Indeed, the first lesson centred on switching on and shutting the laptop down correctly.

The sessions had usually ended in tears; Claire seeing the energy drain from her husband. Paul had been resolute that Claire must learn these skills; he had made it quite clear it was the way the world was turning and she needed to know this 'to stay on'. Claire had listened and over the weeks had picked up enough knowledge for Paul to be satisfied she could cope. Claire had written a note in bold red felt-tip pen which remained on the fridge to that day, simply reminding her of the need to 'CHECK EMAILS TO STAY ON'. 'Stay on' was double-underlined.

It was unlikely that there would be any emails of interest; however, she felt that she should check. Paul would want her to check. She opened the laptop screen and pushed the power button. The fan burst into life and moments later she had entered her password. She was greeted by a screensaver of her, Paul and the boys on their last holiday together ten years earlier. She smiled; it had been a good time. She double-clicked the icon which Paul had helpfully set up to take her straight to her emails and logged in. She had thirty-six new emails. She scrolled down the subject lines, reading and discarding them one by one. The main bulk of the emails were shopping offers, though there was also a Vodafone online bill and a couple of spam emails. It was rather like the post she had opened when she arrived home. There was nothing of interest to Claire, aside from an email from an old friend who was returning to England for a couple of weeks. The friend had moved to Canada more than three decades ago, but she and Claire had kept in touch. Claire read through the message, noting that her friend was to be in England the following month. The friend had suggested two possible dates that they could meet, in between her 'whistle-stop' tour of Great Britain, calling on her own and her Canadian husband's family. Claire clicked to print the email and then clicked the cross in the top right-hand corner of the screen, which returned her to the home screen.

She began to close the laptop lid, and then decided otherwise, choosing instead to double-click the blue lower-case 'e' icon which appeared to be wearing a golden halo. She was immediately greeted by the Google home screen. The cursor flashed, inviting her to search for a subject. Moments later she was on the BBC website, catching up with the news. She had leafed through a couple of discarded tabloids whilst in Spain, but the news they carried wasn't of any particular interest. She had no inclination to read about overly dramatised murder cases, drunken celebrities or supposition about anyone and everyone that would help to sell papers. She scrolled down the website, reading pieces of interest. It appeared that nothing in particular had happened over the past week, nothing that caught her eye. After a few minutes browsing she again clicked the cross and disconnected from the internet. She laid the laptop on the sofa next to her and went to collect the email she had printed.

The washing machine was entering its final spin, whirring and giving off a high-pitched screech as it did so; the sound of a thousand giant, metallic wasps hovering ominously. It moved, banging the sides of the cupboards which stood on either side. Claire reached onto the shelf above the washing machine and retrieved the paper from the printer. She noticed the print was faded, suggesting that she would require new printer cartridges fairly soon. Replacing printer cartridges had not been part of the lessons Paul had given her and she made a mental note to mention it to Neil the following day.

She closed the door behind her to silence the wasps and walked back through the kitchen to the lounge. Collecting her handbag from the chair, she sat back down on the sofa. She unclasped the press-stud and reached inside to retrieve her diary. Rustling around between the various items – hairbrush, purse, make-up – she couldn't seem to find her diary. She lowered the front of the bag to allow more light inside and looked in. It didn't appear to be there. She moved items from side to side with her hand as if stirring soup. Then she lifted out items one by one, beginning a process of elimination. It didn't take long. The first item was her journal, which she pulled from the bag and rested on the taupe scatter cushion next to her. The diary, the smaller of the two books, slid from partway inside the journal onto the cushion beside her. "Ah-ha," she said to no-one in particular, and to make room she lifted her bag down onto the floor by her feet.

She retrieved the diary from the journal, and laid the journal opened face down alongside her. She flicked through her diary, comparing it with the email she had printed, happily finding that she was free on both dates her friend had suggested. She removed the small pen which lived in the spine of her diary, crossed through the dates and noted that she would be unavailable to anybody except her friend.

For a reason that was unclear to her, she circled both the dates on the email as well and placed it on the floor. She would respond to her friend's email in detail over the next day or two, confirming the dates and also updating her with her own news. She replaced the pen and dropped the diary into her bag. Then she collected the journal and turned it to face her. The last four words she had written greeted her. She remembered her last encounter with Michael and retrieved the laptop, logged back in to Google and waited for the cursor to appear.

Although the conversations that she and Michael had shared were brief, Claire could recall almost every detail. She had made brief notes in her journal should she have forgotten, however Michael was not a person that she was likely to forget. There was something peculiar, perhaps even sinister that made him stick in her mind. From their first meeting she had decided that he would be an ideal character for one of her stories. His objectionable temperament would be easy to write about. But it went deeper than that. There was something about his personality that she couldn't quite fathom that gave her the feeling she needed to find out more about him. Something that was repeatedly illuminating in the back of her mind that compelled her to find out more. She typed quickly into the box "MICHAEL SEWELL CAR CRASH MARGARET OXFORDSHIRE SOLICITOR".

She hit enter.

thirty-one

"So you have absolutely nothing for today?"

"No, sir – as I've already said, there are no flights today."

Michael had been standing by the airline ticketing desk for more than half an hour. He had waited his turn as various imbeciles had asked pathetic questions of the man behind the desk. The young, olive-skinned man had answered each question helpfully and greeted each member of the queue with an obliging, almost apologetic smile. The man would answer eighty per cent of traveller's questions by simply pointing them in the direction of the right check-in desk or the way to departures. Perhaps once or twice a day he would meet somebody like Michael. The skill of the job was to keep the scales tipped in the direction of customer care and politeness against an all-out physical assault.

Michael sighed and turned away from the desk, but then he span back toward the man, jutting his face forwards over the desk into his face.

"No flights whatsoever?"

"I already told you, sir," said the man, trying to draw different English words to say the same thing through his Spanish accent, "there are none."

"I want to see your supervisor. Now," Michael spat.

"You can see him, sir. But he will only say the same thing. I'm sorry." The man raised his eyebrows, his mouth curling at one corner. He held out his hands and gave an 'I've done absolutely everything I can' shrug.

"Just get him," Michael ordered.

A queue had formed behind him. The man pushed a button on the phone and after a few moments spoke very quickly down the phone in Spanish. Michael listened, but didn't understand. The call lasted no more than a few seconds.

The man looked up. "He'll come soon. Okay?" The patience in his tone was replaced with dismissiveness. He motioned Michael to one side.

"Next?" The man smiled to greet the next person in the queue.

Although he would never admit it, Michael now regretted the situation he was in. He had spoken to the supervisor at some length and, aside from taking ridiculously long journeys through the airports of various European capital cities, he had to accept that there were no flights to where he wanted to go that night. No flights home. The supervisor had explained the situation to Michael and, despite Michael's rage, assured him 'there was simply nothing further that can be done'. Michael had eventually begun to calm when the supervisor had told him in no uncertain terms that he would call security to remove Michael from the airport. Michael had no intention of being held captive by a bunch of corrupt Spanish police officers, and so he backed down at that stage.

He was now lying on the floor of the airport, using his case as his pillow, with sixteen hours to wait. Sixteen hours before he could begin his journey home.

Sixteen hours to regain control.

thirty-two

Claire was surprised at just how many *Google* pages existed from the search she had typed in. There were tens of thousands of possible pages which appeared. The first being the simple headline 'SOLICITOR'S WIFE DIES IN TRAGIC CAR CRASH'. It had been front page news for the *Oxfordshire Evening Post* three months earlier. She clicked the headline and was greeted immediately by a photo of Michael, smiling broadly, dressed in a dinner jacket and holding aloft some kind of golden award. The caption underneath the photo reading 'WIDOWED: Top Local Solicitor, Michael Sewell'. (The photograph could have perhaps been better chosen. A smiling Michael seemed wholly inappropriate starkly juxtaposed with the headline above or indeed the caption below).

Claire read on. The article went on to describe the events of that night.

Local solicitor Michael Sewell, 59, was last night in a stable condition following a car crash in which his wife, Margaret, 56, was killed. Mr Sewell, a well-known local partner of solicitors Milton, Knight and Haxby, was involved in a collision with a bridge near the village of Westfield Emil, Oxfordshire. The police have stated that the incident has 'all the hallmarks of a tragic accident' and are continuing to investigate. A local man at the scene, who did not wish to be named, stated that 'the weather was appalling and would have made driving very difficult'.

Claire removed the pen that was clipped over the hardback cover of the journal and scribbled down the name of Michael's employers. She then returned to the Google search results and clicked an article a little lower down the page, again from a local newspaper. She noted that the date was six days after the first article. This headline read 'LOCAL SOLICITOR QUESTIONED OVER DEATH CRASH'. When she selected the article she was greeted by the same stock photograph of a tuxedo-clad Michael, this time captioned 'RECOVERY: Local lawyer recovering from injuries after death crash'.

> *Police have questioned local solicitor Michael Sewell over the car crash which killed his wife a week ago. Mr Sewell, 59, was released from hospital on Tuesday after suffering injuries following the crash in Westfield Emil, Oxfordshire. The police are refusing to comment on this development aside from stating that 'this is an ongoing investigation'. There was speculation that Mr Sewell had been seen in the Ring O'Bells public house on the evening of the crash. James Ruppert, representing Mr Sewell, stated that his client 'had not been arrested and was assisting police with their enquiries'.*

Claire continued to click through the stories, but they were mostly facsimile or very slightly amended versions of the same article. As she clicked through the search results to page three, she found the results were in no way connected to the research she was undertaking. These pages were about Michael Sewell, a deceased Los Angeles pianist, or Michael Sewell Recruitment, an agency that had apparently 'been supplying the engineering and manufacturing sectors with exceptional people for more than thirty-five years'. She concluded that there were no articles any more recent than the one about Michael being questioned.

She clicked back to the search screen and tried a number of different searches using information gleaned from the articles. There was nothing.

Claire yawned and shut down the computer. She closed the laptop screen and stowed it away underneath the sofa. The travelling had finally caught up with her: it was time to sleep.

thirty-three

"I think you'd better come in right now," said Martha, eyeing the selection of boxes standing in the doorway of the shop.

"Really?" said Jane. She rolled over in bed, noticing the coldness of Matt's side. The last thing she wanted to do was to get up and go into work, but the urgency in Martha's voice suggested that perhaps she should.

"Yes, darling. Right now."

"Have they arrived?" said Jane, trying to pierce her tired monotone with enthusiasm. She didn't really care about the books or trying to solve the mystery any further. She didn't really care whether her father found the missing text. She knew that whether she found the book or not, she would receive absolutely no appreciation from her father. And neither would Martha. The search for the missing book was simply an exercise that echoed the father and daughter relationship they shared. A miniature version of every moment she had spent with him. The pattern was simple: he expected everything, she gave everything to meet his expectations, whatever she gave was not enough – it never had been; it never would be. It was time to cut ties. Fuck the books, she thought. Fuck him.

"Yes, they have, darling. Boxes and boxes and boxes of them," Martha exaggerated.

There had been four deliveries that morning. The first was a very small selection of new titles which customers would always ask for around the date of publication. Martha had enough contacts to be able to get her hands on a few signed, hardback first editions from her various suppliers. This always pleased her customers. The next three boxes had arrived in two separate deliveries. The first two boxes measured around a foot by a foot square, and Martha had anticipated that there were perhaps four to six books in each, depending on the amount of packaging that had been stuffed inside. The second delivery was of a slightly larger box, perhaps two feet by two feet, which contained exactly sixteen books. Martha could be sure of the number of books because she recognised the supplier's sticker on the underside of the box.

Before Jane could speak, Martha continued: "They're everywhere, darling, everywhere. You must come in, you simply must."

"Okay," replied Jane, sounding just spritely enough so as not to burst Martha's vastly inflated bubble of expectation. Regardless of how she felt about her father, there was no need to destroy the excitement of her friend. At the very least, she could play out this drama the way she imagined Martha had envisaged it to be played out.

"Wonderful. How long?"

Jane glanced at the clock. Eight fifty.

"I'll be there in half an hour."

"Shall I wait?"

"To open them?"

"Sorry. What am I talking about, darling? Do forgive me. Of course I'll wait."

Martha removed her podgy fingers, which had already worked their way beneath the brown tape which sealed the largest box.

"Thanks."

"Hurry, darling. Do hurry."

"I will."

Jane rolled over across the bed, its coldness reminding her that there was something she needed to do first.

Claire fingered her cup of coffee, idly looking through the window of her lounge. It was dull outside, a stark reminder that the brightness of the sunshine abroad was now gone. For a while. The wind blew gently through the conifers which stood in a line where her garden met the pavement outside. The conifers; around seven feet tall and positioned a few feet apart, allowed an intermittent view of the road. A woman appeared, pushing a pram across the top of the drive. She then disappeared behind the first conifer before reappearing again. She was holding her hat with one hand, giving Claire the impression that it was perhaps windier than the sturdy trees were giving away. Claire watched the woman appear and reappear, her hat still in place, until she was out of sight.

The mantelpiece clock had edged past nine, and Claire picked up the telephone and dialled the number scribbled on the back of an envelope alongside. She had found the number on the internet the previous evening. The tone on the telephone repeated itself twice.

"Hello, *Milton, Knight and Haxby*. How may I help you?" sang the voice. It was a young voice, draped in a mock poshness and heavily lilting with locality.

"Oh, hello," said Claire. "I wonder, could I speak with Michael Sewell?"

"I'm afraid not. Mr Sewell is on holiday at the moment."

"Oh."

"Can I ask what it's in connection with, please?"

"Well, it's a private matter actually. I was hoping Mr Sewell could perhaps represent me. Do you have a mobile number I can call?"

"I'm afraid that I can't give out Mr Sewell's mobile number without his permission."

"Oh," continued Claire politely, "that's a shame. I've spoken to Mr Sewell on numerous occasions previously and...well, this matter is quite delicate and quite urgent."

"I'm sorry, we aren't allowed to give out mobile numbers. Will it wait until Mr Sewell is back?"

"No, it won't; I do need to speak to him today. Perhaps if I explain the situation to one of the other partners they might be able to help?"

"Well..."

Claire sensed her indecisiveness. "It is absolutely necessary that I speak to Mr Sewell today. I need his representation immediately in this matter. My name is Mrs Peterson; he may have mentioned me? Can I please speak to somebody who can help me?"

"I understand, Mrs Peterson," said the receptionist. She was flustered now and couldn't remember whether she had heard the name previously or not. "And I really do want to help."

"Well, there must be somebody I can speak to," Claire continued firmly. "I can't tell you how urgent this matter is."

"Look, okay, I shouldn't do this, but as the matter is urgent I'll telephone Mr Sewell and get him to ring you immediately."

It was a fair solution. One that Claire hadn't expected. She thought quickly.

"No, I'm afraid that won't do. I'm travelling at the moment, and my signal keeps going in and out – you know how it does?"

There was a silence which signalled that Claire should continue.

"And I don't want repeated dropped calls with no way at all to get back in touch with Mr Sewell. I *need* to speak with him. It's very important. If I can't contact him, I'll have to find a lawyer elsewhere, which I really don't want to have to do."

"I see, but…"

"Listen." There was a pause while Claire quickly recalled the conversation. "I'm sorry, I don't know your name."

"It's Lacey."

"Hello, Lacey. Now listen to me, please. I must speak to Mr Sewell. Of course you'll know from the conversations you've had previously with Mr Sewell about me that my case is worth tens of thousands of pounds. Probably far more."

Lacey paused again. It was her turn to think quickly.

"Mrs Peterson," she half-whispered, glancing around the large reception area. She was pleased it was empty. "I shouldn't do this, but as the matter is urgent, I'll give you Mr Sewell's mobile number."

"Thank you, Lacey."

"Please don't tell him or anyone else I gave it to you."

"I won't."

Claire jotted down the number on the back of the envelope.

"Thank you so much, Lacey. You've been extremely helpful."

"It's fine, Mrs Peterson."

Claire pressed the button to end the call, and placed the phone next to the envelope on the sideboard. She smiled. Now she just had to speak to Michael again to find out a little more detail. She would question him directly about the accident. Their chance meeting had provided her with an idea which would form the basis of a perfect storyline for her debut novel. It would be a thriller that had everything; mystery, death, intrigue and tragedy. She would call it 'The Page'.

thirty-four

Michael sat idly staring out of the plane window. He had been asleep for just under an hour. The plane made him feel claustrophobic. He hated the closeness of the other passengers. To his right, behind him, in front of him. But, he was feeling better than before they left the runway.

He had walked aimlessly around the airport for hours. To waste time. To try to find a quiet space (though this proved impossible, because each time he became settled the area would soon fill with departing travellers, and they brought noise and clatter and children with them). And to try to escape the feeling in his chest, the butterflies bursting through him. He had restlessly moved from place to place, but each time he got settled his heart would start pumping at such a rate that he needed to move. He hoped that the blood from his heart would rush to his legs as he walked, giving him at least a brief respite from the feeling, the feeling of unparalleled fear. This had led to endless walks around various bars and duty-free shops. He had been tempted to buy a bottle of whisky and sit and drink it. Perhaps he could drown the butterflies? He reminded himself that this was not an option. He needed to stay focused if he was to regain control.

At least the plane was quieter, the dull, monotonous sound of the air-conditioning coupled with the pressure in the cabin subduing the sound of the voices around him. He rubbed his eyes. The feeling in his chest reappeared. He couldn't focus. He couldn't concentrate. He needed to get home, to his usual surroundings.

Once home, he was sure he would feel more in control. He would be able to ensure that whatever grave consequences lay ahead for him, he could deal with them on his terms. Apart from a few brief conversations with Jane he'd had no contact with anyone at home. Nothing from work. No missed calls on his mobile. Being away had made him feel uncomfortable. Anything could have happened whilst he'd been away and likely he'd be the last to know. Maybe on his return the feeling that had plagued him would disappear. It certainly hadn't been evident prior to him flying abroad.

It was the page – ever since he had been unfortunate enough to find it, he had felt trapped. Trapped within his own story. Trapped whilst away on what could not in any way be described as a holiday. Now he was trapped again. Suspended in air, where he could do nothing to make the time pass, to get him home, get him to control. In fact, this was worse than being on holiday because sitting on a plane miles above the earth made him feel that time had completely stopped. They were flying at hundreds of miles an hour yet, looking around him, life felt motionless. Nothing around him gave him the impression they were moving. They were all trapped. All suspended in air. In time.

He brought the detail of the story back to his mind. He had read the page so many times that he could remember it almost word for word. But now his memory seemed to be failing. In his mind the text on the page was beginning to change. He couldn't remember what happened to the Michael in the story. The words 'grave consequences' burst into his consciousness appearing from the corners of his mind and spinning into his thoughts. His mind was playing tricks on him. He wanted to pull the screwed up ball of paper out that minute and re-read the text once again. But, it was locked away in his wash bag, which was stored some metres beneath him in the hold of the plane. He needed to get home and find the book that the page was ripped from. He needed to know what the grave consequences were. He needed to know the fate of Michael and find out whether he shared the same.

The child in the adjacent seat nudged him accidentally. He turned to her. She was looking down toward the tray that fell from the seat in front of her. Long, dark curls concealed her face; only a small button nose was visible.

He looked to where the girl was staring. The ends of her little fingers were covered in a rainbow of colours which ran from her knuckles to the ends of her fingers. In her right hand, she held a yellow felt-tip which she was scratching quickly across the paper in front of her. The picture she had drawn appeared to show the helpless body of a dog lying on its side. There were red and maroon splashes of ink spurting from the brown fur surrounding its neck. Its head (similarly covered in a deep crimson where its neck used to meet its body) was on a grey plate that sat on a partially completed straw-coloured table. A knife and fork were drawn crudely on either side of the plate. Michael frowned.

The little girl looked up and stared into Michael's eyes.

Michael stared back.

Unflinching, the girl continued her stare.

The woman alongside her (which Michael took to be her mother) threw her head back finishing a half glass of wine in one gulp. As she pulled the plastic cup away from her lips, her eyes met Michael's.

"Come on, Mollie, get back to your colouring," she said, her eyes staying fixed.

Silently, Michael turned his head back toward the window, hoping that soon the journey would be over.

thirty-five

"Hello."

"It's me."

"Oh, hi, Jane."

"So where were you last night?"

"I was working?"

"Working."

"Yeah, I told you."

"I don't remember that."

"Yeah, I said I'd be working late."

"Well, tell me when that was, Matt, because I got no messages or calls from you yesterday."

"I told you the day before I'd be late all this week."

"I don't remember that either."

"Yeah, as I was leaving the day before."

"Well, whatever. So you were working so late you didn't even come home?"

"Yeah. We had a huge problem, had to go down to head office about eleven p.m."

"Right."

"And it took hours to fix it. I'm shattered."

"So where did you stay?"

"Er, I just stayed at a friend's. Seemed more sensible than driving back."

"Right. Which one?"

"Which what?"

"Which friend?"

"You wouldn't know them; they're from a different office."

"Try me."

"Sorry?"

"Try me. I may have heard you mention them."

"I don't think so."

"Matt, I'm not pissing around here. Where did you stay?"

"I told you. At a friend's."

"Which one?"

"She's called Hannah."

"Hannah, right. And is she a new friend?"

"Yeah. Well, I've known her a bit – y'know, emails and stuff at work."

"And you thought it better to stay at Hannah's than come home to your wife?"

"It was late, okay?"

"And?"

"And I was absolutely knackered and didn't want to drive."

"Uh-huh."

"And I didn't want to wake you."

"Yeah, right."

"I didn't. Honestly, it seemed stupid to drive two hours home, only to wake you and then get back up at six and drive two hours back."

"So why didn't you ring me?"

"I dunno. Time just flew by. By the time I looked at my watch I figured you would've been asleep."

"You had two hours in the car driving there to ring me. To let me know you were safe."

Silence.

"Why didn't you ring me then, Matt?"

"Listen. I don't know, okay? My mind was full of stuff. I was thinking about work and stuff. I thought I'd told you, okay?"

"No, Matt, it's not okay. Not at all."

"Don't speak to me like that. It's you who's been getting pissed and coming in at all hours."

"One time, Matt. One time."

"Well, this is one time."

"This is different. You decide to stay with some girl I've never heard of. Decide not to even ring to tell me that's what you're doing. And I'm expected to be okay with that?"

"You should trust me."

"What does trust have to do with it?"

"Well, asking me all these questions about where I've been, what I've been doing. You should trust me."

"It's nothing to do with trust. I wanted to know where you were."

"Why?"

"Because we're bloody married, Matt. I'd expect you to maybe wonder where I was if I suddenly didn't come home."

Silence.

"And tell me, Matt. Is it Hannah who likes Strawberry Cheesecake Häagen Dazs?"

"I don't know what you mean."

"You do, Matt. You left it in the freezer."

There was a pause, longer than the previous two.

"Look, Jane, I'm gonna have to go, all right? I'm at work."

"Right. That's good timing."

"Let's talk later? Jane? Jane?"

Jane walked into the studio and knelt down and opened the box and rummaged through the tubes of used acrylic paints. She selected the brightest, most vibrant colours she could find and laid them in a row on the floor in front of her. Cadmium Yellow Hue; Brilliant Red; Phthalo Green; Ultramarine; Crimson; Phthalo Blue.

She smiled.

She then selected two large brushes, their tips flattened at the end. Then two smaller brushes, each tapered perfectly to a point. Not a bristle out of place.

She closed the box and stood facing her easel. It was time for a change. A second or two passed, then she lifted her most recent work from the easel, turned the canvas and laid it against the wall. Her painting out of view.

She would collect a fresh canvas during her dinner break at work later that day. It was time to paint something new, something fresh and bright like the pictures she had painted before life began to throw problems at her. Before her mother died. Before her marriage. She stared down at the colourful tubes on the wooden floor. She imagined the vibrant colours flowing from the tubes twisting themselves around one another in mid-air. Dancing toward her eyes, exciting her with the possibilities of what she could create. Mentally, she began to imagine the picture she would paint. It would be tessellated birds flying from left to right diagonally across the canvas. A hundred of them, maybe more. Each bird would be painted in a bold and vivid colour. The contrasts of colour would cause the observer to have their focus constantly distracted from one shape to another. It would cause their senses to be overloaded with the ever-repeating pattern and the boldness of each individual segment.

And Jane would be the only one who knew the secret that lay behind the painting. The secret that each individual colour had been meticulously hand-picked by her; each representing a specific positive event she drew from her own experience.

thirty-six

Following the phone call with Matt, Jane had got ready and taken the bus into town. The bus ride had been a silent haze, a journey consumed by Jane's thoughts, which were anywhere but on board the bus. Just after she had paid for her ticket and found a seat, she received a text message from her father. This was unusual. Her father never text. It was a simple message. Six words: 'Coming home. Hope you have books.' That was it. When it arrived, Jane was overcome with the temptation to text back her own simple response. Four words: 'So what? And no.' In fact, she had typed them into her phone, but after staring at the send button for more than a minute, she had deleted the words and chosen not to respond.

From then on she had decided that she was not going to waste any more of the journey wrapped up in negativity. Instead she spent her time compiling a mental list of things in her past that brought her joy. It was surprisingly easy. Songs, moments, walks, gigs, weddings, academic successes, births, romantic meals out, books, drunken nights in, hugs. There were so many. Memories jumped into her consciousness, queuing eagerly to be included in her painting. As each appeared she assigned it a colour and stored it away for later use. Outwardly, she was now smiling. The whoosh of the doors swiftly transported her back to reality. A tall red haired man left the bus. Jane looked around and noticed that the bus was empty aside from a lady, who was perhaps in her seventies. She clutched a tartan trolley bag closely to her chest. The woman noticed Jane and returned the smile. The smile radiated from deep within the woman's grey eyes and instantly warmed Jane. She added it to her list. She would allocate it a deep ochre colour. Through the window behind the lady, Jane noticed the bright yellow sign of the local Chinese takeaway. Bold red text exclaimed 'Golden Horse'. She had missed her stop.

Quickly, she reached her arm up the grey pole and pressed the button. From a few feet away a ping sounded repeatedly. The bus driver turned his head and stared at Jane, disinterestedly. He raised his eyebrows.

"This stop please," said Jane.

A few moments later the bus pulled to an abrupt halt and the doors sprang open again. The driver nodded his head in the direction of the door. Jane shuffled to her feet.

"Thank you," she said to the driver. He raised his eyebrows again. Jane hopped from the final step and onto the pavement. It was only a ten-minute walk back to the shop from here.

The piston hiss of the doors sounded and the bus wearily rumbled back into life. The lady continued to smile as she retreated backwards into the distance. There was something about the kindness in her face that reminded Jane of her mother. For a second she wanted to rush behind the bus, begging it to stop. The negative thoughts quickly rushed back in. Her husband. Her father. God, her life was a mess. She knew that just a touch or smile from her mother would go some way towards making her feel less alone. Of course, this wasn't possible. She had spent her entire lifetime holding everybody up and now, at the one time she needed someone to help her from falling, there was no one. Her mother was thoughtful, loving and through her downtrodden life, somehow strong. Yes, she had lived in Michael's shadow for her entire adult life. Tolerant of every whim he may have. On hand when he shouted one simple word from one room to another. No courtesy, no thanks. Simply "Coffee!" Brisk. Sharp. Dutifully, Margaret would stop whatever she was doing and oblige. Jane had often seen this as a weakness but now instead it seemed like a sign of strength. A resolute statement that her mother made a choice to respond in this way. Previously, both Jane and Matt had questioned Margaret about why she would simply comply, with no thanks or recognition. Margaret would simply whisper "Don't" and smile. Yet despite her situation, the smile always radiated warmth. Just like the bus lady. And then Margaret would lower her head and look away. Perhaps out of embarrassment or simple apathy. It just seemed easier for her to do what Michael asked.

Jane walked purposefully up the High Street. It was fairly quiet; market towns such as this didn't really spring to life until late morning. Her head felt fuzzy. She questioned why she was even doing this for her father. She couldn't bring to mind any memory which involved him that would make its way into her painting. Not one. And now *yet again* she was helping him. This time, to find a book that he had suddenly developed an obsession with. And the worst of it was that *he wouldn't even share with her* the reason why he so badly wanted it. She shook her head. *She was such an idiot*. Her thoughts turned again to her mother. In the final two or three weeks of her life Jane had noticed a change in her. Yes, Margaret had continued to conform in every way just as she always had. But she seemed stronger somehow. And she was visibly becoming brighter. Her warm smiles were no longer cut short by a need to look away. Michael's commands were now met with a new vigour. Drinks were still delivered, socks were still pressed and towels were still presented when requested. But now Margaret seemed to be moving with a new momentum. A renewed spirit that Jane had never witnessed before. She was changing; perhaps had already changed. The frightened look which seemed to crease her entire face downwards had disappeared; her reaction to Michael's demands was instead a curled lip which silently shouted one simple word back: *whatever*.

If it hadn't been for Martha's excited smile, it was likely Jane would have walked on past the bookshop to...well, who knows. Martha had been watching the High Street for well over twenty minutes. When she spotted Jane meandering slowly towards the shop, she rushed out onto the stone doorstep to greet her. She stood, arms folded, her enormous breasts escaping from over the top of her yellow bra, which was itself visible above the neckline of Martha's baggy woollen jumper. Horizontal rainbow stripes made their way from the top to the bottom of the jumper, which hung just above her knees. It was an outfit Jane hadn't seen before.

"Janey! You made it, darling!"

"Morning, Martha," said Jane, her eyes following from red to violet and back up again.

"It's new," said Martha. "Doesn't it just fill you with so much joy?"

Jane couldn't help but smile. "It does," she said.

Martha reached forward and pulled Jane tightly toward her. Jane would have reciprocated the hug, but her arms were tightly trapped at her sides.

"Come on," said Martha excitedly, releasing Jane at the same time.

The door chime greeted them as they walked into the shop. Martha swiftly locked the door and turned the card so the word 'OPEN' faced her. Above it, Jane noticed a new sign which Martha had prepared earlier that morning. The bold black text had bled through the paper. 'CLOSED UNTIL TWELVE. NO EXCEPTIONS' it informed the outside world.

Martha grabbed Jane's hand and took her toward the back of the shop. It was dark, aside from a section directly ahead surrounded by shelves of books on three sides. What appeared to be a dark red sheet covered something on the floor. A shaft of light from the overhead spotlights beamed directly down onto the sheet, colouring the surrounding wooden shelves with a deep-red reflection.

"Look," whispered Martha, sweeping her right arm in front of her, "they're here."

Jane stared at the sheet.

"Go on," continued Martha dramatically. "De-clothe them."

Jane looked quizzically at Martha, then stepped forward and pulled at the sheet, uncovering three boxes in the process.

Martha gasped, appearing to be shocked at the sight of the boxes she had covered less than an hour before.

"Let's do it," said Jane, smiling at Martha.

Martha clasped her hands together. "Get the scissors, Janey. Get the scissors."

Jane walked back across the shop and opened a small drawer beneath the till. She rummaged around. Martha stood guarding the boxes, her hands clasped together as if she was waiting to see whether she had won some huge award. Jane located the pink-handled scissors and held them aloft. Martha let out a shriek and clapped her hands together. Moments later Jane was scoring along the brown translucent tape which bound the flaps of the boxes together. She then inserted the scissors at each end severing the tapes attachment to the sides. Each piece of tape gave way with a satisfying 'pop' and the flaps across the top opened slowly unaided. All three were now open.

"Which box first, Janey?" said Martha.

Jane eyed the boxes. She had to admit that this part was slightly exciting. Perhaps it wouldn't have been so without Martha's childlike dramatics.

"This one," she said pointing to the largest. She got down to her knees. Martha followed suit using Jane's shoulders to steady herself. Jane's cheek received a brief flirtation with Martha's right breast in the process. Martha let out a deep breath and then reached her podgy fingers into the box. She removed a large sheet of blank paper from the box and placed it to one side. Beneath was a pile of books. She pulled the first and held it in front of her. A flowery font scrolled itself across the top of the book displaying its name: *Footsteps on Minor Avenue*. The scene on the front was that of two side profiles of what looked like late 19th century women. The lady on the left had long red curly hair which fell to her shoulders. She had a cheeky almost elfish look on her face. She was smiling. On the right was an older lady, with dark black cropped hair above her ears. She didn't look happy at all. In fact, it was fair to say that she was positively scowling. Martha looked at Jane with mock fright as though she was experiencing first-hand the scowl from the dark haired lady. Jane took the book from Martha and read the blurb out loud. It was a tale of an errant daughter who wished to be far away from the spell of her overpowering mother. The girl had lost her father (and presumably the mother, her husband) and she wanted now to be free to follow her own path. It appeared the mother had other ideas.

Jane turned to page 163. She began to scan read the text. It was a love scene. It seemed that Ann was indeed following her own path. A path with Leonard, who seemed to be doing nothing to discourage Ann in her pursuits. Jane felt Martha's eyes burning into her cheek.

"Well?"

"It's a love scene."

"Ooh, a love scene? Really?"

"Yep. Ann and Leonard seem to be," she paused turning to Martha with a cheeky smile, "into one another."

"Ooh. Doesn't seem your Dad's thing."

"No. It doesn't."

Jane put the book on the floor and reached into the box again.

Half an hour later, Jane and Martha were surrounded by books. They had taken it in turns to take a book from the box, glance at the cover and quickly read the blurb before putting it on a pile alongside them. When each pile became unstable with the number of books they started a new one. In total there were thirty-four books spread across four piles. Jane stretched out her legs in front of her and rested on her arms. It was not a position Martha could easily achieve, so instead she sat cross-legged. There was more than a passing resemblance to a rainbow Buddha.

Martha picked a book from the pile nearest to her. This one was by Ed Drewhorn and was entitled *A Time to Talk, a Time to Act*. The front cover was simply a flood of crimson, with the title in a bold white font across the middle. The author's name was displayed in bold black print just beneath it. It reminded her of Joseph Heller's *Catch 22*. It was unlikely that this book would provide the answer that Jane's father required. After all, it wasn't by Dirk Heille. However, it was possible that it was a translation and thus could be the same book. Martha flicked to page 163.

Jane stretched out fully, her head on the carpet. She stared at a small cobweb in the corner above her. A spider made its way to the centre.

thirty-seven

Michael slammed his case down in the hallway. He used the heel of his shoe to close the door behind him. It had been a shit holiday. He should never have gone. He should never have listened to Jane. He threw down his small black bag on top of the suitcase and turned to pick up the letters that had collected behind the door in his absence. He carried the jumble of post through the lounge into the dining room.

The house was empty. But it felt emptier than usual. Michael couldn't work out what it was, but it had deserted feeling about it. Usually, being alone in the house didn't concern Michael. But today there was something sinister in the air. The house didn't feel warm or welcoming. Rather, it was devoid of any feeling of comfort. It had become a house that was no longer a home. An empty shell. Michael got the distinct feeling that the walls and ceilings and floors were aware of a secret. The house knew what Michael's fate was, but wasn't sharing it. He was to be the last to know. The air hung heavy on his shoulders and head. He stood by the table for a moment, staring directly forward, listening. Hoping that the silence would give him a clue to the uneasiness that the house offered. Nothing. The house was keeping its secret close. Michael began to feel that someone else was there with him. He turned and stared through the archway back into the lounge. The room was empty. He frowned and continued into the kitchen, leaving the post on the table.

He opened the fridge to find it as it was when he left. Almost empty. The milk, in a glass pint bottle, had turned from white to an off-yellow, the half-peeled silver foil lid allowing a smell to escape. The bottom shelf housed a lonely packet of Lurpak. The middle shelf was entirely empty. A single bottle of Sauvignon cowered timidly on one side. On the other, two cans of Coke faced one another as if chatting about the temperature. Small drips of condensation clung to their sides. Michael grabbed a can and closed the door. Then he felt it again. The feeling that he was not alone. He was certain that somebody was there with him. Again, he stopped and looked around the kitchen. Like the fridge, it was empty. There was no space large enough for a person to hide. Slowly, he pulled the ring pull back on the can, allowing the tiniest amount of oxygen to collide with the carbon dioxide waiting inside. An eager fizz of bubbles escaped through the invisible gap. Michael pulled the ring pull further, widening the gap. He controlled the sound, allowing a long, almost inaudible hiss. The bubbles would escape at his pace. After cracking through the metal fully and pushing back the ring pull, he drew the can to his mouth and took a sip. He eyed the coving as he did so. He then turned slowly and walked back into the dining room.

"I have absolutely no idea," said Jane. The initial fire of excitement she had felt an hour before was now entirely extinguished.

"It's quite hard, darling, to find the text your father requires when we don't know what we're looking for."

"I know," sighed Jane.

Between them they'd pored through the first nine books now, taking it in turns to read a short section to the other. Within a paragraph or two there was a knowing look from one to the other, followed by a synchronised shake of the head. They had been interrupted briefly by a loud knock at the front door. A man was standing outside, peering into the store, one hand cupped just above his eyebrows to shield his eyes from the glare of the sun's reflection. Martha had turned and impatiently shooed him away with her hand. She then returned to the book in her hand. After reading aloud yet another few paragraphs they both agreed that it was extremely difficult to find the information that Michael needed to see without knowing what the information was.

"Shall we keep going?" said Martha, her voice suggesting she hoped for a negative response. Her interest in pursuing a career as a detective was rapidly waning.

"Seems a bit pointless really, doesn't it?"

"Why don't you ring your father and ask him?"

Jane knew this was coming. She had no interest in calling her father. She didn't want to speak to him, not at the moment. But then, after all the effort Martha had put in to get this far, it wouldn't be fair to simply refuse to call him.

Martha recognised the pause. "Don't you want to, Janey?"

"Er…" She managed enough enthusiastic inflection to entrap Martha once again. "Yes, of course I do. I want to find out as much as you do."

"And then…" said Martha. She paused for effect. "…we shall solve the mystery of Mr Heille and Mr Drewhorn once and for all!"

"We certainly will!" said Jane, standing to collect her phone from her pocket.

Michael stood in the lounge. Still. So still. He listened intently, being careful not to make any sound at all. Although he could feel the beat of his heart, slow and deliberate, it didn't make a sound. He looked around the room, scanning each corner for a place someone could hide. The sofa to his left was pushed against the wall, and the chair opposite was nestled tightly next to a long oak coffee table which separated the two. He moved his head to the left. The space beneath the window was open and there was no place to hide in the corner by the television. The room was empty. In fact, he concluded, the whole of the downstairs of the property was empty. The atmosphere stood heavy. The walls, the pictures, the doors were all watching him. *Someone* was watching him. He craned his head to his side and listened for sounds from the floor above. Nothing. Silence.

A sudden humming sound broke the silence and startled Michael. The tenseness in his body disappeared and he made his way over to where the strange hum was coming from. The leather jumped slightly with each hum as he reached his bag. He unzipped the top and reached inside for his phone. The word 'Unknown' flashed on the screen. He pushed the green button to answer.

"Hello?"

"Michael?" a female voice chirped.

"Yes?"

"Michael, hi. It's Claire."

"Claire?"

"Yes, Claire. We met in Spain, earlier in the week."

What the fuck does she want? thought Michael. His heart opened, freeing a thousand butterflies into the openness of his rib cage. His tone changed; he decided it was wise to add a friendly lilt.

"Claire. How are you?"

"I'm fine, thanks. Nice to be back. Look…"

"Yes, it is good to be back."

"Look, I just wanted to apologise for upsetting you while we were away."

"That's okay."

Where did she get my number from? What does she want?

"Did you say you were back as well?"

"Yes, today."

"Oh, I thought you were staying a little longer than that."

I was. I changed my plans, all right? What the fuck do you want?

"I decided to come back early."

"Oh. Nothing terrible, I hope?"

"No. Just decided it was time."

"Right."

The butterflies continued to enjoy their freedom, battering the inside of Michael's chest repeatedly as if trying to find a way to escape him altogether.

"Listen, Michael, I wanted to speak to you. There's something I need to ask you."

There was a long pause.

"Are you still there?"

"Yes, I am."

"I wanted to ask you about your wife. Margaret, wasn't it?"

Another pause. The hallway seemed to close in around Michael. He stumbled backwards slightly and sat on the second step of the stairs.

"Yes."

"I wanted to ask you about the crash."

"I don't really want to discuss this with you."

"I'm sure you don't, but I need to know something..."

Michael pressed the red button on the phone and placed it alongside him on the step. The butterflies pounded harder and harder. He was suddenly hot. A blistering heat that ravaged first his body and then his head. He was on fire; he needed to cool down. Immediately. He unbuttoned his shirt, fully expecting to see the shape of the butterflies through his skin. He expected to see the giant outline of the mass of his heart visibly stretching his skin taut. Nothing. No movement through the wiry white hairs on his chest. So much was happening inside him: the butterflies, his heart racing, the heat. He was struggling to breathe.

The phone rang again. He picked it up. A single word, 'Unknown', screamed at him.

He pushed the red button.

Silence.

He was being watched.

He could feel it. The house seemed to *know*.

He pulled himself to his feet and pushed the phone into his pocket. He turned and rushed up the stairs. The phone buzzed. He ignored it. He flew into each room, pulling open the cupboard doors, throwing himself to the floor to check under the beds.

One bedroom.

Two bedrooms.

His pocket buzzed. He pulled open another cupboard door, then another. The endless activity of the butterflies urged him to keep going. Faster, faster. Into the bathroom, throwing open the clear shower door. Nothing.

He pulled back the shower curtain that hung above the bath. Nothing. The walls, the ceilings seemed to move in around him, ever closer, crushing him, draining the air, forcing him from each room.

His study. He shoved the leather chair to one side, its wheels catapulting it into the wall; bouncing it back into his path. He was on his knees, under his desk. Nothing.

The next bedroom, onto the floor, under the bed.

His pocket buzzed. He threw open the cupboard door,

sweeping Margaret's old coats and dresses to one side. There was nobody there. The walls were closing in. The air disappearing. He gasped, desperately trying to take in some oxygen.

His pocket buzzed again. The room forced him out, into the last room. His room. His and Margaret's room. The cupboard.

Nothing.

Just clothes.

Onto the floor.

Nothing. There was nobody there. Just him. He stood and steadied himself against the windowsill, staring out on to the front garden below, breathless. And then it was silent.

The atmosphere changed.

The walls stopped moving.

His body cooled.

It was just him.

Just him and…

Nothing.

He spat out the butterflies with each breath, releasing them a mouthful at a time. His heart slowed.

He stood by the window. Watching.

A few minutes passed.

It was now calm.

His pocket buzzed, and he reached into it, ready to press the red button. He pulled out the phone and the screen flashed brightly. It was Jane. He took one further deep breath and answered.

"Hello?"

"Hi, Dad." Her tone was direct.

His stare fixed on two cars which had just pulled up on the street below. One was a non-descript silvery-grey. The other was white with yellow and orange stickers running down the side. It had blue lights on the roof. Huge words were stamped on the side and on the bonnet. The doors opened in tandem. Four men got out. Two were dressed casually in trousers and white shirts. No ties. The other two were dressed in uniform.

"Dad?"

The men marched down the path toward the front door. Michael recognised two of the men. The taller of the two looked up at the window and nodded at him. Michael stared. They banged loudly on the door.

"Dad, are you there?"

"Jane, I'll have to call you back."

"I need to speak to you now."

"I'll call you back. There's someone at the door."

about three months earlier

thirty-eight

"For Christ's sake, Michael!"

Michael could hear the fear in his wife's voice. The tone had changed from her earlier cries for him to slow down. It was now pure fear. Fear that in seconds everything around her could shrink into a tiny white dot and then disappear. The old television would turn off for the last time and everything would be black.

Michael turned slowly toward his wife and smiled.

"What?" she screamed.

The rain continued to beat its staccato rhythm on the roof as car lurched around yet another bend. Michael calmly pushed his foot toward the floor, and the car eagerly accelerated as they came onto a straight stretch of road.

Margaret sobbed heavily, gasping for breath, as dark trees appeared and disappeared in quick succession.

"You're going to kill us both!"

Michael continued to drive, swinging the car from side to side as they made their way to his destination.

"Don't you care?"

Michael remained silent, enjoying the panic that filled the car. They were nearly there. Less than a few miles to go.

"Michael?"

Margaret took her hands away from her face and turned toward her husband. "Why won't you answer me?"

The car screeched forward, spraying loose gravel out through the exhaust smoke.

Nearly there.

She began to beat her fists against her husband's left arm and shoulder, both blows hitting in tandem.

"For God's sake, Michael."

Again, no reaction. Michael sped ever faster along the straights, braking heavily around bends causing deep puddles to spray against the side of the car, coating the windows in brown sludge. As the wheels made contact with the water the car felt momentarily out of control, and Margaret's stomach flipped. She looked physically sick.

Michael continued to drive. It wasn't much further. He slowed and took a left turn down a thin lane. There was only enough width for one car; the hedgerow cocooning them. They sped on, locked in pure darkness. He knew the country roads extremely well, especially this road. He had made this exact journey more than a dozen times in the last week alone.

Margaret screamed again.

"For God's sake, Michael. What are you doing? Slow down. Oh God. Oh God. Oh God," she sobbed, resting her head against Michael's taut arm. "For Christ's sake. Oh God. For Jane's sake…"

"You're rambling," said Michael, pushing his elbow out to move her away from him.

Two more bends, one right turn, and they would be there.

The car swerved again and picked up speed as it left the first bend.

A deep puddle. The wipers threw the muddied water back down toward the road. Margaret sobbed.

Into the last bend. They were close now. It was darker than the previous times Michael had made this journey, but he knew the way from here. He sped up again, lifting the clutch slowly to make the engine scream for effect.

Margaret curled herself into a ball, head in hands, facing toward the passenger-side window.

Just a moment or two now.

Michael hit the brakes. In daylight it would have been possible to see the signpost announcing that a right turn would get them to Westfield Emil in two miles. Michael followed the sign making a final turn into a slightly wider road. The car was going much slower now. Margaret felt the reduction in motion and turned her head slowly, daring to peek at her husband through her fingers.

Michael removed his hand from wheel and felt in the darkness for the button down to his left. He found it easily, just as he had practised, and pushed it firmly down. Margaret's seat belt released with a satisfying click.

The car quickly gathered pace again, and veered slightly to the right. He checked his mirrors, to the side and behind. There was nobody else around. Then he concentrated hard, ensuring the speed was perfect as he crossed the white line that ran across the middle of the road.

Slightly faster.

As the car headlights lit up the small bridge in front of him, he braked suddenly and made the final turn of the wheel before impact.

Michael had believed Margaret would die instantly. As he stood in the cold river water beneath the canopy of the weeping willow, he could still not tell whether his wife was dead. He could hear noises coming from the road which stretched several metres above him through the woodland area. He tried to listen but the pounding rain and gushing of the river made it difficult to make out the sounds clearly.

He pushed Margaret's foot, forcing her closer to the darkness of river's edge. Out of sight, hidden beneath the trunk of the tree that bent solemnly over the water. The moonlight trickled through the leaves which held off much of the strong rain from above. A few branches gave way to rain, creating three or four tiny waterfalls which streamed into the river.

He heard the sound again. It sounded like voices.

He turned Margaret toward him so he could see her face. It was too dark to see properly and he used the density of the water to turn her clockwise. He manoeuvred her shoulders so her face was in the moonlight and stared at her. Her eyes were closed.

He held his ear to her mouth. Feeling and listening for air at the same time. There was a breath. Shallow. It came from her nose.

He brought his head up and stared at her, holding her head firmly between his hands. He then moved his ear over her face to ensure he wasn't imagining the breath.

Again, it was there. Shallow. Almost indistinguishable. But there.

The sounds from through the woodland were getting much closer. Michael shot his head around toward where the noises were coming from. They were definitely voices.

Michael looked down at Margaret and then pushed his hands firmly beneath the cold water. He didn't have long. Water covered her forehead and eyes, before fully submerging her face. As the water entered her nose her head momentarily moved to the side. Michael pushed her further under.

He heard the voices again. They were very close now. One belonged to a man, the other a women.

Michael continued to hold Margaret under the water; her brown hair floated on the surface, dancing around his wrists. She gave no resistance. He was instantly reminded of the day that

Thomas died. It was much the same. There'd been no struggle, no resistance. Only in the case of Thomas, he'd instead had to use a pillow to stop the breathing. Quick and easy. Simple.

And then the voices were on top of him.

No more than ten metres away.

He released his grip, letting Margaret float on the surface, and quietly dragged himself out of the water and onto the river bank.

acknowledgements

Writing this book has been a difficult task which at one stage took me, quite literally, to the edge of the precipice. It is not easy to sufficiently describe the gratitude I feel for those who brought me back in line and inspired me to finish this book. You should know who you are. However, special thanks must go to my good friend, Harry Dunn whose inspiring late night emails made me dust myself down and get back to writing. And to my editor, Charlie Wilson who helped me to again find my 'happy writing place'. Thank you.

Thanks to Terry Compton, Jeremy Thompson and everyone at my publishers, Troubador for their patience and understanding. To Robert Weston for his invaluable and meticulous input. Once again, thanks to Stephen Lee and Matt Niblock for again providing art that is truly worthy of that title.

about the author

M Jonathan Lee was born in 1974. He lives and works in Yorkshire, England.

His first novel, *The Radio* was nationally shortlisted for The Novel Prize 2012.

The Page is his second novel.